Dead Ground in Between

A DETECTIVE INSPECTOR TOM TYLER MYSTERY

MAUREEN JENNINGS

McCLELLAND & STEWART

Library and Archives Canada Cataloguing in Publication
is available upon request
ISBN: 978-0-7710-5055-8
E-BOOK ISBN: 978-0-7710-5056-5

Cover art: © Stephen Mulcahey / Arcangel Images
Cover design: Leah Springate

Typeset in Adobe Caslon by M&S, Toronto
Printed and bound in the USA

McClelland & Stewart,
a division of Penguin Random House Canada Limited,
a Penguin Random House Company
www.penguinrandomhouse.ca

1   2   3   4   5   20   19   18   17   16

Penguin
Random
House

To Iden, as always, and also to Howard Murphy,
who found the treasure in the first place.

There may be dead ground in between and I may not have got
The knack of judging a distance; I will only venture
A guess that perhaps between me and the apparent lovers
(Who, incidentally, appear by now to have finished,)
At seven o'clock from the houses, is roughly a distance
Of about one year and a half.

– Henry Reed, from the poem *Lessons of the War,*
part 2, "Judging Distances"

HE BEGAN TO PACE OUT THE DISTANCE BETWEEN THE
hawthorn saplings that marked the corners of the fallow field. Forty
paces due east. Every movement sent a stab of searing pain through
his chest but, except for a sharp intake of breath, he ignored it. He
had to. He had no time to lose.

He'd chosen the spot hastily. The field beside the road was a short
distance from the barn. He thought it was as good as any other place,
shielded from the farmhouse by the hedgerow surrounding it.

At the sapling, he reversed and counted twenty paces back west.
He halted. With the rounded top of Clee Hill behind him, just visible in the gathering darkness, he struck a straight line directly south.
Ten paces. Here he dropped to his knees, gasping at the agony in his
chest. He knew his ribs were broken. Roundhead, Roundhead.
The jailer, an ardent Royalist, had spat out the word over and over
as if it was vile upon his tongue, each time accompanied by a kick
with his heavy boot. He'd lain in that dark cell for at least three days.
Finally he'd been released, why he didn't know. They could have
killed him easily, with no one to protest the injustice of it. No one
but his mistress, and now she was almost as helpless against them as
he was. How hard she'd pressed the purse into his hand. "Go, dear
friend, for that is what you are to me, my dear friend. Go. Deliver
this to my husband. He waits at London. War will be upon us before
we know it. Our soldiers must be paid. May God keep you safe."

Like any man born to Eve, he'd been curious about his commis-
sion, and when he'd left his mistress he'd opened the purse. Silver
coins. Many of them. He'd considered keeping one or two for his
own travail but didn't. Coins wouldn't protect him against the men

who were pursuing him. They wouldn't be bought off with a couple of ducats, and he'd see them in hell before he'd let the money fall into their hands.

Dusk was falling fast, lengthening the shadows across the field. He might yet escape into the darkness if he was quick. Fortunately, the ground was still soft from summer and it was easy to scrabble out a shallow hole with his dagger. He'd found a discarded clay pot near the barn and he dropped the leather purse into it, then placed them into the hole, smoothing over the soil so it looked untouched.

He struggled to his feet and paused, lifting his head like an animal that smells its death fast approaching.

The light breeze carried the sound of jingling spurs and bridles. The dragoons were close. If he were caught he knew they'd show him no mercy. They were the King's men.

Roundhead. Roundhead.

Fast as he could, his breath harsh, he returned to the gap in the hedge and thrust through to the path. His mare was grazing nearby and he mounted quickly, jerking her head around to face the way he'd come. She balked, not willing to be ridden again, tired from their long journey. So he allowed the reins to droop, drew his sword, and waited. Not long. The riders appeared over the hill, trotting two abreast. Half a dozen at least, dusty and travel-weary.

He stood up in his stirrups and cried out. "I'm here, you scum of the earth. God's despised ones. I'm here. The Roundhead is here."

The captain didn't hesitate and he gave the halloo. As one, they all plunged forward into a gallop. They drew their swords, which keened through the air as they swung them aloft. Their spurs raked the flanks of their horses.

He called again. "Take me if you can. I defy you!"

The first two were on him in moments, and they cut him to pieces as a butcher slices the deer's carcass. The others joined in. He fell bleeding to the earth not far from the small grave he had dug for the pot with its precious contents.

MONDAY, DECEMBER 7, 1942

A GUST OF WIND FLUNG HARD PELLETS OF SLEETING
rain against the windows. The police station was ancient, the
window frames ill-fitting, and a cold draft blew down Tom
Tyler's neck. He shivered. The creaky old radiator gave off
barely any heat, making little impact on the chill of the office.
Sergeant Oliver Rowell was a good manager and tried to make
sure they stayed within their coal ration, but sometimes Tyler
wished he would splurge a little. Especially on mornings like
this. He could hardly remember when the sun had last shown
its face. He contemplated the rain-dark window.

"Blimey. At this rate I'll be needing to sit in my overcoat."

He took a sip of the tea that Rowell had brought in a few
minutes earlier. It was weak and already tepid. No biscuit
redeemed it – that had to be saved for his afternoon tea break.

Another blast shook the window frames. There was a tap on
the door and Rowell came in. He had a sheet of paper in his
hand and he gave it to Tyler.

"This is the case order for tomorrow's court, sir. Thought
you might want to know what you've got to deal with."

Tyler groaned. It was normally the job of the chief constable
for the county to attend the magistrates' court, but he was down
with the flu. As detective inspector for the Ludlow station,
Tyler had to attend in his place. It was not a thing he enjoyed,
as it tended to make him despair of human nature.

"Read it out to me, Oliver."

Rowell took a spectacles case out of his pocket, removed the
glasses, and perched them on his nose. They were rimless, and

wearing them in that way gave him a peculiarly Pickwickian air. He saw Tyler's expression and ducked his head sheepishly.

"I should have got these months ago. Didn't want to admit I was getting older, I suppose. I just use them for reading."

"Sounds like a good idea."

"Right." Rowell consulted the paper. "First up is a charge of unnecessary travel against Sir Edward Spence of Clee village."

"Really? What's his story?"

"He says he went to visit a farmer in Wem. He claims it was in the course of his duty as magistrate. Wanted to make sure there was nothing untoward going on."

"Such as?"

"He didn't specify, sir. But I happen to know said Wem man breeds hawks and kestrels. Before the war, Sir Edward was a keen falconer. I'd wager he went to buy a bird."

"Ha. You never know. Those hawks might have cameras attached to their legs. Secret spies." Tyler scowled. "Truth is, Spence is one of those arrogant sods – excuse my language, Sergeant – who seems to think rules of wartime don't apply to them."

"You're right about that. Sir Edward is Old Family in these parts. Doesn't see why he has to change his ways."

"Was it young Mady? I'm glad he had the gumption to wave him down and see why he was on the road," said Tyler.

Rowell chuckled. "Apparently, he stood his ground when Sir Edward pulled rank. It's a wonder he didn't threaten to clap Mady in irons and throw him in the dungeon."

"It's a good thing for my mental health that most people in this county are responsible and conscientious about following the new laws," said Tyler. "I'd wonder what we were fighting for if they were all like him."

"Unfortunately, Arthur Desmond is the chief magistrate tomorrow. He's not going to come down heavy on one of his own."

"Who's working with him?"

"Wendell Hare. He's a retired solicitor, sort of fancies himself an expert in the law."

"That could be good for our side."

"Not necessarily, I'm afraid. From what I've observed, Mr. Hare is a dyed-in-the-wool conservative toady. He won't challenge anything Desmond says. It's my guess Sir Edward will get off scot-free. Those boys stick together."

Tyler wagged his finger at the sergeant in mock reproach. "Oliver, that is quite a subversive remark. You should know your place. These men are our betters, don't forget."

"Are they, sir? Could have fooled me."

Tyler laughed. "All right, what's next?"

"Two men charged with bicycling without proper lights and using abusive language to an officer of the law."

"Good heavens. What did they say?"

"According to the constable's report – Biggs, this time – one chap said, 'Don't worry, Officer, we can see perfectly well in this moonlight.'"

"That doesn't sound abusive to me."

"It was the second chap who got rude. He called Constable Biggs a silly arse and an effing moron. Biggs says both were under the influence."

"How the heck did they get enough booze to get themselves drunk? These days, shortages are sending three-quarters of the population into enforced sobriety."

"Probably not a bad thing, that." Sergeant Rowell had strong views about the destructive nature of liquor.

"Regardless, they can't be allowed to flout the law. Drivers and bicyclists must have sufficient lights to be seen by pedestrians. And let's follow up on the source of their liquor supply. Might be black market."

"Will do."

"Who are the two inebriates?"

Rowell read from the sheet. "A Timothy Oldham and a Samuel Wickers. They're both farm labourers and work at the Mohan farm just outside of Bitterley. Ages given as twenty-three and twenty-two respectively."

"If they're like all the other lads in reserved occupations, they're fretting about not seeing any action," said Tyler. "Makes them throw their weight around . . . I'm going to ask for a ten-shilling fine for each of them. I'm not going to let any riff-raff show disrespect to one of my constables. I don't care if they are languishing heroes."

"Noted, sir."

Rowell scanned the rest of the page. "Now this is a rather interesting case from the sound of it, sir."

"Read on. I could do with some excitement this morning."

"Mr. Walter Delderfield, who is the manager of the Woolworth's store, caught two boys stealing. His statement is included. Shall I read it as is, sir?"

Tyler waved his hand.

"'When I confronted the two boys, one of them in particular went half wild and kicked down a shelf holding a new consignment of cups and saucers, breaking several of them. This was particularly damaging as they are intended for Christmas sale and are not easily replaceable. The boy's language in front of the female customers was foul. When I told him to desist, he lit out and punched me in the lower stomach. As I have to wear a truss due to an ongoing hernia problem, this caused severe pain.'"

"Ouch. I bet it did," said Tyler, wincing in sympathy. "Who are these little thugs?"

"Apparently both boys are evacuees. They are billeted with a Mrs. Nuala Keogh, who resides on Lower Broad Street.

She is a widow." Rowell gazed at Tyler over the top of his glasses. "Her statement is also included. Shall I read it?"

"Yes, please. Poor old thing. She probably had no idea what she was getting herself into by taking in evacuees." He'd heard many stories about the children who'd been evacuated from the cities. Often the problem arose from a serious clash of cultures. There were children with head lice, who wet the bed, wouldn't eat anything "strange," and who had somewhere acquired the foul language usually employed by England's fighting forces. The goodwill of the locals was being stretched to the breaking point in many cases.

"She says, 'I don't know what came over the boys. Up to now they have been no trouble whatsoever. I believe that the manager overreacted and the boys in turn became frightened. They struck out in self-defence.'"

Tyler whistled through his teeth. "That's a very kind view of what happened. It'll be interesting to see what the magistrates decide."

"That's all for tomorrow, sir. It'll probably take up most of the morning."

There was a sound from the front hall and a voice called out. "Post."

"I was wondering where that had got to. McBrearty has been complaining about his lumbago. He's been getting later and later," Rowell said.

"Maybe it's Father Christmas coming to ask me what I want in my stocking."

The sergeant grinned. "I already sent in my request. My chilblains are killing me. A nice pair of fleece slippers would be gratefully received."

He left and returned with a small bundle of letters, which he placed on the desk. "Can I warm up your tea, sir?"

Tyler handed him his cup. "Thanks, Sergeant."

There was another rattle of rain against the windowpane.

"It's blowing up for a gale," said Rowell. "I could probably eke out another lump of coal for the boiler if you like, sir."

"No, don't bother. We'll only have to make up for it later. Just bring me that hot tea."

"Oh, to remind you, sir. You have that appointment with Mrs. Hamilton at noon tomorrow."

"No, I didn't forget, Oliver. I hope I'm not wasting her time and mine."

"I'm sure you're not."

The sergeant left and Tyler reached for the letters. He started to riffle through them. Nothing too exciting. Then the very last one made his heart leap. The familiar handwriting that he looked for with every delivery. Finally a letter from Clare. In the two years since she'd been sent to Switzerland on government service, as the War Office put it, he'd received only four letters, all of them far too brief, all scored through by the censor. She had addressed this letter to the police station in Whitchurch, which was where he'd been when she'd left. They had forwarded it on to Ludlow.

He tore open the envelope, his hands shaking a little. He couldn't help it. The date at the top was six months ago.

June 8, 1942

My dear Tom,

I will get straight to the point. It has been two years since we have seen each other. I have no idea when I will be able to return to England. Perhaps when the war is over. And who knows when that will be?

I cannot bear to think of you waiting for something that

*might never happen. I am releasing you from any
promise, actual or in essence, that you might consider you
have made to me. That we have made to each other.
Please, I beg you, go on with your life. Give your love to
somebody else. I am sorry, but I know this is for the best.*

Clare

The door opened and Rowell came back in.

"Good heavens, sir. What is it? Bad news? Has somebody died?"

Tyler looked up at him. "You might say that, Oliver. You just might say that."

***

What time was it? Jasper really had no idea. There was the merest lightening of the eastern sky so he assumed it was getting close to dawn. He was wearing his rubber boots and his overcoat but he could see that underneath the coat he was in his pyjamas. He didn't remember getting undressed for bed but he must have. He had a lantern with him. It cast a pool of light ahead of him, which he followed. "We all need a guiding light," Gracie had said to him more than once. "You're mine," he'd replied with a kiss.

He could take only short steps and had to keep the hedgerow close at his side for guidance. He had no gloves, and his fingers felt so stiff he was afraid he'd drop the lantern any minute. What was he doing on this road? He thought that the barn was just around that bend but he wasn't sure. Perhaps it was the opposite way. He couldn't remember. The storm was blowing his thoughts away, tugging at him no matter which direction he turned. It felt as if the wind was trying to pull his treasure case from beneath his arm, and he clutched it tighter. He had to get it out of harm's way as soon as he could.

He shouldn't have said anything about his find. He frowned. Had he told them? Or did he just think he had? Never mind. He wasn't going to reveal the place where he'd found the treasure. No siree. Never. Nobody had seen him. Or had they? There had been boys, he remembered. On the road, spying on him. He'd yelled at them and chased them away. They'd disappeared into the fog. Were they real boys? Sometimes he thought he saw shadowy riders coming along the lane but they always vanished when they got closer. He heard them, though. Talking and laughing, the horses snorting, bridles jingling. He'd mentioned it to John, but his son had looked so alarmed that Jasper had ended up shrugging it off. "Must have been the fellows who work on Mohan's farm."

He'd been ploughing in the east field when he found the treasure.

That morning, Susan had put up a fuss when he'd proposed to do some work in the field. She'd said it was Sunday, the Lord's day, and he should come to church with her and John. What would people think?

He'd told her the ploughing had got to be done soon so they'd be ready for spring planting. "Farming don't bend itself to suit us. We bend to suit it." She'd shut up at that. She wasn't from the country and didn't like it when he reminded her of the fact.

John hadn't said much, as usual, except that they could work tomorrow. The Itie could help them.

"Nope, I'm doing it now," he'd said. "I don't take my orders from a woman." And off he'd gone to harness Ollie, relishing his little victory.

But after an hour's hard work, he was hungry and his shoulders were aching. A wind was blowing up strong from the west, and thickening wet fog was drifting down from Clee Hill.

Bump.

Damn. His plough had jolted hard on a rock. He couldn't afford to have it bent or broken. He pulled up the horse so he could take a look. This field was worse than a gravel pit.

Something was nestled into the unearthed rock, almost hidden, but even in the gloom it was glinting softly. Stiff at the knees, he knelt and brushed away the covering soil. There was a small clay pot, no bigger than a teacup really, open and cracked down one side. Inside was what looked like a leather purse, which had almost disintegrated. Inside that were two or three stacks of silver coins. It was they that had caught the light. He could tell at once they were very old.

He pulled out his handkerchief and spread it on the ground. Tenderly, as if it were a wounded bird, he lifted out the pot, which was heavy, and placed it on the handkerchief. The wafer-thin coins were stuck together but not hard to pull apart. One by one, he began to count them. On some of them, he could just make out the dates. One roll was from the time of Elizabeth Regina. The latest had the date 1643 and the head of Charles I stamped on one side.

He scratched at the back of his mind, trying to recall dry-as-dust history lessons in school. English Civil War. Roundheads and Cavaliers.

Jasper wiped his wet face now with the back of his sleeve. He started to retrace his steps. There. He was on the right track again. He hadn't gone too far out of his way after all. His lantern showed him the entrance to the barnyard. He knew exactly where he was going to hide his box. But wait. Didn't the POWs sleep in the barn sometimes? Were they still here?

Perhaps they'd gone back home to Italy. He couldn't remember if peace had been declared. Somebody had died in that war. His mother had cried for days. Or was it Grace who had wept and wailed? No, it wasn't her. He was fairly sure his son was alive. He'd seen him recently.

He hadn't seen at first that there was gold amidst the silver. He kept back three coins from the pot; one gold, two silver. They felt as smooth and silky as if the metal were the pelt of a little animal.

He replaced all the remaining coins in the pot and returned it to its shallow burial place, covering it again. He'd have to think about what do. It was his treasure, nobody else's.

Ollie shook his harness and whinnied. He probably wanted to get back to his stable. Jasper stood still. He mustn't forget where the treasure was buried. He had to register his bearings. "Whoa," he called to the horse, and he walked over to one of the big hawthorns that stood at each corner of the field. With the eastern one as his marker he strode off forty paces. Back to the midpoint, twenty paces. Clee Hill at his back to the north. The soil where he'd buried the pot was a raw circle. He reached it in exactly ten paces forward in a straight line.

Not bothering to finish the ploughing, he guided his horse out of the field. He kept repeating the measurements to himself so he wouldn't forget. He'd have to think about what to do next. He must find Grace and tell her. She'd know what to do.

A sudden gust of wind slapped at Jasper's cheeks, driving the rain into his face. Where was his cap? Had he worn it when he'd left the farmhouse, or had it blown away along the road? Water was dripping down his nose. He was so cold.

It was because of Susan that he'd decided to move his treasure box. He knew she liked to snoop in his room. Claimed she needed to clean, but he knew that wasn't the truth.

—

Jasper thought of the case as his treasure box but it contained private things rather than things of value in the world. The medal he'd won as a boy for perfect attendance at Sunday school. A photograph of Grace taken just before they married: she was standing at a trestle table holding a large soup ladle, in front of her a bowl of some kind. A church picnic, probably. He'd put the picture and the medal together with the leather collar from his old beloved dog, Moss, into the case. He had taken some scraps of silk from Grace's sewing box and kept them to wrap his special things, like his wife's wedding ring. He'd added to it from time to time. Things he found in the fields, mostly. Stones that were beautifully marked. A man's steel watch with the time forever stopped at a quarter past eleven. It wasn't expensive, by the look of it, but he liked it, liked the solidity, the clarity of the numbers.

Now he chose a piece of blue silk, wrapped the gold coin, and put it in the box. The silver coin he'd put in his handkerchief and shoved it into his pocket. He'd find a hiding place for it. He vaguely recalled he'd taken three coins from the little pot. Was there a third somewhere? Another silver one? He must have dropped it.

Another gust of wind almost blew him over and he had to bend double. Somehow, he seemed to have gotten lost. He must have turned left at the farmyard gate instead of right. He was already soaked through, his hair plastered to his face. "You'll catch your death of cold." That's what Grace always said if he was running out without his cap or his muffler. "You'll catch your death, Jasper," she said. "Then what will happen to me? I have no desire to be a widow."

But she'd gone first, and it was him who was left alone.

Where was she? Would she be at the farmhouse waiting with a towel she'd warmed at the fire and a pot of soup on the hob, the way she usually did on winter days when he came in from the fields? She'd be at the window. "You're soaking wet, Jasper. A dog has more sense. Come in out of the rain this minute."

He should turn back. He could hide the box tomorrow.

His stash had grown steadily since Grace had died, but after Susan and John had come to live with him he'd kept his box hidden. His daughter-in-law would throw everything away as rubbish, he thought resentfully. He wasn't going to let her, no siree. He'd better return to the house or else Susan would scold him. She could be sharp with her tongue, that woman could. Most folks thought she was sweet as pie – John was lucky, they said – but Jasper knew better. He knew what she was really like. And she never made soup that he liked. Tasteless most of the time.

Thank goodness, here was the gate. He shoved it open and trudged across the yard to the house. He turned the doorknob. It was locked. Was it not his house, then? Had he acciden-tally gone to the Mohan house down the road? No, that was smaller than his, and their door was green. He remembered that. He knocked. No answer. Again, this time so hard he hurt his knuckles. Nobody stirred. He stopped. Susan would be angry if he woke her up.

The wind worried at his ears. Angry wind. He might as well go to the barn. It was always warm in there with the cows. But had he brought them in from the fields?

He must have. It was winter now.

Wait till he showed Grace the coins. She'd be thrilled about the treasure too. They wouldn't tell the landlord. He'd want to take it for himself. But Jasper wouldn't let him. It was his. He found it. Worked hard for it.

He plodded back to the gate. *Go right.* He continued on down the road as far as the barn, a darker mass against the night. Not far. His lantern swung in the wind as if he were on a ship. *The ship of life*, he thought to himself. *I'm being carried along by the sea. There are dangers all around. Vicious creatures from the depths. Pirates, always pirates. But the harbour is in sight. Grace will be waiting for me. She always is.*

He lifted the bar and pushed open the barn door. It was dark inside, but the warmth and shelter reached out to welcome him. The reassuring smell of the cattle.

Somebody called out. "Who's there? Who's that? Identify yourself."

SAM WICKERS OPENED THE BEDROOM DOOR TO THE sound of the alarm clock shrilling away unheeded. Sam and Tim had a small room at the back of the Mohan house. There was only one sagging double bed, which they had to share, and the meagre furniture was scruffy, but boarding with Mrs. Mohan suited them.

He walked over to the alarm clock and switched it off. Then he leaned over Tim and shook his shoulder, hard.

"Come on. Get up. We've promised rabbits to at least six people and we don't want to disappoint them."

"Sod them," muttered the other man, opening one eye. "It's not even bleeding daylight yet. How come you're dressed already?"

Sam pulled away the blankets. "Get up! Now!"

Tim curled up tighter. "Please, Sam. I can't go. My ankle's killing me. I can't even get my boot on. Let me sleep just a bit longer."

Sam stood over him for a moment. "All right, you lazy sod. I'll give you half an hour. I'll go and lay the nets. But when I get back, no mithering or moaning. You'd better be ready to go."

"I will," muttered Tim. "I promise."

"Half an hour. That's all. Don't forget we've got to show our ugly mugs in court later this morning."

But his pal had already fallen back to sleep.

Sam paused for a moment to listen. Mrs. Mohan was elderly and slept in the front room of the farmhouse as she had trouble with the stairs. She was also hard of hearing, which made their coming and going in the wee hours of the night much easier. Mrs. Mohan didn't seem to be stirring yet.

Sam left the room, closing the door quietly behind him.

***

Tyler woke too early, unrefreshed and miserable. He'd hardly slept at all. Painful, angry dreams had tossed him around. *Storm outside, storm inside* was how he thought about it. The gale had worsened, and you could sail a ship in the draft coming in around the window frame. His bedroom was freezing. He'd slept in his socks and dressing gown and was reluctant to leave the snug warmth of his bed. But as soon as consciousness came flooding in, all he could think about was Clare's letter. *Give your love to somebody else.* How could she say that? If she had offered him words of love he would have waited till hell froze over. But she hadn't. Sure, it was hard, but thousands of people were going through separations. You just got on with things, and you waited. After a while the pain numbed. The ache in the arms at night subsided. That was how Tyler had been dealing with missing Clare for the last two years.

She's right, you know, whispered a traitorous voice in his head. *It's been too long.*

She might never be able to come back to him. Who knew how the war would end? Who would die and who would live? Then what? He didn't think he was cut out for permanent bachelorhood. But who could ever replace his love? The girl he had fallen for when they were children together. She'd left him once before, and he'd bounced into a marriage doomed from the start to be unhappy. Then, for a brief, brief, glorious season two years ago, she'd returned. To his arms, to his bed. A tantalizingly short time together.

Give your love to somebody else. Yeah? Who? Who could replace Clare?

He slid out of bed. Christ, it was perishing. Usually he heard the friendly sounds of his sergeant as Rowell trotted around the kitchen preparing breakfast, but not even that early bird was up yet. Tyler knew he was getting spoiled. Every morning, Rowell made the toast, had the kettle on the boil ready for tea. Almost as good as a wife but without the intimacy of sex. Sex! He'd practically forgotten what that was like. *Give your love to somebody else.* At this moment, it almost felt like good advice.

He hopped over to the window, his toes curling against the cold of the linoleum, and pulled back the blackout curtain. Rain fell in sheets past the window. He wondered if the weather was this bad where Clare was. Probably not. Probably Switzerland was bright and sunny with a blue sky and crisp white snow. If that's where she was. He didn't even know that for sure. She might have been reassigned to another country. She might even have been back in England and just not able to tell him. Perhaps the truth was that her love had died, and this dismissal was just a ploy to get him off her conscience.

No, in spite of his distress, he believed the letter. He trusted in Clare's loyalty. For whatever reasons, she was pretty sure she wouldn't be coming back for a very long time.

He leaned his forehead against the icy windowpane. He hoped she was at least safe. *Give your love to somebody else.* How the hell could he do that unless he knew what had happened to her? He dropped the curtain and skittered to the wardrobe. Might as well get dressed and make himself useful.

Not for the first time, he made a mental note to do something about cheering up his living quarters. His bedroom was pretty basic in terms of furnishings, but he'd hung up two pictures after he'd moved in. One was a photograph of Jimmy and Janet taken on the boardwalk at Rhyl, where they'd all gone for a holiday one summer. They were skinny kids in bathing suits, sand still clinging to their legs. Jimmy had lost his front teeth but it didn't stop him grinning like a Cheshire cat. They were happy.

The other was an oil painting he'd discovered in the Whitchurch market two years ago. It was a portrait of Clare done by an artist she'd met in Europe. He'd bought it on the spot when he'd recognized her. Moving into this house had given him his first opportunity to actually hang it. He regarded it for a moment. Perhaps he should take it down, stuff it in the wardrobe. Why torment himself?

***

Tim awoke with a start. The oil lamp was lit, and he could make out Sam on his hands and knees on the floor.

"What're you doing?"

"I decided to check our earnings," said Sam. He slipped the chamber pot out from under the bed.

They never used it for its intended purpose but kept it to hold the profits from their little business. Mrs. Mohan never came into their room, and wouldn't have checked the chamber pot if she had. Sam removed the lid and upended the contents on the coverlet.

"Do you want to count it, Timmy, or shall I?"

"You. I trust you."

Sam glared at him. "What do you mean, you trust me? What the hell do you think I'm going to do? Slip a couple of shillings into my pocket?"

Tim raised his hands in a placating manner. "Keep your shirt on. I was only joking. Go ahead and count away. Shall I get up?"

"In a minute."

"Did you lay the nets?"

Sam shook his head. "No, I didn't. The wind was too fierce. It'll need both of us."

He stirred the pile of notes and coins in the pot. Tim pulled the blanket up under his chin for warmth and watched.

"Ten pounds all told. Well, ten pounds, two shillings, and ten pence. Mrs. Cooper gave us a shilling tip, she was so pleased with that big buck we sold her."

Tim peered at the money. "What we going to do with it all?"

"I've been thinking," answered Sam. "I know I said we could save it to start our own business, but I've changed my mind."

Tim frowned. "Not again."

Sam began to gather the notes together. "We'll buy a car first. How can we be proper businessmen without a car? Now would be a very good time to buy us a car. There's dozens of them these days sitting up on blocks getting rusty. People would be more than happy for us to take them off their hands. Some poor widow, for instance, whose old man has kicked the bucket, and she don't know what to do with that darned old Bentley sitting in the garage." He raised his voice into a falsetto. "'Of course you nice boys can have it.'" He knuckled his forehead ingratiatingly. "'Thank you, missus. There's an awful lot wrong with it but I'll give you a fair price.' 'Oh I know you will. You have such an honest face.'"

"Bollocks," snorted Tim. "Nobody's going to do that. It'll cost a lot more than ten quid."

"We'll get it."

"We won't get permission to drive."

Sam returned the money to the chamber pot and shoved it back under the bed.

"Leave it to me. There are ways."

Tim laughed. "And you knows all of them, don't you?"

Sam punched his pal on the arm, not too gently. "Good thing for you I do. You'd be as good as an unweaned calf without its teat if it weren't for me. Now come on. We can't stay out too long, we've got to be in court at ten o'clock."

Tim swung his feet out of bed and tentatively stood up. "Ow."

"Don't be such a baby. It's sprained, not amputated."

Tim hobbled over to the chair where he'd piled his clothes the night before and, shivering, started to get dressed.

"Shite. I hope we don't get a fine. You should have kept your temper, Sam."

"It was that bleeding pansy of a constable that got my goat. He could have looked the other way. We weren't doing nothing."

Tim grimaced. "I suppose you might say that. If you discount what we'd got hidden in our baskets."

"Good thing the stupid ponce didn't think to look. He was just too excited at writing down my naughty words."

Tim pulled his heavy jersey over his head, muffling his voice. "You're a misery this morning, Sam. What's the matter? Her husband come home early, did he?"

"None of your business," snapped Sam.

Tim emerged from the jersey. "Pardon me for asking. I'm your pal, don't forget." He dragged his boots out from underneath the chair and gingerly pushed his right foot into one, wincing as he did. He stood up. "Right, I'm ready."

The wind pounced on them as soon as they stepped out the door.

It was pitch-dark. It could have been the middle of the night. Sometimes when they went out on mornings like this, Sam fantasized that the world had stopped turning and there would never be daylight again. Perpetual darkness. Wicked things happened in the darkness. That's when animals killed their prey.

"Blimey, it's a bloody gale," said Tim.

There was a large rabbit warren in the copse that ran from the crest of the rise along the north perimeter of the Cartwright farm. Tim and Sam had been there before but, according to Tim, rabbits reproduced at such a rate that there was an almost endless supply for the picking.

"It's good to keep them culled. Makes the survivors healthy and stronger," he said solemnly. "It's a rule of nature."

Sam snorted. "If it's a rule of nature, it should apply to people as well, but I can't say I've noticed. Healthy men are being killed off by the hundreds, and them that's left don't seem stronger. The opposite. They's all old and decrepit."

Tim thought for a moment. "But that includes us, and we ain't old and decrepit."

Sam switched on his torch and led the way to the disused shed where they kept their ferrets. They both suspected Mrs. Mohan knew they kept the animals in there, and why, but she had never challenged them. If a rabbit appeared as a special gift for her to make into a stew, she accepted their feeble explanations. They'd come across the poor thing out in the field. A dog had got to it and they'd put it out of its misery. At least four such unfortunates had come to that end while they had been staying there. She didn't question them, just made tutting sounds at the disgraceful behaviour of the dogs that the farmers insisted on keeping.

Sam pushed open the shed door. The strong smell of the ferrets sailed out at them. They had three, a hob and two jills. One of the jills was pure white and a good hunter. Tim took her out of the pen and dangled her in his hands.

"How's my girl, then? Ready to go and chase some little bunnies for your dad?"

"Weeping Jesus," said Sam. "One of these days, the bloody thing is going to answer you."

"Ferrets are sensitive. They pick up mood just the way dogs do."

"Well, I'm rapidly getting into a bad one, so get a move on."

"I think Snowflake should stay at home. She's been off her feed a bit."

"She's probably knocked up again. Mr. Blizzard there is as randy as a goat . . . or a ferret. He won't stop until he keels over."

Tim returned the jill to the cage. "You might be right. I'll give her the time off. She can put her feet up."

"Lord help me," said Sam. "Will you please hurry up?"

Tim removed the brown male and put it in its carrying box. The remaining ferret reared on its hind legs, its nose twitching.

"You want to come, Digger?" Tim said. "All right then."

He stroked its long back gently then placed it in the other box.

"Let's go. Bunnies, prepare to meet your Maker."

***

Even though it was only a local court and dealt with lesser offences, the courtroom was intended to intimidate. It had been built at least four hundred years ago, when peasants knew their place and were made to realize the power and majesty of the law. The panelled walls were dark with age, the wooden benches shiny from use. The magistrates' seats were on an elevated platform, and the bench in front of them was massive and solid. Behind them, high on the wall, was the county coat of arms, and next to that a large clock. *Tempus fugit. And don't you miscreants forget it.*

Below the platform sat the two clerks of the court. The courtroom was not much warmer than the police station and

one of them looked quite padded. Tyler thought he was probably wearing a wool jersey or two underneath his official black
gown. The other clerk was a woman. The two could have
been related, Tyler thought, both elderly, both grey-haired and
rather stooped. She was typing rapidly. Facing all of them was
the defendants' dock, lower than the magistrates', of course.

Tyler had been directed to a bench at the side of the room,
positioned close to the magistrates – he was an upholder of the
law, after all. This was where the plaintiffs and any witnesses
sat. Across from them were two more benches for those who
were up on a charge.

The usher called out, "All rise," and the two magistrates
entered through the rear door. Tyler knew Desmond, the chief
magistrate, but the second man, a stringy fellow in baggy
tweeds, was a stranger to him. He had to be Mr. Wendell Hare,
retired solicitor. They took their seats and, with much rustling
and fidgeting, the other members of the court also sat down.
The male clerk handed a sheaf of papers to Desmond, who
popped a gold-rimmed pince-nez on his nose. Tyler thought
such visual aids had gone out of style decades ago, but obviously not.

Desmond said something to his colleague, who nodded vigorously. Rowell had read it correctly, Mr. Hare was going to
defer to the other magistrate on all matters.

Desmond was a local landowner, a member of the minor
gentry. He was a little shrimp of a man whom Tyler had met
at previous county sessions. Whether from some obscure set of
principles or from sheer bloody-mindedness, he never seemed to
consistently follow either common sense or fairness. Sometimes
he awarded maximum fines for minor offences and extolled the
work of the police; sometimes he went in the opposite direction, scolded the police officer who had laid the charges for
being overly zealous, and sent off an obviously guilty accused

scot-free, or with a negligible fine. You could never predict which way he would jump. Tyler found him intensely irritating. He and Rowell privately groused to each other. "He's Hitler's secret weapon, if you ask me," said the sergeant. "Keeping us all off balance."

The usher brought in Sir Edward Spence, who went to the dock. At least that was egalitarian, although Sir Edward's frown made it obvious he considered it an insult. He had a prominent beak nose, and Tyler wondered if that had anything to do with his affinity for hawks and kestrels. Perhaps it had grown that way as his passion developed . . .

His reveries were interrupted by Desmond's reedy voice. "My colleague, Mr. Hare, and I are in agreement. We see no solid evidence that Sir Edward was violating the law by taking the journey he did. As he has explained, he was investigating the possibility of using birds of prey for carrying messages, in much the way we have made such good use of pigeons."

Tyler couldn't believe any grown man would buy such a story, but Desmond was acting as if he believed it. Hare nodded.

Desmond appeared to be suffering from a heavy head cold and he blew his nose before continuing. "A man in Sir Edward's position has to be always aware of what is happening in his jurisdiction. Resourcefulness in these dangerous times is what we want at all levels of society. He was right to go and inspect those birds."

He turned to young Mady, who was standing in the witness box ready to present his case.

"Constable, I think you were overstepping your bounds when you charged Sir Edward with making an unnecessary journey. Case dismissed." Desmond smiled at the burly man in front of him. "On behalf of the court, Sir Edward, I apologize for taking up your time. Especially on a miserable day like this."

"Not at all, your worship. Justice must be served."

Spence's voice was unctuous and as greasy as lard on a frying pan.

Tyler growled to himself. *Well, don't get too comfortable, Sir Edward bloody Spence. We'll nab you on something else, sure as shooting, and I for one will make sure it sticks.*

He caught the eye of his young constable and gave him a reassuring nod. Poor lad looked as if he wished the floor would open up and swallow him. But he'd been quite right to nab the self-satisfied lunk currently preening himself. If Tyler had his way, he would fine the bugger ten pounds for wasting *their* time.

Sir Edward stepped out of the box and walked out of the courtroom with a tip of his head to the two men at the magistrates' bench.

The next case up was that of the two drunk and foulmouthed bicyclists.

The court clerk got to his feet. "We have next Timothy Oldham and Samuel Wickers, both of the parish of Bitterley, your worship. They are charged with operating a bicycle without proper lights on the night of Saturday, December fifth, contrary to bylaw L243. In addition, Samuel Wickers is charged with uttering rude and offensive language to a police officer on the night in question."

The usher went over to the two young men and indicated that they should go into the dock. One of them limped rather badly, but otherwise they seemed typical farm lads, sturdy and weather-beaten. At the same time, Tyler noticed an attractive, dark-haired woman enter the courtroom and take a seat on the witness bench. He wondered who she was. She was smartly dressed in a grey wool costume and jaunty green felt hat. She seemed too young to be a mother to either of the two young men, too old to be a girlfriend. His eye caught hers and he shifted his gaze, not wishing to appear overly curious.

Constable Biggs went into the box just vacated by Mady, ready to give his evidence. The two young men shuffled into position. They were dressed in the usual farmer fashion: tweed jackets, brown corduroy trousers, heavy boots. Both were holding their caps in their hands. The taller of the two was twisting his nervously. The other, however, had his head up and was glancing around the courtroom with a nonchalant air that verged on being cheeky. There was no acknowledgement between him and the woman who had just entered. Not related, then.

"State your name and occupation," said the clerk.

"Tim Oldham, farm worker," mumbled the nervous one.

"Sam Wickers, farm worker," said the other.

Desmond took over. "Well, you two, what do you have to say for yourselves? You're charged with being a menace on the highway. Riding a bicycle without proper lights, then having the audacity to insult a police officer who was doing his right and proper duty by apprehending you. According to our good constable here, you, Wickers, used offensive and obscene language. Is that true? What do you plead, guilty or not guilty?"

They both hesitated, then Oldham shot a quick glance at his pal before turning back to the magistrate. "I'm sorry, your honour – "

"That's not the way to address me." Desmond's head cold appeared to be making him particularly testy. "I'm not 'your honour.' You have to address me as 'your worship.'"

"Yes, worship."

Desmond sighed. "Continue. Were you under the influence?"

"I suppose we were," said Oldham.

"No supposing about it. Had you been drinking?"

"Yes, worship. But only cider."

"No difference. Drunk is drunk. You, Samuel Wickers, do you plead guilty or not guilty to the charges as read?"

"Guilty, with extenuating circumstances."

Desmond peered at him over the top of his pince-nez. "Good lord. Do I have a solicitor here before me?"

Hare chuckled at the brilliance of the joke.

"No, sir," said Wickers, not smiling. "I simply wanted to offer an explanation."

Tyler had to bite his own lip to keep back a smile. *The lad's got bottle, that's for certain.*

"Proceed," said the magistrate. "What is your explanation?"

"The battery on my lamp had run out. I tried to replace it but you know how scarce they are these days. We weren't going far, just up the hill from the Angel to Sandpits Lane. It was bright as day out and there were no pedestrians on the road, so we weren't going to hit anybody."

"Did you or your friend swear at the constable?"

"I'm afraid I did, sir. He grabbed hold of my handlebars so that I almost went arse over teakettle. I beg pardon, your worship, I meant to say I almost fell head first. I didn't know who he was, you see, sir. Could have been a fifth columnist. In the heat of the moment, it is likely an expletive jumped from my lips."

Tyler noticed the woman on the bench duck her head, presumably to also hide a smile. Desmond, however, was not amused. He sneezed violently, wiped his nose, and glared. Hare also frowned.

"Did it indeed? Well, I think doing a bit of time with hard labour might keep those so-called expletives under control."

Wickers nodded solemnly. "That is possible, your worship, although it is a problem I've had all my life."

Don't push him, my lad, he's got all the power in here, not you.

Tyler got to his feet. "Might I address the court, your worship?"

The magistrate looked at him in surprise, glanced at his colleague, and then nodded.

"Very well."

Tyler walked to the bench. He had to look up at the two magistrates. Desmond leaned in closer.

"Yes, Detective Inspector. What is it?"

"My constable was doing his duty, and he was quite right to charge these lads. But there has been no harm done, and they might be better employed elsewhere than in jail. They are both in a reserved occupation, after all. Could I ask for a remand of sentence and that they be released into my recognizance?"

Desmond screwed up his face. "We can't have youths like these flouting the law and getting away with it. I know their kind. They'll probably be the heroes of Sandpits Lane."

"That is not out of the question, sir. But there is work I can put them to around the station. It will save the council money, for one thing, both by not incarcerating them and by getting necessary repairs done."

Desmond turned to the other magistrate. "What's your opinion, old chap?"

Hare sported a straggly walrus moustache, which accentuated his rather lugubrious expression. He twisted one end of it.

"I think the inspector has a good point."

"Do you indeed?" Desmond tapped his pen on the blotter in front of him.

Go on, you tight-assed dinosaur. Give them a break. You were quick enough to let Spence go free when it was so obvious he was guilty.

"Perhaps in the spirit of the upcoming Christmas season, sir?" said Tyler.

Desmond looked around the courtroom. All eyes were on him. He went for magnanimity.

"Very well." He addressed the two young men. "Samuel Wickers and Timothy Oldham, consider yourselves lucky. I am hereby remanding you over to the recognizance of Detective Inspector Tyler for three weeks. When your case is brought back to this court, he will give a report on your conduct. In the event that you are foolish enough to further offend against the laws, I promise you, I will throw the book at you. Is that clear?"

"Yes, worship," said Oldham, who looked frightened.

"You will report to the inspector at the conclusion of these proceedings," continued Desmond. "Now, you may step down. You can wait in the next room."

Wickers' expression didn't change. Not exactly grateful apparently for Tyler's intercession, but Oldham ducked his head and beamed. The usher beckoned to them and they walked out.

"Next," snapped Desmond.

The clerk consulted his docket. "Mr. Lawrence Delderfield is in court to claim redress of losses. He is the manager of the Woolworth's store, sir."

"Bring him forward."

A round, middle-aged man stepped into the plaintiff's box. His hair was combed across a balding head and he was neatly dressed in a dark suit, although it was a bit on the tight side. He made Tyler think more of an undertaker than a store manager. He stated his name and occupation slowly and deliberately, as if the court clerk were hard of hearing.

Desmond flapped his hand impatiently. "I understand you have already given a statement about your reasons for appearing here today. However, for the purposes of the record, please repeat it to the court. Begin by stating the date and time of the offence."

"Yes, your worship. The offence took place five days ago. Thursday, December third. It was near closing time so that would place it about a quarter to five. In fact I was about to usher out the last customer and lock the door.

"I had seen the two boys come in some minutes earlier. Usually I keep an eye on youngsters who are unaccompanied because you never know what they will do. Some of them can be quite light-fingered, especially these days. I recognized these two from previous visits and, frankly, I've always been a bit suspicious of them. They're not local. However, I was called to help Mrs. Meadows, who had a rather heavy shopping bag and needed help carrying it out to her pram." Delderfield paused. "Mrs. Meadows uses a pram for conveying her goods rather than an, er, an infant."

Desmond hissed at him. "I would appreciate your getting to the point a little sooner rather than later. We don't have all day."

The Woolworth's manager turned pink with embarrassment. "Of course, your worship, my apologies. Well, when I returned to the shop, I saw the two boys were in one of the aisles. They didn't see me coming up behind them. One of them was handing an object to the other, who stuffed it into his coat. I immediately asked them what they were doing. They both looked very guilty and refused to answer. I repeated the question. Again no reply. I decided to investigate for myself, but when I attempted to open the coat of the younger child, he screamed, loudly. As I tried to get a better hold of him, the other boy began to kick at me. You can see the bruises on my legs, your worship."

He paused again, but Desmond showed no desire to see said wounds. Delderfield continued.

"All the time this one, the bigger of the two, was yelling the most vile obscenities. Very loud he was too. Well, in the ensuing struggle, we collided with the shelf where there was a display of china cups and saucers. They had been brought in from London especially for Christmas sale. The shelf collapsed and most of the china was broken. I have estimated the cost to the store at between ten and twelve pounds. I would like to be reimbursed for that cost, and also to see that these young hooligans are punished. They have no business being given the freedom and privilege of wandering about our streets. It is my belief they belong in a reform school."

Desmond pursed his lips and addressed the clerk. "The note here says they are evacuees, and the billeting matron is here to speak on their behalf."

"Yes, your worship. She is in court now." He nodded in the direction of the public bench.

She must be the smart-looking woman in grey, thought Tyler.

"Call her up. I'll hear what she has to say."

The clerk beckoned and the woman made her way to the witness box, stepping in through its little gate. She was taller than Tyler had first thought, and she walked straight-backed with a certain air of confidence. Not a woman to be easily intimidated, law court or no law court.

"Please state your name and address."

"Mrs. Nuala Keogh. I live at number two River Close, off Lower Broad Street." She spoke with an Irish lilt.

Desmond frowned, as if he had a personal grudge against the Celts. "Madam, you've heard Mr. Delderfield's statement, I presume."

"Yes, your worship. I have indeed. I have myself made a statement about the incident."

Desmond took a moment to blow his nose. Not a pleasant sound. "I have read that statement, madam, but in this instance I must give more credence to the evidence of Mr. Delderfield."

"Why is that, your worship? Perhaps you could be so good as to enlighten me."

Her voice was cool. *Oh dear*, thought Tyler, *this could get tricky.*

"He was directly involved in said incident. You were not."

She looked as if she was about to speak, but he lifted his hand to stop her.

"I realize you feel a certain sympathy and responsibility for these boys, madam, but we cannot tolerate such atrocious behaviour in this town. I have a good mind to send them off to a reform school where they can learn some proper manners."

From the flush that had suddenly appeared on Mrs. Keogh's cheeks, Tyler thought she must have the reputed Irish temper to match her accent.

"I don't think so, your worship. That would not only be cruel and unusual punishment, it would also be rather stupid."

Desmond stared down the length of his red-tipped nose at her. "I beg your pardon, madam. Did I hear you correctly?"

"I'm sure you did. I do not for one moment think these boys deserve to go to any such place. If you ask me, the manager overstepped his authority. He should not have grabbed ahold of the boy like that. His brother was only defending him."

The two court clerks were watching the proceedings with great interest. Tyler had the feeling that even in this lower court the magistrate had established a brutal authority that nobody questioned.

"According to Mr. Delderfield," continued Desmond, shaping his words with knife-edged precision, "not only was one of the boys stealing, he also inflicted considerable damage on valuable property. Do you understand?"

"Completely. But there is no proof that he was stealing. He'd had no opportunity to go to the till and pay for the goods – a bar of chocolate worth tuppence, I might add. The manager made a totally uncalled-for assumption."

"Hardly that – "

"Excuse me, sir, an uncalled-for assumption. As for the breakage, as Mr. Delderfield himself has admitted, that was an accident. Surely the damage to some cheap cups and saucers is hardly comparable to the damage that might occur to the minds of these two boys if you send them to be among true juvenile delinquents."

Desmond sat up straighter. The woman was standing only a few feet away from him, and Tyler was reminded of a standoff between two angry cats. If they had each had a tail, they would have been lashing them.

A moment elapsed, and the magistrate leaned back in his chair. Backing off a little? Hare was chewing on his lip.

"If you think it would be so detrimental to these boys to go to a reform school, then I, perforce, shall have them returned to their parents."

"You can't."

"I beg your pardon, madam. I can and I will if I think it necessary."

Mrs. Keogh's eyes glinted. "What I meant to say is that you *can't* because we have no idea where their parents are. The boys were sent over to England with the Kindertransport. I assume your worship is familiar with what that is?"

"Of course I am, madam," said Desmond. "Children were brought here from occupied Europe by a charitable organization. It was thought their lives were in danger."

"Not just 'thought,' your worship. They were indeed in danger."

Her voice was sharp and Desmond was momentarily taken aback.

"As I understand it, the majority of the children were German. Are these boys German?"

"No, they are Dutch of Jewish heritage. Their parents foresaw the catastrophe that was about to befall Holland and secured a berth for them on the very last boat to leave from Amsterdam."

"I see." Desmond's expression appeared to be softening.

"That was two years ago," continued Mrs Keogh. "Their parents stayed behind, and they have not been heard from for over a year. We don't know if they are alive or not. The boys were sent to London initially but, given the severity of the bombing there, they were forthwith evacuated to Wales. Unfortunately, that family was not able to keep them for health reasons. They were relocated to Ludlow. To myself."

"And when was that?'

"September of this year."

Desmond wiped his nose and looked at the Irishwoman through the mask of his handkerchief. "My dear madam, I commend your generosity in taking in these children. But we have been taking in many children since the war began, who are in similar circumstances who do not play Old Harry with our townsfolk if they are thwarted."

Mrs. Keogh wasn't backing down for a minute. "I don't think 'thwarted' accurately describes what happened, your worship. Jan has told me that he and his brother were in Woolworth's to buy some Christmas presents."

"Rather early for that, don't you know," interjected Hare.

Desmond nodded. "Quite so."

"They wanted to see what was available. They have saved their pocket money for that purpose. They were not stealing anything, just trying to make a choice. However, the manager immediately assumed they were shoplifting. According to Jan, Mr. Delderfield grabbed his brother, Pim, by the collar. He is a large man, and Pim is a small boy who has been severely traumatized by past experiences. He became frightened and cried out. Jan went to his aid and a struggle ensued, in the course of which the display of china was knocked down."

The magistrate pursed his lips. "Mr. Delderfield says the boy attacked him, as well as releasing a torrent of foul language that no customer should have to be subjected to."

"I heard what Mr. Delderfield reported," said Mrs. Keogh. "But I don't know how he can say for certain it was foul language. When they're upset the boys sometimes speak Dutch or Yiddish. Mr. Delderfield could have misunderstood what was said. Jan thought his brother, to whom he is most attached, was being threatened."

At this point, the manager, who had returned to his place on the bench, jumped up. He gave a little wave in the magistrate's direction.

"Yes, Mr. Delderfield?"

"Beg pardon, your worship, but I beg to differ with this lady. There is no doubt that the words the one lad was using were pure Anglo Saxon. I can repeat them, if you wish."

"No, I do not wish," said Desmond. "We won't sully the ears of this court." He wiped his sore nose, which was getting redder by the minute.

"Mrs. Keogh, what is your response to what Mr. Delderfield just said?"

"It is possible. Their first foster home was not the best. They did hear words that are not acceptable in polite society. I have been talking to them about this."

"It doesn't appear to have sunk in," said the magistrate irritably.

She shrugged. "In the excitement of the moment, I presume Jan resorted to some old habits. As we all might do."

Desmond shuffled his papers as if would have liked to shake her out of them. Hare stroked his moustache.

"The older boy seems to be the leader. Perhaps it would be better if they were separated as being together seems so easily inflammatory."

Tyler saw Mrs. Keogh inhale deeply. *Don't lose your temper, lady. You won't get anywhere with this moron if you do.*

To his surprise, she turned her head and her eyes met his. Whatever he was conveying, it seemed to help her, and when she spoke again her voice was less belligerent.

"I assure you, your worship, any separation of these two boys would be disastrous. To all intents and purposes they are orphans. The only family they have in the world is each other."

Tyler had the feeling that Desmond was not going to be swayed by any appeal to the milk of human kindness. He was right.

"That is all very well, madam, but these young hooligans who have been dropped in our laps must learn that they are in decent society here, even if it is not what they are used to. Who is going to pay for the damages and expenses incurred by Woolworth's?"

"I would assume that an American company as large as Woolworth's would have allowances for a certain amount of breakage, but, given the circumstances, I myself will cover the cost to replace the china that was destroyed."

Desmond sniffed. "What guarantee do we have that these boys will not reoffend in perhaps an even more violent way? According to you, they have come from a situation that might in itself have affected the balance of their minds."

Another deep breath.

Hold on.

"Shall I remind your worship that we are talking about a boy of fourteen and a boy of ten? We can hardly determine that they are unbalanced, no matter what unimaginable experiences they have gone through. They have both expressed much contrition over what happened in Woolworth's. I'm sure it will not happen again."

Although, with much effort, she had kept her voice even, her contempt for the magistrate was palpable.

"We can't just sweep this incident under the carpet."

Tyler had had enough. He got to his feet.

"May I address the court?"

Desmond didn't look too happy but he nodded. Tyler approached the bench.

"Excuse me, your worships, but perhaps I could offer a solution here."

"Yes, what is it, Inspector?"

"I would like to suggest we remand the case."

"Not again. This is getting to be repetitious."

"I don't think so, your worship. These are very different situations. If you will release the boys back to the care of Mrs. Keogh, I will personally take it upon myself to speak with them and to keep an eye on them. Make sure they will not be a danger to the community."

The magistrate pursed his lips. He turned to Hare. "What is your opinion, Wendell? Shall we allow it or not?"

The other magistrate hesitated.

Trying to see which side your bread is buttered, are you?

However, he whispered something to Desmond that Tyler couldn't hear, and the magistrate nodded.

"Very well." He flapped his hand in the direction of Mrs. Keogh. "Approach the bench if you please, madam."

The clerk jumped up so he could open the little gate of the witness box and she walked forward until she was shoulder to shoulder with Tyler.

"Mrs. Keogh, did you hear what Detective Inspector Tyler is proposing? I have the good of this town to take into account.

It's an assessment by the inspector or off to Borstal with them. Take your pick."

If it was possible for her back to get straighter, it did. "Needless to say, I will choose the assessment," she said. "I have to trust that the inspector will proceed with sensitivity. The boys are highly strung."

Desmond rapped his gavel on the desk with some force.

"I am remanding the case until January 4 of next year, when court will resume. Madam, you can speak to the clerk before you leave about the recompense to Woolworth's, and you can deal with the detective inspector here about setting up the interview." He checked his watch. "Court is now adjourned."

The clerk got to his feet. "All will rise."

The magistrates both stood up. With his ledger tucked underneath his arm, Desmond led the way through the rear door.

Mrs. Keogh started toward the clerk, but Tyler caught up with her.

"Excuse me, madam, I'll need to arrange a time to talk to the young lads."

"It's bloody ridiculous," she said. "The boys got frightened and what happened was an accident. Blathering on about reform school is utterly lacking in common sense. Not to mention compassion. What's wrong with the man?"

Her eyes were brown, and right now they were dark with anger.

Tyler had no answer to that. "I do sympathize, madam. Perhaps it's his bad cold bothering him today. His head's stuffed, as it were."

She blinked at him and allowed herself a little smile. "If I'd known that, I'd have brought him some camphor to inhale."

It was Tyler's turn to smile. "I suggest the sooner we get the interview over and done with the better for all concerned. When would be a good time?"

I'd like to see you again.

He was surprised at himself. Given the circumstances and his recent letter, it was not a thought he'd expected to have, but it had come unbidden. Nuala Keogh was brown-haired where Clare was fair, round where she was skinny. But there was something about her that reminded him of Clare. Maybe the way she'd gone to bat for her charges. Her directness and refusal to back down. On the magistrates' docket she had been listed as a widow. Not the grey-haired matron he'd anticipated, but then, he should have known better given the times. There were too many young women being made widows. He wondered what her circumstances were.

"We can be available after school today," she said. "But I'd like them to have their tea first. Will that be all right, or are you off duty by then?"

"No, that sounds good. Why don't I come to your house? It might be less intimidating for the boys to be in more familiar surroundings."

She smiled. A nice smile. "Thank you. I'm sure it will be." She turned to leave. "They really are good children, Inspector. They have had a worse time in their young lives than we can ever imagine."

"And they're lucky to have you for an advocate," said Tyler impulsively.

She raised her eyebrows in surprise, then nodded and walked away.

Tyler refrained from watching her and was saved from further self-admonishment by the rotund clerk who came hurrying up, his clipboard clutched in front of him like a shield.

"Detective Inspector, the two young men are asking if they can leave. I assume you will want to have a word with them before they go."

"Right. I do. Where are they?"

"In the anteroom, sir. This way."

Tyler followed him.

"Dreadful weather we're having, aren't we, sir?" he said over his shoulder. "What with these gales and the war, I don't know what the world is coming to. Dreadful."

Gales, war, and lovers who don't want you anymore. Dreadful indeed.

***

It had been well over a year now since he'd been captured. He could still remember the English soldier who'd taken him prisoner. He had a suntanned face, dusty khaki uniform, and Angelo noticed an inflamed sand ulcer on his shin. He stood over the trench where Angelo had taken shelter and waved his rifle at him. "Hands up." He jerked the rifle upward but the words needed no translation. Angelo shot his arms into the air.

Time froze. He'd wondered if this was to be his last moment on earth. Then what? No prayer sprang to his lips then, no feeling of where he might be going. His eyes locked with the Englishman's. What a strange intimacy passed between them. Potential killer and potential victim. There was no hatred in the other man's eyes. Is that what hell really is? To have hatred the last thing you ever see? And the opposite is to die looking into the eyes of love.

He'd climbed out of the trench, his legs so shaky he could hardly stand, but it was a physical fear only. He could not feel anything except this strange stillness of time. This exquisite connection with the Englishman. There were others on the sandy strip outside of the trenches, his fellows. They were all silent, only the English shouting. Excitedly shouting. Not quite serious, posturing really, but dangerous nonetheless. His captor waved the rifle to indicate that Angelo should walk over to the group, and he did, his hands still in the air. With his back to the Englishman, he could no longer see his face and for the first time he felt fear, an engulfing fear that both emboldened and weakened him at the same time. He had the sensation of losing his bones, as if the very skeleton of his body was melting. He was amazed his legs were still capable of moving.

He saw that the other captives had been told to sit down, hands on their heads. "His" Englishman gave him a prod in the back. Not hard, but enough. He was not a friend, don't fool yourself. Angelo looked over his shoulder and again their eyes met. He had brown eyes, the Englishman. He looked far more Italian than Angelo himself did, with his blond hair and blue eyes. Angelo actually smiled, as though his captor were a pleasing acquaintance. Much later, when it became clear his captivity was irrevocable, he thought about that smile. He could hardly think of anything else. Why had he smiled in such a manner at this enemy? When he saw the cold, hard eyes of other English soldiers as they rounded up the prisoners, when he saw the way they knocked them with their rifle butts, or kicked them on the legs, he understood why he had smiled. "His" English soldier had not hated him. He supposed he might have been afraid as most of them were afraid but it wasn't just that which had diluted the rage of the other, it was because he had seen Angelo as another human being. Another man like him, forced to be a soldier.

"Crying comes after laughter as sure as night follows day. It is God's will."

This was one of his Nonna's favourite sayings, said in a hushed voice, as if she were speaking for God himself. Angelo hated it. It was like an insidious poison eating away at joy.

He had known such joy last night. But afterwards had followed sorrow. Just as his grandmother had said it would.

***

Tyler found Oldham and Wickers waiting in the anteroom. Oldham was sitting on a bench, leaning forward with his head in his hands. Wickers was standing next to him, smoking a cigarette. Even the way he dragged on the fag revealed his pent-up anger.

"Right, you two. In case you didn't catch it first time round, my name is Tyler. Detective Inspector Tyler to you. We need to have a bit of a chinwag before you scarper."

Wickers blew out smoke, keeping it just barely within an acceptable distance from Tyler's face.

"We've got to get back to work, we do. We can't hang around here all day. There's always jobs to be done."

The young man was good-looking, Tyler thought, with tanned skin, wavy fair hair cut short, and blue eyes. He had the compact muscular frame of a man used to hard physical work. But there was an expression of shrewdness in his face that Tyler hadn't expected. For a minute, he wondered if the defiance and bravado weren't more of a pose than anything.

"Look, Wickers," said Tyler, "we're at war, in case you hadn't noticed. My constables have got plenty to do making sure nobody's cheating honest folks in the black market, never mind the everyday misdemeanours that thick lads like you think are funny. I don't give a toss if you're stupid enough to ride around in the pitch-black without your lights on. If you end up with a broken neck because you fell off your bike, that's your business. Mine is to enforce the rules, which are made for ignorant blokes like you. When you're out at night, you have to have some light on your vehicle. That includes bikes."

Wickers shrugged, not intimidated in the least by Tyler's rant. "Like we said, we could see well enough. We live here. We know the roads."

"I heard all that," said Tyler. "But I tell you what, Wickers. And you too, Oldham. What really ticked me off was the fact that you used bad language to my constable. You were almost ready to take a swing at him, according to his report. Now that, in my book, is a serious offence. You're lucky the magistrate listened to me. He could have had you both sent down for three months hard. That would have been really tough on the cows, I would imagine."

Oldham was staring at him in dismay, but Wickers only lowered his head a little while he stubbed out his cigarette.

"Cows? What cows?"

"I was under the impression you had urgent work to do. The only job that urgent is milking cows."

"No. Mrs. Mohan don't have cows. We're general handy-men, you might say."

Tyler could feel the younger man's tension. Wickers was a man who talked with his fists first.

He raised his voice slightly. "That's good to know. So you can report to the police station by one o'clock this afternoon. You'll spend two hours every day for the next week doing some work there."

"What sort of work?" asked Oldham.

"The station hasn't been given a good scrubbing for years. We'll start there."

"Christ. Scrubbing?" exclaimed Wickers. "Don't you have painting or fixing we can do? That's more up our alley."

"You've got to clean before you can paint and fix. Scrubbing it will be. And no swearing. We have a rule around the station. Anybody heard using the Lord's name in vain or any other profanity has to put a shilling into the Spitfire Fund." In fact, Tyler had just instituted this rule on the spot. "Got that?"

"Yes, sir," answered Oldham.

"Wickers? Got that? What I just said?"

The young man nodded.

"Say the words for me, Mr. Wickers. Say you have understood what I just said."

Wickers stared at him, but he was the one to look away first.

"I understand what you just said."

"I understand what you just said, *sir.*"

"I understand what you just said, sir."

"Good. That wasn't so hard, was it?"

Tyler knew that Wickers would rather have swallowed glass than wrap his tongue around *sir*, but the young man was obviously wily or experienced enough to know who had the upper hand.

"I'll see you at the station at one, then."

Oldham stood up, keeping his weight carefully on one leg. He was taller than his mate, brown-haired, but with the same husky build. At the moment, he looked so woebegone that Tyler almost felt sorry for him.

"What'd you do to your ankle?" Tyler asked.

"Twisted it in a rabbit hole."

Tyler didn't miss the flash of anger that his mate sent Oldham's way.

"At least, I – I think it was a rabbit hole," stuttered Oldham.

"Do what you can, then. Your pal here might have to do the lion's share of the work. All right with that, Wickers?"

"Course."

"Go on, then. Off with you."

"Come on, Tim," said Wickers. "Let's get out of here."

Tyler let them go a few paces. "Oh, by the way, boys, you were obviously three sheets to the wind on Tuesday. I was wondering how you came to be so inebriated given the shortage of booze these days. It's almost impossible to even get tipsy with what they are serving at the pubs."

Oldham answered. "We was drinking cider. Powerful strong stuff, that is. Called Stun 'Em Dead. You don't need much of that, I can tell you." He grinned. "Cheaper that way. Two pints is all we need."

"Good to hear that. Because I wouldn't want to think you'd been trafficking with somebody who's selling black market liquor. I'd expect you to turn him in, if that was the case. National interest. Selling on the black market is a serious offence, but so is buying."

"We know that," interjected Wickers. "We're very patriotic, aren't we, Tim?"

Oldham nodded vigorously.

"And where was it you imbibed this Knock 'Em Dead cider?" asked Tyler.

Oldham hesitated for a moment, but Wickers gave him an almost imperceptible nod. "The Feathers. And the proper name's *Stun* 'Em Dead, not *Knock* 'Em Dead."

"Right. Same result, presumably. And the publican's name?"

"Mr. Harold Johnson."

"He'll vouch for you then, will he? Just two pints of cider?"

Oldham shifted slightly. Wickers was the one to answer.

"It was a busy night. He might not remember."

"I'll ask him anyway. These chaps usually know exactly what their customers are up to."

Tyler was sure they weren't telling the whole truth. Didn't mean Johnson was crooked, but he might have turned a blind eye if the lads had brought in their own illicit booze. Men did it all the time in order to get around the regulations. Beer wasn't rationed but the supply was limited. Two strapping young men like these would need a lot of cider to get drunk. He didn't for a minute buy the excuse that they didn't have heads for liquor. Most farmers made their own strong cider and quaffed it down like water.

"All right then, boys, you'd better go and tackle your important chores. See you at one o'clock. Sharp."

The big clock on the mantelpiece bonged out the half hour as the men made their escape. Crikey. He'd almost forgotten his appointment, in spite of Sergeant Rowell's helpful reminder. Somewhat against his will, he'd arranged to meet with a Mrs. Hamilton, a purveyor of "sincere introductions for the single." Rowell had talked him into it only last week. Given the letter he'd received yesterday, he didn't know if this was perfect timing, or the opposite.

"Won't hurt, sir," Rowell had argued. "You know how difficult it is for men in our line of work to meet suitable prospects. At the very least, it'll make you get out a bit more."

"What if I don't like these women? Or they don't like me, for that matter?"

Rowell had shaken his head. "That's why Mrs. Hamilton is so good. She knows how to match people up so they're compatible. Look how well I've done with Dorothy. I'd never have met her without Mrs. Hamilton."

Two months earlier, Rowell had been introduced to a widow, Dorothy McPhail, through Mrs. Hamilton's service, and they'd got along like a house on fire. Where formerly all he'd talked about was his deceased wife, now Rowell's conversations revolved around Dorothy, what she thought, what she said. Tyler thought she was a sweet, placid sort of woman, who was a perfect match for his lonely, anxious sergeant.

Should he cancel the appointment? He had work to do at the station, but he didn't like to back out at the last minute. Better follow up and see what the lady had to say. He wouldn't have to take it any further if he didn't want to.

***

The two boys had managed to huddle into a corner of the school assembly hall. It was playtime, but because of the foul weather the children had not been allowed outside. The girls had remained in the classrooms but the boys had been sent to the hall so they could run around, and the noise in the close confines was deafening.

Jan and Pim were ignored. Jan had already shown he could react quickly if threatened and, in spite of his skinny build, his blows hurt. None of the other boys were willing to risk taunting them, and nobody was generous enough to coax them to join in the wild games of tag that sprang up spontaneously. Even though at least half a dozen of the children were evacuees from London and Liverpool, they had arrived shortly after the outbreak of the war and were now pretty much assimilated. They weren't sympathetic to these newcomers either. The brothers kept entirely to themselves. Pim never fought but he simply wouldn't join in. He stuttered badly, and he mostly hovered in the background, looking miserable. It didn't help that the boys had learned English in the East End of London when they'd first arrived in England. A lot of the other children couldn't understand them. Or professed not to.

Pim leaned in closer to his brother so he could make himself heard above the din of screaming schoolboys. From the beginning, Jan had insisted that they always speak English except in a dire emergency. Pim had almost forgotten how to speak his native language.

"What's g-going to h-happen, Jan? They won't send us to a camp, will they?"

He was on the verge of tears, and his brother patted his arm.

"Stop asking that. I've told you and told you, they don't have camps in England."

"Yes, they d-do. Carl Stein's uncle is on an island. He's been there for t-two years. He's an alien."

"That's different. That's the Isle of Man, and it used to be a holiday camp. He's in the lap of luxury."

"Why's he stuck there then?"

"He must be a communist."

"I don't th-think so."

"Well, even if he is, they won't kill him. The English won't do that."

Pim's voice was tremulous. "They might. You n-never know. Carl is a Jew."

Jan glanced around to make sure nobody was watching them. The bigger boys had started a game of leapfrog and two lines had formed down the length of the hall. Two teams, both intensely competitive.

Furtively, Jan pulled a small brown envelope from his pocket and opened it.

"Don't forget we've got this. It's our treasure. We'll get to see Queen Wilhelmina with this."

He picked out a thin, blackened coin, which he rubbed with the sleeve of his jersey until the silver edges shone softly.

"That's all v-very well, Jan," muttered Pim. "But who'll b-buy it? We don't even know if it's w-worth so much as sixpence."

"Don't be thick. Course it's worth more than sodding sixpence. First off, it's a piece of silver treasure. I showed you how old it was. *Regina* means Queen. This is a coin from the time of Queen Elizabeth. Whoever was king or queen was the one whose head they put on the money. Like now, it's King George."

Pim liked the King because he'd heard him speak on the radio, and he tended to stutter as well.

"Besides, the reason it's so valuable is because they's very, very scarce."

Pim regarded him dubiously. "What if everybody thinks we s-stole it?"

Jan had read more books than his brother and he knew a lot about treasure. "You don't bleeding well *steal* treasure, lummox. You *finds* it. Somebody else must have stole the frigging gold and silver and hid it. Then they made a map – which they lost, else they'd've found it again."

Pim raised his hand as if he were in the classroom.

"Christ. What?" Jan asked impatiently.

"Why'd they lose the map, Jan?"

"How the bloody hell do I know? They's scared some sod's after them. So they bury the treasure, see, but they have friends and they want them to know where it is in case something happens to them – "

"Like a b-bomb falls on them or something? Or they g-get taken away?"

"Don't interrupt. There weren't bombs in the Middle Ages. But they could have got killed by a sword or an arrow or some-thing like that. Somebody else finds the map and they's the ones who figure out where the treasure is."

"We didn't find no m-map, Jan. The old m-man must have dropped that coin on the road."

"I know that." Jan thumped his brother hard on the arm. "You're such a bloody drip sometimes. You have no imagination."

"Ow. You don't need to wallop me. I'm j-just asking is all. Besides, one c-crummy silver coin isn't exactly treasure."

"I know, I know. You don't have to bloody tell me. We might have to go on a treasure hunt soon."

"You m-mustn't swear, Jan. You said *sod* before. You know what Mrs. K. said about that."

"I didn't. I said *sot.*"

"Didn't sound like th-that."

"Never mind. Nobody heard. In fact, I'm thinking we should go back to the hideout and put this coin in a safe place until we can get out of here and go talk to the Queen."

"What if the old man sees us?"

"We ride off fast as the wind. Like we did on Sunday. He couldn't catch us, could he?"

Pim frowned. "Do you think he kn-knew we were Jews?"

"What! Of course he didn't. How could he? First off, it was foggy. Second, we look just like anybody else now."

Suddenly tears came to the younger boy's eyes, which he wiped away with the edge of his sleeve.

"Why're you sniffling?" asked Jan.

"I don't know if I want to be a J-Jew any more."

Jan drew in his breath sharply. "Don't be stupid. It's not something you can put on or off like a coat. Buck up. Things'll look better when Pappa and Mamma get here."

Pim rubbed at his eyes. "I think they're dead, Jan. I don't think we'll ever see them again."

***

A neatly printed card reading "MRS. W. HAMILTON" was pinned above an electric bell in a doorway next to the ironmonger's shop in Castle Square. Tyler pressed the bell, but then quailed. Was he ready to even think about meeting women – "suitable prospects," as Rowell had referred to them? Maybe he could pretend he was shopping at the ironmonger's and had got confused. He was on the verge of turning tail to flee when a woman's voice called to him from the top of the stairs.

"Come on up, Mr. Tyler."

He obediently tromped up the uncarpeted stairs to meet the purveyor of "Sincere Introductions."

Rowell had never described Mrs. Hamilton, and for some reason Tyler had expected a motherly sort of woman with apple-dumpling cheeks. But if Moira Hamilton had seen forty yet he'd be surprised. Her hair was dark and drawn up into plump, sausage-shaped rolls on top of her head. The only things about her that were in any way dumpling-like were her full, round breasts, which pushed against a snug, pink mohair jersey.

She must have caught his covert glance. "Most people are surprised when they first see me," she said with a smile. "They think I'm going to be some old dear in a shawl. But I've been a happily married woman for ten years, and what better credentials are there for bringing together people who are looking for love?"

Tyler could see her point but he almost winced. He wasn't yet ready to admit he was indeed looking for love. Not from anyone but Clare, that is.

Mrs. Hamilton stepped aside so he could enter the flat. It was warm, and there was a fragrant smell of cinnamon in the air.

"Give me your hat and coat," she said. "You must be perishing. Why don't you go and sit down. I'll make us some tea. The kettle just boiled."

"Something smells delicious."

Moira Hamilton herself had a nice flowery scent. He hoped she didn't think he was referring to her.

"I've been baking some pies with the last of the apples. I'm going to keep one and give the other to the church fete next Sunday. They're raising money for the rebuilding of Coventry Cathedral."

The flat was really one large room with a kitchen at one end. The sitting area was a grouping of stuffed chairs arranged around a tiny electric heater.

"I'll only be a jiffy," said Mrs. Hamilton. "Take that wingback. It's the most comfortable for men."

Tyler did as ordered and sat down in the brocade-covered armchair.

There was a faux mantelpiece against the wall with the heater in place of a hearth. He could see several cards, most of which seemed to be early Christmas greetings. One had the words *Thank You* in large letters crusted with silver glitter. Presumably from a grateful customer.

He took a fast look around. There wasn't much more furniture, just a table and two more chairs near the kitchen area. A small rag rug in front of the heater was the only concession to comfort. The most impressive feature was a mahogany rolltop desk standing against the wall between the two deep front windows.

Mrs. Hamilton wheeled a tea trolley over and manoeuvred it into position next to his chair. She removed the knitted cozy from the pot and poured out the tea into his cup.

"Milk? Sugar?"

He accepted both.

"I do find the tea ration above all is so difficult to manage, don't you, Mr. Tyler?"

Not being much of a tea drinker he actually didn't, but he agreed politely.

She poured a cup for herself and sat down in the chair across from him. She kept her knees decorously together but she had good legs and was wearing a skirt that looked to him a bit shorter than the prevailing fashion.

She gazed at him over the top of her cup. "I've made myself hold out until now. This is only my second cup of the day, and I do so enjoy it."

He sipped at his tea, willing himself to relax. This was shaping up just the way he'd dreaded. Awkward as all get-out.

You can leave. Say you've just remembered an urgent appointment. This isn't for you.

But before he could act, Mrs. Hamilton placed her own cup and saucer on the trolley.

"Well, I'm sure you don't have a lot of time, so why don't we get straight down to business?"

He sighed. "Of course. Let's get right to it." He swallowed down the rest of his tea.

Moira gave her knees a little slap. "First, then, is the matter of my fee."

"Fee?" Rowell hadn't mentioned a fee, but of course nobody would go to all the trouble of running a dating agency from the sheer goodness of their heart.

"I charge one pound for the initial interview," she continued. "Non-refundable. If we agree that you are a suitable candidate, you will pay a further three pounds, which will entitle you to three introductions with women chosen for you especially by me. If, after sincere attempts, none of these introductions work out for the long term, then you are allowed one more free introduction."

Tyler raised his hand in protest. "Just a minute, Mrs. Hamilton. Let's be clear. I don't consider myself to be in the marriage market, and from the way you are describing your, er, service, that would seem to be the goal of all and sundry."

She didn't answer but jumped abruptly to her feet and went to the desk. All of her movements were brisk and decisive. She would have made a good private secretary, Tyler thought. She returned to her chair holding a ledger that surely belonged in a law office.

"I specifically state that my job is to provide sincere introductions to single people. What you do with yourselves after that introduction is entirely up to you. Some people have found marriage partners, some have found good friends." She smiled. "Some are content to be, shall we say, lovers."

Oh God. He had one lover and that was Clare Somerville. Currently far from him. Perhaps forever.

"How long have you been . . . in this line of work, Mrs. Hamilton?"

"Five years now. We were living in Manchester when I started. My husband has trained as an engineer and he travels a lot. I was bored and lonely so I thought I should take up some kind of suitable work. He was only too happy to support me. 'Keep you out of mischief, my girl,' were his words."

Tyler wondered if Moira was prone to getting into mischief, and of what sort.

"Anyway, even back then I could see that people some-times needed help finding a partner they could get along with. Now, with the war on us, it's even more difficult. You think it wouldn't be what with all the dances happening. But let's face it, they tend to be for the younger crowd. But my clientele are rather more mature. A little nervous about jumping into the melee of the jitterbug. I must say, my business has thrived since the war began. Walter was afraid it would drop off with the current loosening of moral standards. Who needs a match-maker when you can pick up a girl at any time in the local pub or dance hall? Fortunately, that has not been the case. More than ever, people seem to need a compass in the sea of uncer-tainty that surrounds us."

Aptly put. Not to mention the poetic turn of phrase. Me, I'm barely keeping my nose above the waves.

Mrs. Hamilton was wearing cherry-red lipstick, which emphasized her full lips. She had a way of pouting those lips when she was making a thoughtful point.

"Does your husband still travel a lot?" Tyler asked.

"He's been conscripted into the Royal Engineers," she said with a sigh. "Fortunately, he's too valuable to be sent to the front lines so he's stuck behind a desk down in London. I don't even know what he does. It's all terribly hush-hush. He can only get away every couple of months."

"That must be hard on both of you."

She beamed at him. "Let's just say it makes our reunions that much more delightful."

Tyler wrenched his imagination away from the luscious Moira reuniting with her doting husband in a delightful way.

She opened the ledger. "Are we all right with the fee, then? Shall we go ahead?"

"Yes, of course."

"I like to get payment in advance. You'd be surprised how many men get cold feet."

"No, I wouldn't be surprised at all. But I didn't come prepared with that amount of money. Can I drop it off to you later?"

"Certainly you can. Cash or bank draft is fine. Besides, you are an officer of the law. If I can't trust you, whom can I trust?"

"Precisely."

She turned to a blank page in the formidable ledger.

"Righty-o. I'll need to get some information from you." She began to write. "Age?"

"Forty-four."

She didn't comment. Neither the flattering "You don't look it," nor the chilling opposite – "Only forty-four?" – which was what he half expected these days.

"Marital status?"

"Divorced."

Pity. Not everyone wants to commit to a divorcé.

"One failure already, is that the idea?"

"In a way, although the issue is more that the first marriage can cast such a shadow over any new love."

Her eyes met his. She had pretty blue eyes and long eyelashes, he noticed. "Who was it, if I may be so bold as to ask, who left the marriage?"

Tyler hesitated. "I'd say it was a mutual decision."

When Moira spoke next her voice was soft. "I'm sorry for my next question, Mr. Tyler, but I am obliged to ask it. Are you still in love with your ex-wife?"

"Good lord, no." Seduced by her expression of kind under-standing, he added impulsively, "I probably never was."

She wrote something in the ledger. "Any children?"

"We had a boy and a girl. Only my daughter is living. My son was killed two years ago."

"I'm so sorry to hear that. A casualty of war?"

"Yes, you could say that."

She looked at him, obviously waiting for him to expand on his statement, but Jimmy's violent and untimely death was not something he wanted to talk about.

She returned to her ledger. "Now, just a few questions about yourself, Mr. Tyler. How would you describe your personality?"

"Not sure what you mean."

"Well, would you say you are generally a cheerful, optimistic sort of person? Or do you have trouble feeling hopeful about the future?"

"These days, only fools would be always cheerful, wouldn't you say, Mrs. Hamilton?"

She gave a little shrug. "You have a point. But we can't suc-cumb to despair, either, can we? I'm sure Herr Hitler would like that. It is not an emotion that I myself subscribe to."

But you have a loving husband who can't wait to get home so he can take you in his arms and caress those full breasts and thighs.

"Mr. Tyler?"

"Sorry, just thinking. Ask away."

She did, and soon filled the page. Some questions were easy to answer. What kind of music did he like? Vera Lynn got to him every time. He enjoyed Gracie Fields. Glenn Miller was a toe-tapper. Who was his favourite comedian? Tony Hancock. What writers did he like? Lots of them. Shakespeare, for one. A lift of the eyebrow at that but it was true. Graham Greene. George Orwell.

A more thought-provoking question came next. What sort of woman did he enjoy being with? "Depends." A little more probing and he offered the answer, "Clever women, I suppose. Honest. Straightforward." She seemed to like those answers and underlined them in the ledger.

"My final question, Mr. Tyler, and a rather important one. Do you enjoy intimacy? Of the physical kind, that is."

He wanted to cry out, "You bet I do! I haven't had sexual relations for two years." However, he settled for a more decorous, "Definitely."

"Splendid. That's all for now." She took another piece of paper from the folder. "Here is my standard contract. It guarantees you three introductions. There will be no refunds. If there are unexpected circumstances that mean the introduction is not completed I will replace that introduction with another at my discretion. Clear?"

"What might be a circumstance of incompletion?"

She pouted her lips in a rather mischievous way. "One of my clients considered herself to be a widow and was ready to meet another man . . . when her husband returned."

"Not dead, then?"

"Not at all. Reported to be missing in action in North Africa but he was only wounded."

"You removed her from your list?"

"Good heavens, yes. It was a most joyful reunion, I must say."

Mrs. Hamilton seemed to admire reunions, thought Tyler.

"Just sign on the bottom line, if you please." She stood up and went back to the desk. Tyler kept his eyes firmly fixed on the piece of paper that might or might not be determining his future. She returned with a folder. "I currently have three women on my list who, in my opinion, are most suitable candidates. I will make the initial contact, give you a little introduction, as it were.

Then I will send you a letter with the place and time of the first meeting. I always recommend you make an appointment to meet first of all in a public place. At the pictures, or a restaurant, for instance. A dance can be too intimidating initially. Many men do not consider themselves to be Fred Astaires on the dance floor and things can get off to an unnecessarily awkward start."

"That's me for sure," said Tyler.

"It might be worth taking some proper lessons."

"Maybe."

"Pictures or restaurant, then?"

"I think it'll be the pictures."

"Good choice. There's an American comedy playing at the Clifton. It's quite amusing. I would like you to come in again after each meeting and let me know your impressions and so forth. The women will do the same."

Wow, this is indeed a business, thought Tyler. *I didn't expect to be marked.*

"What happens if I am completely satisfied with the first woman I meet? Do I have to make a date with the other two?"

She nodded. "I always advise it. Hedge your bets. But do be honest with them. You don't want to deceive anybody, do you? No broken hearts, thank you. We've got more than enough of those to go around these days."

She picked up the teapot. "More tea?"

He flapped his hand. "No, thanks. That was more than sufficient."

"I'll get your hat and coat, then." She paused. "The reason I asked you about your wife, Mr. Tyler, whether or not you were still in love with her . . . I had the impression that your feelings had been badly hurt, and that it might be difficult for you to give your heart to somebody else."

For a moment, Tyler could only gape at her. Then, "Don't worry about me, Mrs. Hamilton," he said. "I'll be all right."

***

Playtime was over and Miss Lindsay was ringing the handbell with great gusto, the signal for the children to line up ready to return to their classrooms.

Jan grabbed his brother's arm. "Soon as school's over, we'll ride the bike to the hideout."

"Why?"

"We've got to put our treasure in a safe place, for one thing. We don't want anybody taking it from us. We've got to check on our supplies as well. Soon as the weather lets up we'll be able to go to London."

"Jan, I don't w-want to get into any more t-trouble."

"We won't, I promise. I'll ask Wally Green to tell Mrs. K. we've had to stay behind at school."

"What if she checks up on us?"

"She won't. She told me, 'cause of going to court this morning she has to stay late at the library. She won't be home until seven. We'll be back by then. If she does find out, we'll say we were all cut up about the manager accusing us and we needed to be alone. She's a softie. She won't rag us."

Pim chewed on his lip. "I dunno, Jan. Besides, it's p-pissing down with rain. We'll g-get soaked."

"We ain't made of sugar. And we've got those macks Mrs. K. bought for us."

"What if we get hungry?"

Jan reached into his pocket and took out two small bars of chocolate. "We've got these. We can have one today and keep the other for later."

Pim covered his brother's hand with his own. "Don't let anybody see them. We'll really g-get sent away then."

Miss Lindsay gave the bell another a vigorous shake.

"Playtime's over now, boys. Let's start lining up. No tarrying. No more talking."

"Stay here," said Jan, and he scurried over to the line that was slowly forming and pushed in behind a small boy with pinched features. Wally Green was an early evacuee from Liverpool. So far, no amount of country air and better food had fattened him up.

Jan tapped him on the shoulder. "Hey, Wally, do me a favour, will you?"

"Depends what it is."

"I want you to take a message to Mrs. Keogh."

"What sort of message?"

"Tell her Pim and me have had to stay at school for a bit. Say we got detention."

"Is it true?"

"Course it isn't. We just don't want to go home right away."

"Why not?"

"Doesn't matter why not. Will you do it? It's on your way. She'll be at the library."

"I don't like fibbing for other people. What if she don't believe me? Then I'll be the one in trouble."

"No you won't. I'll never tell. Come on, Wally. That's not a lot to ask of a mate. I'll give you me new comic. It's a *Beano*."

"I've got a *Beano*."

"A *Beano* and me best marlie."

"I don't – "

"And I won't tell the teacher you took a leak against the school gate yesterday."

"I did not," said Wally, full of indignation.

"I saw you. Both me brother and I did."

The other boy hesitated. "I was caught short."

"I believe you, but the dragon won't. Is it a deal or not?"

The harsh bell clanged again.

"Those who aren't in line by the time I count to ten will get a detention," called out Miss Lindsay. She'd been evacuated from London with her class and she'd brought her city ways with her. Detentions, previously unheard of, were one such innovation.

The local children both feared and hated her and did what they could to defy her whenever possible. Delaying tactics at the end of playtime was one small way they could get back at her.

"All right," muttered Wally. "A *Beano* and your best marble? No welching, and no blaming me if she finds out the truth."

"Spit on my hand, cross my heart, and hope to die."

"I thought you was a Jew. Jews don't cross their hearts."

"Course we do. It's all the same."

He suited his actions to his words and pressed his palm against Wally's. Then he hurried back to where his brother was waiting.

"He'll do it."

Pim looked worried, but he followed his brother to the line that was now moving slowly in the direction of the doors.

***

Sergeant Rowell was seated behind the reception desk when Tyler entered the police station.

"How'd it go?"

"Fine. Good. She's a shrewd woman. Very pleasant too."

Rowell beamed. "I told you so."

"You didn't tell me she was also a nice bit of crumpet."

The sergeant threw up his hands. "I wanted you to go to the meeting with no preconceptions."

"Nor did you mention I had to pay."

"It's worth every penny. You'll see. You're going to follow up on it, I hope."

"For three pounds, you bet I am."

Behind a low glass partition was the common area, and Tyler glanced toward the young constable sitting at his desk. Even from a distance Tyler could see Constable Mady's eyes were alive with curiosity. He leaned closer to Rowell.

"Oliver, if you so much as breathe a word to anybody about this I'll skin you alive."

"I wouldn't dream of it, sir. It's your own private business." He grimaced. "I did mention to Dorothy that I'd recommended Mrs. Hamilton to you, but that's all."

Tyler sighed. It would be all over town before he knew it. He might as well have put an announcement on the BBC: *Lonely, sexually starved copper, divorced, seeks understanding woman. No strings attached.*

"Remember, Oliver – loose lips sink sergeants."

"Yes, sir."

"All right. Now, let's get back to being coppers, shall we? Did those remand lads come in yet?"

"Not yet. But while you were away, I took the opportunity to send young Mady to have a chat with the publican."

"And?"

"He says the boys had a couple of pints of cider. All legal and above board. He was too busy to notice their level of inebriation."

"Just a couple?"

"Apparently."

"Perhaps the stuff is as strong as they claim."

Rowell pointed to the waiting area. "There's a lady come in who wants to speak to you urgently."

If he hadn't said it was a woman, Tyler wouldn't have known. She was standing with her back to him, looking out the window, wearing a nautical sou'wester and a shapeless heavy black waterproof.

"Her father-in-law's gone missing," continued Rowell. "Old chap. He hasn't been seen since last night. She's worried something might have happened to him. Especially in this weather."

"What's the name?"

"Cartwright. She's Susan. Father-in-law is Jasper."

At that moment, the front door crashed open and Sam Wickers and Timothy Oldham came in. Blew in was more like it. A gust of wind snatched at the door and took the cap off the younger one's head. He chased it down quickly.

"Come in, why don't you, lads," said Rowell. "Make yourselves at home."

Mrs. Cartwright turned round at the ruckus and Tyler saw that she was younger than he had first thought. Despite her rough-and-ready apparel, her features were rather delicate.

"I'll be right with you, madam," he called over to her. He nodded at his sergeant. "Take her into my office. I'll just get this lot sorted."

Rowell came around the desk and ushered the woman into Tyler's office. In the meantime, the two young men were shaking out their wet caps and generally making loud *brrr* noises.

"All right, you two," said Tyler, "I get the picture. It's cold and wet out. Don't worry, I'll give you something to get your blood flowing. You'll be warm in no time." He pointed to the hooks on the wall. "You can hang your things there."

He turned to the constable, who had been watching the proceedings with great interest. "Mady. Come here, will you? Constable, this here is Sam Wickers and his chum Tim Oldham. One of our fellow officers, Constable Biggs, had the misfortune to be doing his duty when these two decided to not only disobey him but to disobey with foul and abusive language. Now, as upholders of the law, we take a very dim view of that sort of behaviour, don't we, Constable?"

Mady nodded. He was a skinny, round-shouldered young fellow with a squint in one eye. That, together with his flat feet, had meant he hadn't been conscripted.

"What do you want for us to do, Inspector?" asked Wickers. "You said two hours' work. We've got chores piling up on the farm so we'd like to get going."

"How nice to see you so eager," said Tyler. "All right. First off, this floor needs a good mopping."

"It's pouring rain out," said Wickers with a jerk of his head. "People are going to be tramping in and out in their muddy boots."

"All the more reason to stay on top of it, then. We don't want the public to think we police officers live in a pigsty. Oldham, you can start with the floor. Wickers, you can tackle the wc It's been getting a bit whiffy of late."

"That's skivvy work," snarled the young man.

"Is it now? Well then, good thing you're here because we don't have a skivvy." Tyler placed a hand on Mady's shoulder. "You'll answer to Constable Mady. If I hear one peep of disrespect coming out of your mouths, I will personally lay charges. And you won't get soft treatment this time, I promise you."

He knew that Wickers would love to have protested further, but all he could do was glower.

"All right then. On the double. Even you, Oldham. Hop if you have to. Constable Mady will show you where to get your mop and brush. I will inspect the job before you leave. If it's not satisfactory, you will do it again. The cows will have to cross their legs."

Mady started for the rear door and the two men began to meander after him.

"I said *on the double!*" Tyler yelled. They jumped and quickened their pace.

Rowell had come out of Tyler's office and seen most of this display.

"Brazen pair, aren't they."

"Wickers is. Oldham is just a follower. Well, I'd better speak to Mrs. Cartwright."

"I warn you, sir, she's in quite a tizzy. She wants us to go out and search for the old man right away."

"Fat chance of that. We haven't got the manpower. Who's on duty besides Mady?"

"Biggs is doing some sorting in the storage closet. Chase called in sick, he's got the flu."

"Constable Mortimer?"

"She's over at the school. The headmaster asked if we'd send somebody to talk to the nippers about safety during the blackout. She should be back soon."

Tyler went into his office and took a seat behind his desk. Mrs. Cartwright had removed the sou'wester, revealing greying hair smoothed into a bun at the nape of her neck.

"Good afternoon, madam. My sergeant tells me that you're concerned about your father-in-law."

"Yes, I am. We haven't seen him since last evening. I'm afraid something might have happened to him. I want to report him as missing."

"Has he ever disappeared before?"

"Yes, but never for more than three or four hours at a time." Her gaze shifted. "We didn't miss him right away. He doesn't always come down for breakfast, you see. Depends on how he's feeling. So this morning I didn't bother to check on him. Then he didn't answer to the midday dinner call, and that isn't like him. I sent my son up to take a look and he could see that Jasper – Mr. Cartwright – must have gone out in the early hours. He hadn't even got dressed. There were no sign of his pyjamas, you see, and his daytime clothes were still on the chair."

Tyler looked at her. "That doesn't sound too good. Dreadful weather last night. Any reason you can think of why he'd go out in his night clothes? Do you have an outdoor privy, for instance?"

"No, we've got a proper indoor one. He didn't have any need to go outside." She clicked her tongue. "My father-in-law is not himself is the problem. He gets confused."

"Do you think it's possible he's taken shelter somewhere – with a neighbour, perhaps – and is waiting out the gale?"

"Any neighbours would have come and let me know. They'd know we'd be worried."

"Where did he go when he wandered off before?"

"Usually he just goes to the fields or to the barn, but then he forgets how to get back. My husband has had to go fetch him more than once." She took a handkerchief from her pocket and wiped at her eyes. "I'll never forgive myself, Inspector, if something has happened to him. He's an old man. He shouldn't be out in this weather."

Tyler tapped his fingers on his desk. He hardly had enough men for a search party. On the other hand, he couldn't in all conscience leave matters unexplored.

"Have you made any attempts to find him yourself?"

"Of course we did. When we realized he wasn't in his room, both John, my husband, and my son went out to look for him. They found his lantern in a ditch alongside the north field but no sign of him. So I said we'd got to get the police in on this."

"You say his mind is going, but how is he physically?"

"Fit as a fiddle. Been a farmer all his life. Tragic it is, really. He's a proud man. Hates the fact that he isn't what he was. I do my best. We all do. This is my second marriage, you see, but from the start I've tried to be a daughter to him. But he can be very trying."

Something about the way she said that made Tyler think she wasn't presenting the situation as bad as it was.

"Where do you live, Mrs. Cartwright?"

"We're on the Old Pike Road just outside of Bitterley village. I drove here in the lorry. I can give you a lift if you want."

"Let me just check with my sergeant. I'll be right back."

Tyler went out to the desk.

"Oliver. It doesn't look too good concerning the old chap who's missing. I'm going to have to take a look for myself. I'll register a report if necessary. I'll leave Mady with you but Biggs can come with me."

The front door slammed open again and Constable Agnes Mortimer entered. She saw Tyler and grabbed the handle so she could close the door more quietly.

"Sorry, sir. Wind caught it."

"You came just in time, Constable. I'm going out to check on a missing person. His daughter-in-law is the one making the report and she's pretty upset. The old fella may be sitting by the fire by now smoking his pipe, but given this weather, I'd rather get out and see for myself. I want you to come with me in case we need to take a look around the farm."

Rowell sucked in his breath. "Just remembered, sir. The Austin is in the shop again. A problem with the starter motor. Won't be fixed until this afternoon."

"Damn. I keep telling you, Oliver, we need to invest in some reliable Percherons."

"Does that mean the motorcycle and sidecar, sir?" asked Mortimer.

"For you it does. Mrs. Cartwright has offered me a lift in her lorry. You can bring Biggs. And for God's sake, don't go too fast."

"I won't, sir. We'll follow behind you."

"All right. Let's go."

—

Tyler considered his young female constable to be a mad driver, but she was positively sedate, he thought, compared with Susan Cartwright. The battered lorry had lost a lot of its suspension and swayed wildly at every curve, so that Tyler expected they might skid into the ditch at any moment. The driving rain obscured the view through the windshield, which sported a long vertical crack. This did not impede Mrs. Cartwright, who drove at breakneck speed. She didn't speak until they had passed Bitterley and turned onto a dirt road.

"We're just over the hill."

Tyler looked over his shoulder. The motorcycle and sidecar had kept close behind them, although he could have sworn that Mortimer had taken a couple of the turns on two wheels. He pitied Biggs.

The lorry turned off the road and jolted through an open gate and across a muddy, cobblestoned yard. The farmhouse was old, and probably in sunlight, in summer, with roses climbing up the trellis, it would be charming. Now it was bare and tired-looking, and the white-painted walls seemed dingy.

As the lorry pulled up, the front door opened and immediately a man came out. He was clearly a farmer, and Tyler guessed this was Susan's husband. A younger man, smaller and slimmer, stood at the threshold. He could tell by their expressions they'd had no luck in finding Jasper Cartwright.

John Cartwright had an umbrella, which he opened after a tussle with the wind. He came around to the driver's side and his wife rolled down the window. The younger man stayed in the shelter of the doorway.

"Anything?" Susan asked her husband.

"Not a sign. Can't imagine where he's got to."

Mrs. Cartwright indicated Tyler. "This is Detective Inspector Tyler. He's come to take a look. He's got two constables with him in that there motorcycle. Apparently, that's all the man-power he could muster up, and one of them's a lassie."

"Come in't house," said Cartwright. "We can do a reccy where it's dry, at least. Wait there a minute, sir. I'll bring the brolly."

He ran around to the passenger side of the lorry, leaving his wife to make her own way. Tyler climbed down stiffly. He would have liked to rub some feeling back into his buttocks but thought it might look undignified. John Cartwright held the umbrella over his head and they dashed to the house.

Constable Mortimer had switched off the motorcycle and was helping Biggs out of the sidecar. She had covered herself in a long waterproof for the drive, but Biggs looked thoroughly chilled. Tyler beckoned to them to follow.

***

Riding into the strong headwind was hard work and the cold rain was ferocious. It took the two boys more than half an hour to get from school to their hideout. They had only one bicycle, so Jan pedalled and Pim rode on the crossbar. But the sturdy mackintoshes and caps that Mrs. Keogh had bought for them kept them warm and dry enough. The year before they'd left Holland had been one of considerable hardship, and they con-sidered the new clothes the height of luxury.

Finally, panting hard, Jan slowed down and stopped on the side of the road at the bottom of the hill.

"We'd better walk to the hideout from here. We don't want anybody to see us. Let's go and dry off a bit. We can have some rations."

"What if the old man comes out? He'll have our h-hides."

"Miserable sot. We weren't doing nothing wrong."

"I suppose he thought we'd t-trespass."

Jan shook his head. "I told you, he was hiding something. I bet it was the treasure and he was afraid we'd see him. But we'll find it."

Pim hung back. "I d-don't feel like going around in circles, Jan. I'm soaked."

Jan looked around. Early-winter darkness was coming in on the back of the rain.

"All right. We'll come back when the light's better."

"Maybe it wasn't t-treasure," stuttered Pim. "Maybe h-he was just getting rid of a stone or something."

"I tell you, Pim, he'd no need to chase us off the way he did if he didn't have something to hide. He was in a real funk if ever I saw one."

"Perhaps we should tell C-Captain."

"We will if we see him. All right, hop off."

Pim dismounted, and Jan dragged the bicycle over to the hedge and shoved it under the branches. He stood still for a moment, searching the landscape.

"Coast is clear. Come on. We won't stay long, I promise."

From the crest of the hill, the ground sloped down sharply to the east. Here was a small field, and around its perimeter was a low, thorny hedge. Almost out of sight in the north-west corner stood an old cattle trough. The boys scuttled off in that direction.

"Keep your eyes peeled," Jan said.

"There isn't a soul in s-sight," answered Pim. "We're the only ones st-stupid enough to b-be out."

"Stop mithering. We'll just stash our treasure and head back."

At the trough, Jan leaned over, brushed away some sodden dead boughs from the bottom, and pulled up on the central strut. He had to tug hard, but suddenly a grill underneath dropped open, revealing a square opening into a wide chimney.

"I'll go first," he said. "Give me the torch."

Pim handed it over, and Jan climbed over the lip of the trough and turned so he was entering the chimney feet first. There was a metal ladder fastened into the side wall, and gripping it with both hands, he carefully descended. The torch was tucked under his chin.

Pim leaned over, waiting for his signal.

"Oh bleeding Jesus."

Before Pim could react, his brother's head reappeared abruptly in the opening. He was sheet-white.

"What? What's the m-matter?" asked Pim.

***

Entering the Cartwright kitchen felt like stepping into the past. The low ceiling, the dark wooden beams, and the open fireplace looked as though they had been there since Jacobean times. Tyler almost expected to see a pig roasting on a spit over the fire. An uncarpeted flight of stairs led from the corner of the room. Functional, not in any way grand. There was a large oak cupboard beside the sink crammed with cups and plates, and a massive iron stove took up most of one wall. Brightly coloured cushions and shiny brass ornaments arranged along the pelmet showed what Tyler's mother would have called "a woman's touch." Two or three oil lamps gave off soft pools of light. A lingering, delicious smell of recent baking hung in the air. A scrubbed wooden table took pride of place in the centre of the room.

Susan removed her outdoor things and immediately put on a print apron.

"Please, have a seat, Inspector. I'll make us a pot of tea." She began to fuss at the stove.

"Give me your hat and coat," said John.

Tyler sat down at the table, and the young man who had been standing in the doorway pulled up a chair opposite.

"I'm Ned Weaver," he said to Tyler. "Susan's son."

He seemed to wink at Tyler, who was startled for a moment. Then he realized that Weaver had a sporadic twitch in his left eyelid.

John Cartwright joined them.

Tyler took out his notebook. Not that he really needed it – there'd been nothing to record so far – but he'd learned that people were either reassured or intimidated by seeing a policeman take notes. His two constables, Mortimer and Biggs, were standing quietly by the door. They had not been invited to sit, but at least John had relieved them of their wet outer garments.

Susan hurried over with the tea tray and cups and Tyler waited while she poured cups of strong, dark tea. She took the chair next to her husband.

"Where have you searched so far?" Tyler asked.

"Me and Ned went through all the outbuildings," answered John. "He's not in the cow barn nor the shed. We walked down to the Mohan farm just t'other side of hill, but he's not there either. They haven't seen hide nor hair. We went as far as the Bitterley road but no sign."

"What about the woods?" Tyler asked.

"I don't think he'd have gone off the road," said John Cartwright. "No reason to."

"Unless he was seeking shelter. You said he could get confused," said Tyler.

"Not that confused. You can hardly go more than two feet in those woods. They're too dense."

"You said the last time you saw him was when you all turned in at about half past nine last night."

Susan jumped in. "We all go to bed early. Early rising. We have a farm to run."

"Yes, of course. Did Mr. Cartwright go to his room?"

"Yes."

"And he seemed all right?"

Susan shrugged. "As all right as he ever is these days. He goes into some kind of state. Like he's seeing things that aren't there. He was in the Boer War as a young man, but he gets the wars all mixed up so you don't know which one he's referring to half the time. If you ask him what he's talking about he gets right snippy."

"You know how it is, older people get set in their ways," said John, his voice apologetic. "My ma passed on in '38, see, and there was just two of us, Pa and me, for nigh on three years." He gave his wife a quick smile. "Then I met Susan just last year and, well, we took to each other, and before you knew it, we'd decided to get wed."

Susan took up the tale, as though she didn't trust him to get it right. "At first, we thought we'd live in Market Drayton, in my house, but John's pa started going downhill. Very fast it was. Doctor thought he couldn't look after himself any more." She shook her head. "What can you do? John thought it best if we move in here."

To Tyler's surprise, Agnes Mortimer now stepped forward. "Excuse me, sir. I wonder if I might ask a question."

"Ask away, Constable."

She addressed Mrs. Cartwright. "I couldn't help but notice there are six chairs at the table. Does anybody else live here?"

Good girl, thought Tyler. He had to admit he hadn't really registered that detail.

It was Ned who answered. "We have a billet. A Land Girl."

Susan Cartwright continued. "John hurt his shoulder during harvest and we needed an extra pair of hands. Ned helps out when he's able but it's a lot of work, and John's pa wasn't doing anything to speak of by then. He just wasn't reliable."

Tyler had been taking notes. "What is the young lady's name?"

"Edith Walpole. We all call her Edie."

"She's a good worker is that young lass," said John. "We'd have been hard-pressed to get in the harvest without her."

"Where is she now?"

"She's gone to Mohan's to see if Pa has turned up there. Ned and me already went there but we thought it would be best to check again."

Mortimer gave a little cough.

"Yes, Constable," said Tyler.

"Excuse me, sir, but as I understand it, Mr. Cartwright has additional helpers from the Italian POW camp."

Tyler had not immediately thought of that, but he knew that the men who were waiting out the war in a camp on Sheet Road were encouraged to work on the farms if they wanted to. Extra labour was a blessing these days.

"It's just winter work now so we've only got one fella at the moment," answered John.

"Weather was so bad last night he had to stay over. He slept in't barn . . ." said Ned with a wink

Susan interjected. "They're allowed to do that if the weather is bad or they work really late. Typically they bike over. We rang the camp to let them know. The Captain said it was all right but we had to make sure he was locked in. Which he was."

"What time was that?" Tyler asked.

"After we'd had our supper. Ned walked him over about nine thirty," said John.

"Do you all usually eat together?" asked Tyler.

"Part of the agreement with the camp is that we provide three meals a day," answered Susan. "Breakfast, dinner, and supper."

"Given who they are, them Ities don't do so bad," said Ned.

John gave a little shrug. "Angelo works hard. It's only fair to do right by him."

"So everybody was present at breakfast except for Mr. Jasper Cartwright, the Land Girl, and the POW?"

"That's right," said John.

"Like I said earlier, John's pa doesn't always join us," interjected Susan. "Nobody thought anything about it that he wasn't up. Sometimes he stays in his room until late. It's not worth my life to disturb him if he's in one of his states. Sometimes he gets the Ities mixed up with the Boers and he can be right nasty."

"Doesn't happen all the time," said John. "Just on occasion."

His wife frowned at him. "He's been getting worse, John, and you know it."

"You said you didn't realize he wasn't in the house until you were about to serve the midday meal. And that was when, exactly?" Tyler asked.

"It was just after eleven. I always have the meal ready for eleven," said Susan. "He hadn't shown hide nor hair of himself so I gave him a call. When I didn't get an answer, I sent Ned up to fetch him. He weren't there."

"He hadn't got dressed," said Ned. "When we checked downstairs, we saw his mack was gone and his wellies but not his cap nor gloves. And he'd taken one of the lanterns."

Tyler made a note. "So, at the moment, we have no idea what time he left the house, but it must have been between half-nine last night, when you all went to bed, and when you checked at eleven this morning."

Again Susan interjected. "Like I said, he would often sleep through breakfast so I wasn't concerned right off the bat."

John Cartwright took a briar pipe and tobacco pouch from his pocket and began to fuss with filling it. "Then by afternoon he still hadn't shown up and we was starting to get real worried. We probably should've started to search much sooner. I was working in the shed all morning so I didn't even know he was out."

He glanced over at his wife and Tyler saw the reproach. So did she.

"He's been and done vanishing tricks before, and this didn't seem any different," she said quickly. "That's why we waited as long as we did."

"By then the weather was worsening," said John. "Ned and me went out to search and we found the lantern, and it was still lit, but there was no sign of Pa."

"We thought we'd better report it to the police," said Susan.

"I assume your other helper, the POW, knows that Mr. Cartwright is missing," said Tyler.

John nodded. "He offered at once to help look for him. He's a good lad."

Tyler noticed an expression on Ned's face that he couldn't quite decipher. With the man's disconcerting wink he couldn't be sure, but he had the impression Ned wasn't as enthusiastic about the POW's virtues as his stepfather was.

"Did he? Help you search, I mean?"

John grimaced. "The captain at the camp can be strict about what they're allowed to do or not do. As prisoners of war, that is. So I thought it best if Angelo stayed where he was and Ned and me would take a look around."

"Where does Mr. Cartwright sleep?"

"He's got the front room upstairs," answered Susan. "It was his bedroom from before and he refuses to leave it. Makes things cramped for all of us. My Ned had to take the small back room and Edie has to sleep in the parlour."

Tyler addressed the three of them. "I gather nobody heard any sound of Mr. Cartwright going out or moving around during the night?"

"No. Nothing," said John.

"My husband sleeps like a log," said Susan. "We all do."

"Mr. Weaver?"

The young man winked twice. "Nothing."

Tyler put away his notebook. "Perhaps the best thing – "

He was cut off by a frantic rapping on the front door.

"Maybe that's news," said John, and he jumped up to open it.

On the threshold stood two boys, wet, bedraggled, and obviously terrified.

"Sir. Sir. We just found a dead man. I think somebody kilt him."

The members of the little party hurrying after the boys were drenched almost as soon as they stepped outside. Jan and Pim were leading the way to the place where they'd found the body. The woods were pressing in on the road and the trees were being tossed so violently by the wind that Tyler half expected one of them to snap in two. Pim, the smaller of the boys, looked so white and shaken that Tyler was just about to offer him a piggyback ride when they reached the crest of the hill and Jan pointed to the field on the right.

"He's in there."

"Where?" asked John.

All they could see was a bare, muddy field on the other side of the hedgerow. Jan seemed to be pointing at a rusty old cattle trough in the far corner.

"Where?" John asked again. "Where do you mean?"

"The trough. It's a hideout," said the boy. "You have to go down into it. I'll show you." He turned to his brother. "You stay here."

He started off to the hedgerow and pushed through a gap into the field. The others clambered behind him, except for Pim and Agnes Mortimer, who laid her hand gently on the boy's shoulder to keep him back.

Jan jogged up to the trough and stopped.

He bent over and pointed. "Down there."

Tyler could see a metal ladder leading into a dark hole.

"What is this?" cried Susan.

Nobody answered, but Tyler knew exactly what they were looking at. This was a hideout built by members of the Auxiliary Units.

How had a troubled old man come to die in a top-secret bunker, known only to a very few?

"Is there any chance we could have a cuppa, Miss?" Jan put on his best smile. "My brother here had such a fright and it would perk him up."

When he'd understood the situation, Tyler had sent the boys back to the farmhouse with Constable Mortimer in charge. She had made them sit as close to the kitchen fire as possible. They'd agreed to remove their outer garments and their socks and shoes but balked at taking off their trousers, even though the legs were soaking wet.

"We'll be all right, miss," said Jan.

Mortimer had to be content with borrowing a couple of towels from the warming cupboard and wrapping them around their legs. Pim was pale and still shivering.

"Let me see what I can rustle up," she said to Jan. Strictly speaking, she didn't have permission to requisition any of the Cartwright tea ration, but she considered this something of an emergency. She hoped the inspector would agree with her. The boys tugged at her heart, although she had a sneaking feeling that Jan, the older boy, knew this and played it for all he was worth. Both boys were undersized, dark-haired, and sharp-featured. Pim's scalp was scarred from what looked like a previous ringworm infestation and his hair was patchy. He looked like a newly hatched chick.

There was a set of canisters on the counter, each conveniently labelled – *TEA, SUGAR, FLOUR, BISCUITS* – and she was relieved to find the tea canister was almost full. She spooned three generous helpings into the teapot and added hot water from the kettle on the stove.

"Pim likes his sweet, miss," said Jan. "He can have my helping of sugar if there's not enough."

"Don't worry, we'll manage," said Mortimer. The sugar canister was only half full but she thought two spoonfuls would hardly be missed. She plopped a tea cozy on the pot and brought it over to the table. The two boys watched her quietly, alert as hungry dogs. She went to the cupboard for some cups.

"What were you doing out bicycling on a day like this?" she asked casually. She didn't miss the look they exchanged.

"We had to be in magistrates' court this morning," said Jan. "Nothing serious, just a mix-up, really, but Pim got all nervous about it. I thought a bit of exercise after school would do him good. He's highly strung, you see."

Mortimer poured the tea into the thick mugs she'd found in the cupboard.

"Would you like milk?"

"Yes, please, miss. Thank you. Say thank you, Pim. Where's your manners?"

"Thank you, m-miss," mumbled the other boy.

Biscuits? She wasn't sure if she was pushing the assumed generosity of Mrs. Cartwright too far but she opened the canister anyway. Mrs. Cartwright must have baked recently because it was full. She handed each of the boys two biscuits and sat down at the table.

They almost simultaneously dipped them into the tea, then stuffed the soggy morsels into their mouths.

"You're evacuees, I believe?"

"Yes, miss," Jan answered.

"When did you come to Ludlow?"

Biscuits disposed of, both boys took big gulps of the tea.

"About three months ago. We was in London first, but the house was bombed out and our foster mother had a nervous collapse. We was sent up to Cardiff, but the mum there got ill and couldn't keep us, so we come to Ludlow."

"Poor chaps. You have been all around the Wrekin, haven't you? Where were you living before you were evacuated?"

The younger boy lowered his head and concentrated on his tea. Jan answered her.

"We was in Amsterdam. We come over with the Kindertransport." He paused. "You know what that is, don't you, miss?"

"Yes, I do. Brave boys. Do you have any relatives in England?"

"No."

"That must have been hard."

Jan shrugged. "Not really. Pim and me have each other, see."

"Are your parents still in Holland?"

"That's right, miss. They haven't got out yet." His voice was flat.

"Have you heard from them?"

"Not for a while."

"I'm sure they'll be all right."

"Yes, miss." Jan's voice didn't hold much conviction.

"We're staying with Mrs. Keogh." Jan wiped the back of his hand across his mouth. "She's nice. Like you, miss."

"Thank you, Jan. What about you, Pim? Do you like Mrs. Keogh?"

The other boy smiled shyly. "She's smashing. She's been ever so g-good to us."

Jan drained his mug of tea. Agnes hesitated, then went back to the canister for two more biscuits. They smelled so fresh and tasty she was almost tempted to take one for herself, but, unlike the boys, she didn't need sustenance for a case of shock.

Uninvited, Jan reached for the teapot and refilled both mugs. More biscuit dipping.

Mortimer sat down again. "It's amazing you found that hideout."

"Yes, miss. We're Boy Scouts, though. Have been a year gone. Always prepared."

"Did you ever see the man before, Jan?" Agnes asked. "The man who died. His name is Jasper Cartwright. Did you ever come by the farm when you were out riding around?"

Something happened in Jan's eyes at the question. They went dead, as if a shutter had closed across a lens. "Oh no, miss. We discovered it today. Sheer chance. Pim saw the rabbit holes first. He was the one thought they looked sort of funny. We saw they was glassed over. So we scouted around. Didn't we, Pim?"

"Yes, m-miss, that's what we d-did."

"We're always on the lookout for signs of fifth columnists, miss. Hidden mines and that sort of thing."

"When can we go b-back to Mrs. Keogh's?" Pim asked. "She'll be awful worried." His voice was on the verge of a sob. Agnes smiled at him.

"I'll tell you what. Let's move ourselves into another room. The others should be coming back any minute now. Inspector Tyler will want to ask you some questions. Same sort of thing I've been asking you. When he's done that I'll take you home. I came on a motorcycle. It has a sidecar. It's a bit on the chilly side but it'll be better than your bike. We'll get that later on."

"Are we going to get in trouble, m-miss?" whispered Pim.

Jan cut him off. "Don't be such a twerp. We ain't done nothing wrong, have we, miss?"

DEAD GROUND IN BETWEEN   83

"Not that I can see. It was a good thing that you found the hideout when you did. Nobody might have discovered Mr. Cartwright for weeks."

"He would have been very smelly by then, wouldn't he, miss?"

Jan's voice was matter-of-fact and she was startled by the candour of his remark. And what it revealed about his experience. She decided to probe a little further.

"Jan, when you came to the door, you said that somebody had killed the man you found. Why did you think that?"

The boy looked at her and his eyes had the same blank expression she'd noticed earlier. He shrugged. "I seen dead people like that. All of them was killed."

"By whom?"

"Nazis. Who else?"

Tyler left Biggs at the site to stand guard until the coroner arrived. The rest of them returned to the farmhouse. The walk back in the driving rain was utterly dismal. Nobody said a word. John Cartwright led the way. His wife attempted to put her arm through his but he didn't respond, and she put her hands in her coat pockets, walking silently beside him. Ned Weaver trailed behind all of them.

When they reached the farmhouse John dragged off his wet coat and sat at the table, putting put his head in his hands. Susan and her son took the chairs on either side of him. Nobody spoke for what seemed like a long time, and Tyler didn't try to break the silence.

Finally, John pressed his knuckles into his cheeks as if he could shove back his grief.

"Didn't deserve to die like that, did he? Unless I'm mistaken, he'd been dead for some time."

John had been the one to climb down into the bunker after Tyler and identify the body.

"How'd he end up in that place?" Susan asked, her voice sharp. "I never knew it existed. Did your pa ever mention it to you, John?"

Her husband shook his head. "Not a word."

"Ned? What about you?"

"Nothing, Ma. Never saw it before." The persistent involuntary wink almost made a mockery of what he said.

"Inspector? What was it used for? Why is it such a big secret?"

"I can't say at the moment, Mrs. Cartwright."

"Can't or won't?"

"Let's say it's a matter of security. It's very important that you don't talk about it outside of the bounds of this family."

Susan stared at him, her expression incredulous. "And what am I going to tell people when they ask us where he was found?"

"Susan, all we have to say is that he'd wandered away, took a fall. That's all."

"Exactly, Mr. Cartwright," said Tyler. "These days, people are accustomed to, shall we say, circumspection."

"Speaking of which," said Weaver. "I think I should fetch Edie. No point in her spending her time trying to find him any more. That all right, Inspector?"

"Yes, of course. Just don't give out too much information."

Ned got to his feet, hovered briefly behind his stepfather, and then, with a barely audible "I'm sorry," he left.

Tyler addressed Susan. "I'd like to use your telephone to ring the coroner."

"It's in the hall just outside the parlour. When do you think he'll get here?"

"I hope it won't take him more than an hour."

"In that case, I'd like to go upstairs for a while," said John.

"Do you want me to sit with you?" Susan asked.

"No, thanks. I feel like being by meself for a bit."

"But, John – "

"Leave me be, will you, Susan? I just need a bit of time."

He shuffled off up the stairs, moving slowly, as if he had aged suddenly.

Susan flushed at the reprimand, and Tyler could see she was on the verge of tears.

"I'll make that call first, Mrs. Cartwright, then I'm going to have a word with the laddies. I'd like to send them off home as soon as possible. They've had quite a shock."

"Haven't we all," whispered Susan.

Tyler was able to connect to the coroner's office immediately. Dr. Murnaghan's secretary, Winnie, said he was in the morgue doing some tests. Whatever he was up to, Winnie clearly didn't approve. "It's too cold down there," she said. She agreed to fetch Murnaghan while Tyler waited on the line.

When the coroner answered, Tyler explained the situation as succinctly as he could.

"I can leave at once, Tom. Not doing anything important here. Give me directions."

Dr. Murnaghan was supposedly retired, but medical doctors were in short supply and Tyler knew he was only too happy to be called to a job. One of these days, Tyler imagined, he'd need the coroner and would find he was just too busy.

He made one more call, to Sergeant Rowell, to tell him they'd located Jasper Cartwright's body.

Agnes Mortimer had found a *Boy's Own Annual* and she was reading to Jan and Pim when Tyler entered the parlour. Despite the circumstances, the boys were paying rapt attention. It seemed to be a story about Cavaliers and Roundheads.

"Since the early days of October the Roundheads had shut us up in our own house. But we had kept them to the opposite bank of the moat, although . . ."

She stopped and started to stand up, but Tyler gestured for her to stay where she was.

"Sorry to interrupt. I just want to ask the boys a few questions."

"Miss already done that," said Jan.

Seeing their drawn faces, Tyler couldn't help but recall what Mrs. Keogh had said about them. *Unimaginable experiences.* That was the term she'd used. Poor kiddies.

He flashed what he hoped was a friendly smile. "I realize you've already given your story to Constable Mortimer, but let's just go over it again, shall we?"

Jan did all the talking, and he was polite enough. Just out for a ride to settle themselves down after being in court, he said. He paused there to see if there was any reaction from Tyler.

"I know all about the court, son. Go on. It's what happened just now that I'm most interested in."

No, the weather hadn't really bothered them. No, they hadn't been that way before. It was just chance they got off the bike where they did. No, they didn't disturb anything. No, they didn't touch the body.

"You didn't unbutton his coat, did you?"

No. Absolutely not. He was dead. He weren't going to touch no corpse. He and Pim just ran to the farmhouse fast as they could.

Tyler wrote this all down. "Thanks, lads. You've been plucky chaps. Now I have to say something very serious to you. You must not tell anybody where you found Mr. Cartwright. Nobody.

Not the other kids at school. Not even Mrs. Keogh. Nobody. It's all right if you say you found him, but if they ask where, just say it was near his house." He looked at their solemn faces. "Do I have your word? Scout's honour?"

Both boys nodded.

"Let me see you swear, then. Scout's honour."

They raised their hands in the Scout salute.

"Good. Excellent. I'm asking you to do this for security reasons. We don't want anybody becoming curious about that hideout. It's a secret place. All right?"

Again, solemn nods from both of them.

"Now, I'm just going to have a word with Constable Mortimer, then she's going to get you home." He fished in his pocket and took out a sixpence. "Here. Buy yourself some sweeties."

Jan accepted the coin but didn't relax his wariness. Tyler nodded to Agnes to join him in the hall. She closed the door behind them.

"What's your impression, Constable?" Tyler asked. He spoke quietly.

"I don't think they're telling the whole truth," said Agnes. "But for the life of me, I don't know what they're hiding. Maybe it's just boys' stuff."

"Might not be anything," said Tyler. "They've just had a run-in with the authorities. That might be making them extra cautious. Keep your eyes and ears open, regardless."

"You don't think there's anything suspicious about Mr. Cartwright's death, do you, sir?"

"Being a copper gives you a suspicious nature, Constable. What the hell was he doing in that bunker? I didn't detect any obvious signs of foul play, but we'll see what Dr. Murnaghan has to say."

"Yes, sir. Shall I come back here after I've dropped the boys off?"

"Yes, we might need you."

"Not to just make a pot of tea, I hope, sir."

Tyler stared at her for a moment, not sure if she was joking or not. She wasn't.

"Why'd you say that?"

"That seems to be the role women police officers are assigned, sir. It's not that I mind, exactly, but I do prefer something more challenging in the line of police work."

"Point taken, Constable. I shall keep that in mind. In the meantime I hope you don't object to taking those boys back home. Not too demeaning just being a driver, is it?"

"No, sir. Not at all."

"That's a relief. They're billeted with a Mrs. Keogh. She lives at number two River Close. It's off Lower Broad Street. Tell her I'll come to the house later on. You'll have to say something about the death, but keep it to a minimum."

"Yes, sir."

As she turned to go back into the parlour, Tyler spoke again.

"Constable Mortimer. Good work. I'm glad you joined the police force."

He was a little surprised when she turned bright red. His compliment obviously meant something to her.

"Thank you, sir. I am too."

When Tyler got back to the kitchen, Ned Weaver had returned and was sitting at the table with a young woman who Tyler assumed was the Land Girl. She was dark-haired, very pretty, and dressed in the Land Army uniform: dark-green jersey, beige shirt, corduroy breeches.

Susan Cartwright was at the stove stirring a large pot. The air was fragrant with whatever it was she was cooking. Stew of some kind. John was not present.

Tyler addressed the girl.

"Hello. I'm Detective Inspector Tyler, Shropshire constabulary. I take it you are Miss Edith Walpole?"

"That's right, she is," said Susan. "We've told her what's happened."

"Poor Mr. Cartwright," said the girl softly.

"We were wondering what to do about the POW," said Susan to Tyler. "Somebody should inform him, I suppose."

"Nowt to do with him, is it?" burst out Ned.

"He knows Mr. Cartwright was missing," said Edie. "It's only fair not to leave him hanging."

"I wouldn't mind having a word with him myself," said Tyler. "He might be able to fill in some of the blanks."

Susan frowned. "Blanks? What blanks?"

"What time your father-in-law left the house, for one thing."

"Angelo wouldn't have heard anything," said Edie. "He was down in the barn."

Tyler didn't respond. She was probably right. On the other hand, he'd meant it when he said he wanted to fill in some of the blanks.

"How's his grasp of English?"

Edie answered. "Not bad, considering. He's been studying all summer."

"You can say that again," said Ned with a wink. "We're not supposed to talk to them any more than necessary but he loves to practise. Seizes every chance he gets to ask Edie questions. She has the patience of Job. Not me."

"Why shouldn't I help him when I can? What if I wanted to learn Italian?"

"Italian?" said Susan. "Whatever for?"

Tyler intervened. "Where is he now?" he asked Ned.

"In the barn. At least that's where he's supposed to be."

"Did you want to ask *me* anything?" Edie piped up.

"The inspector wants to know if you heard John's pa going out the door last night," Susan Cartwright answered for her. "Perhaps he thinks you would have just ignored it. You know, who cares if a senile old man goes outside to catch his death of cold? Obviously that's the way of this household. John and I didn't give a toss."

"Of course I wouldn't have let Mr. Cartwright go out on such a night," said Edie. She appeared genuinely upset.

"Mrs. Cartwright, I have said no such thing," said Tyler. "I'd like to determine exactly what happened. Please understand this is part of my job."

"I'm sorry," she muttered.

Tyler turned to the girl. "Miss Walpole, did you hear anything out of the ordinary at all last night?"

She shook her head. "Nothing. None of us knew Mr. Cartwright was even out until we came for our midday break." Her eyes filled with sudden tears. "I'm so sorry. It's dreadful that he would die that way."

Ned reached across the table and put his hand over hers. "Don't cry, Edie, there's a girl. I've heard dying from the cold is a peaceful kind of death."

"Is it, really?" None too gently, she extricated her hand from his.

So that's the lie of the land is it? thought Tyler.

"Why don't you take the inspector down to the barn, Ned," said Susan, "seeing as how he's keen to have a chinwag with the Itie." She returned to tending the stew. Her back was stiff with anger.

Tyler got his hat and coat from the hook and followed Ned out into the chill wind.

—

The inside of the barn was gloomy, only a single oil lamp burning. There was a warm, musty smell of animals and hay.

"Hello? Hello? Angelo?" called Ned.

Tyler saw a young man at the far end of the barn. He was mucking out one of the stalls. He turned but didn't move toward them.

"Hello," said Ned again. "Can you come over here for a minute?" He beckoned. "Over here."

The Italian was wearing the obligatory brown overalls of the Italian prisoners of war, with the two distinguishing orange patches on the legs of the trousers. He was fair-haired with pale skin, probably in his early twenties, medium build, wiry and fit-looking.

"This is Angelo," said Ned. "Don't ask me for his last name because I can't pronounce it."

Tyler had already got the surname from John Cartwright. It was Iaquinta. Not that hard, really.

Ned pointed. "This, Inspector Tyler," he said in a loud voice. "He wants to ask you questions. *Comprende?* Questions. About Mr. Cartwright, senior. The old man. We've found his body."

Angelo froze. "His body? Mr. Cartwright is dead?"

"Yeah. We just discovered him about an hour ago."

The only places to sit were the hay bales stacked against one wall of the barn. Tyler went and sat down.

"Join me," he said, emphasizing his words with a gesture.

Angelo leaned his pitchfork against a stall and came over. Behind them one of the cows mooed loudly.

"I am very sorrowful that Mr. Cartwright is dead," said the Italian. "Please accept our best wishes."

Ned didn't even try to hide his guffaw.

"He was found in the area of the north field, not too far from the barn," said Tyler. "I am trying to determine – to find out – how he got there." He paused. "All right so far?"

Ned jumped in. "*Comprende?* Do you *comprende* what inspector say?"

The Italian nodded, although Tyler thought Ned's mangling of both languages might be difficult to follow.

He continued. "Did you see or hear Mr. Cartwright at any time last night?"

"No. I was – were – locked into the barn for the night. After supper. Perhaps half past nine o'clock."

"That's right," said Ned. "I brought him over myself. Barred and shuttered, as we're supposed to do with these fellows. Don't want them running around the countryside wild and free, do we? Who knows what they might get up to? No woman would be safe, would they? Not with them Italians."

Angelo's hands clenched. Tyler could see that the man was taking in everything Ned Weaver said.

"Private Iaquinta, when did you know that Mr. Cartwright was missing?"

"When I went to house for meal. A discovery was made that he not in room. Not in *his* room." His English was almost better than Ned's.

"You speak English very well," said Tyler.

"Thank you, sir. I am studying since I am a prisoner. No, I should say I *have been studying*, should I not?"

"Hmm. I suppose that is correct. And there was nothing unusual or out of the ordinary last night?"

To his surprise, his question seemed to bring a rush of colour to the man's face. His fair skin couldn't hide it.

"It was not usual for me to spend the night here. Only occasional. But weather was very bad. Too bad to bike. Other than that, there was nothing. Nothing at all."

"All right then." Tyler got to his feet. "Continue with what you were doing."

Angelo addressed Ned. "I shall assume you will need me on tomorrow?"

"There's always work to be done," answered Ned. "Cows won't milk themselves, will they? So you'd better be here. Or somebody should be."

"Thank you, and again I must say I am most sorry at the news of Mr. Cartwright."

Ned shrugged. "He was old. He'd lived his life. We've all got to go sometime."

Tyler walked with Ned back to the farmhouse. He was tempted to give the young man a dressing-down about his treatment of the Italian but he didn't think it would do much good. He guessed it wasn't just the fact that Angelo was Italian that was riling Ned. A pretty girl was in the mix somewhere.

In spite of the delicious odours emanating from the stove, the atmosphere in the kitchen was as cold as the weather.

"How was Angelo?" asked Edie as soon as they entered.

"Fine, I think," said Tyler. "He sent his condolences to you, Mrs. Cartwright."

Susan didn't answer and Tyler wasn't sure she'd even heard.

He headed for the door. "I'll get out of your way and wait for the ambulance in the parlour."

Edie called out to him. "There's a paraffin heater in there, Inspector. You should probably turn it on. That room can get very cold."

Susan focused on her stirring.

The parlour was indeed decidedly chilly but Tyler didn't light the heater. He could tough it out as good as any farmer.

Perhaps for a previous generation this room would have been fairly grand, with its big, heavy furniture, flocked wall-paper, two or three ornately framed oil paintings on the walls. Ancestors? Hard to tell. There were a couple of hooked rugs on the wooden floor. Placed across the far corner was a wooden screen, the kind modest Victorian ladies used to dress behind while their lascivious husbands waited impatiently in the marriage bed. There was a towel hanging over the top of it, and Tyler guessed this corner was where Edie slept. It was certainly neither luxurious nor particularly private.

Rubbing his hands hard to get some circulation going, he walked over to the settee and sat down. It was as uncomfortable as it looked, but at least there was a colourful wool throw draped across the back. He tucked it around his knees, feeling decidedly octogenarian.

Mortimer had left the book that she'd been reading to the boys on the side table, and he reached for it. There was a marker at the place where she'd left off. The story was called "Cavalier Christmas." Lots of plucky action involving plucky young lads of the age likely to be reading the annual. It was all romantic claptrap, really, but in spite of himself, he was getting quite absorbed when he heard the sound of a vehicle arriving. He left the Cavaliers eating roasted boar's head washed down with tankards of ale and went out to meet Dr. Murnaghan.

It was about three-quarters of an hour later when Tyler returned to the house. They'd lit more oil lamps against the gloom. Susan was once more at the kitchen counter, and Edie was at the table, darning a sock. Ned was nowhere to be seen. John Cartwright looked up from the large book he was reading, and Tyler realized it was a Bible.

"Have they taken him?" John asked.

"Yes, they have."

"When will we be able to bury him?"

"There'll be a post-mortem, and the body will be released to you after that."

"Thank you, Inspector. We'd better start making arrangements."

"I should be getting back to the station. I'll be in touch as soon as possible."

Edie put her darning into a basket by her side. "Shall I drive the inspector back to Ludlow, Mrs. Cartwright?"

Susan nodded.

"I'd appreciate that, if you really don't mind," said Tyler. He was being a trifle insincere. Unless he requisitioned the horse, he actually had no other way to get back to Ludlow except on foot. Constable Mortimer had already left on the motorcycle, with the boys in the sidecar, and Biggs had followed after them on the boys' bicycle.

Edie pushed back her chair. "I'll get my things."

She left the room and the heavy silence descended again.

Then John said, his voice low, "Just last week, Pa said he wanted to be buried in the old cemetery in Bitterley. My ma is laid to rest there, and my granddad and grandma. Strange he should be talking about it so recently."

Susan made a scoffing noise. "Your pa was always talking about dying. Where he wanted to be buried. Who he was leaving his money to. Not me, for sure. He never stopped. Every second day, he'd bring it up. 'Now when I go, I want a proper funeral, good pine coffin. And I want to be put in the family plot. Right beside my Grace. If you don't put me right beside her she'll follow me beyond the grave to nag me.' Come on, John. You know how he was."

John's face wore a wounded expression.

Edie came back into the room wearing her overcoat.

"I'm ready when you are, Inspector."

"Right. Mr. Cartwright, Mrs. Cartwright, please accept my condolences."

"Thank you, Inspector, you've been very kind." John glanced at his wife. His eyes were full of unhappiness, but she'd already turned her back and was fiddling with something in the sink.

—

Night had fallen, and the vehicle headlights, with the manda-tory restricting strips, gave out only a feeble light. The rain had stopped, but a low-lying mist had come up, intensifying the impenetrability of the darkness. Edie seemed familiar with the road, and didn't drive too fast

She steered the lorry carefully around a sharp curve, then said, "So, Angelo was all right when you talked to him?"

"Yep. Seemed like a decent chap. His English is good, all things considering."

She smiled. "He's a fast learner. I hope talking to you didn't get him all worried."

"Worried?"

"Well, you know, the Italians are our enemies at the moment. The men here could be accused of anything, at any time."

"Not if I have a say in the matter."

"What did you think of him? As a person, I mean."

Tyler thought he would test the waters a little. "Good-looking lad."

"Yes, he is, isn't he? You don't usually see somebody that fair who's Italian, but he's got northern blood in his veins. They're all blond in the north, according to him, and some of his ances-tors must have come from there. And those Italians are real hard workers, let me tell you. We arrived at the Cartwright farm at the same time in fact. Angelo asked me to help him with his English, so we've had lots of chats." She shot a questioning glace at Tyler. "To tell you the truth, Inspector, sometimes it's hard to see them as enemies, if you know what I mean. Not when you're working together in the broiling sun and they do their best to make some of the jobs easier for you. They didn't have to do that but they did. I know we're not supposed to fraternize, but how can you not talk when you're working together for hours and hours?"

"I'm sure it would seem unnatural."

"Before the war, Angelo was a dairyman in Italy. He's really helped us with the cows. Even old Mr. Cartwright listened to him."

"I thought Mrs. Cartwright said Jasper didn't like the POWs. He was rude to them."

"Oh, he'd get into bad moods with everybody. He wanted to talk about soldiering but their English wasn't good enough, and that frustrated him. But I wouldn't say he was exactly rude. Not the way he was with Ned. Blimey, he could be rotten to him. Said he was a coward because he'd been discharged from the army."

"The army? I'd assumed he wasn't called up because he was in a reserved occupation. Do you know what happened?"

"I'm not entirely sure. It's a touchy subject. Near as I can make out, something occurred when he was in training camp and he was invalided out." She caught Tyler's questioning look. "I don't know what the problem was. He wasn't hurt or anything like that – at least not in any way that shows – but apparently he had some sort of nervous breakdown."

"Is that why his mother said he only helps out when he can? I wondered about that."

"I think she mollycoddles him. But it's true, every so often he goes prostrate. He spends a lot of time lying down in his room. Bad headaches or something." She bit her lip. "Honestly, I feel sorry for him. He must have been teased a lot when he was a boy. You know, that funny twitch in his eye. Almost makes you want to giggle sometimes. I do know being booted out of the army was devastating to him. He really wants to be a soldier. He knows more about what's going on in the war than anybody else. He's got a big map in his room and he marks out every battle."

They bumped along the road in silence for a while, then Edie blurted out, "Angelo thinks Italy will surrender soon."

"Does he now?"

"Mm-hm. He says nobody in his country really wants to fight. Mussolini pushed them into it. After all, they were our allies in the Great War, weren't they?"

"Yes, they were indeed."

"He had no choice, you see. He was conscripted. Fight or be killed – that's what he was told."

"As you say, not much choice there."

"He's a very intelligent man. He really would like to be a teacher. In fact, you might not believe it but he writes poetry."

"In English?"

"No, in Italian, but he translates them for me."

Love poems, Tyler had no doubt. He sighed. The age-old story. Warring families, Montagues and Capulets. Two young people caught in the middle.

"I can see you've grown quite fond of Angelo."

"What? Well, not really. It's just that . . ." Her voice trailed off.

"It's hard to think of him as an enemy?"

"Yes, I suppose that's it. I would have been quite lonely without Angelo," she said. "Initially, I wanted to be billeted in one of the hostels. But our chief said I was needed at the Cartwrights' and I would live in. I didn't like being on my own and I was going to ask for a transfer, until the POWs arrived."

She frowned, leaned forward, and rubbed the condensation off the windshield.

"This weather gives me the pip. Poor Mr. Cartwright. Not the best way to go to your maker, is it? Dying out in the cold like that." She frowned. "Ned was quite mysterious when he came to tell me. He said Mr. Cartwright was found in one of the upper fields by two Boy Scouts. Is that true?"

Tyler nodded. He wasn't prepared to enlighten her fully at this point.

"What on earth were boys doing out on such a day?"

"They said they were just riding around on their bike."

"Really? How odd."

Tyler silently agreed but said nothing.

Edie's shoulders slumped. "I know the family feel bad about not finding him sooner, but Mr. Cartwright could be a stubborn old cuss. If he got it into his head he wanted to go out, out he would go. Mr. John had to go looking for him more than once. And he was definitely getting more and more confused."

Tyler clucked sympathetically. "Must have been hard all round."

"It certainly was."

"How was he with you?"

She shrugged. "All right, really. I don't think he approved of us Land Girls at first but he knew they needed help with the farm. I passed the test. Ready to work hard, bring him his tea, listen to his stories." She slowed down to negotiate another turn. "But I really did like listening to him. It wasn't put on."

"You Land Girls have been a godsend. I hate to think how we'd have got by without you."

"Thanks, Inspector. It's nice to be appreciated. We had to win over quite a few of the old-timers, especially when they saw us in breeches."

"Where is Ned in the equation?" Tyler asked. "I got the feeling he was fond of you."

She chuckled. "He's not had much experience with girls. Perhaps that's why."

Tyler thought she wasn't doing herself justice. She was an extremely attractive young woman and, experienced or not, he could see how a single man like Ned might be infatuated. They had turned onto a wider road now, still dark but easier to navigate. Tyler peered out the window.

"The POW camp is on the right, isn't it?"

"Yes, it is. They all live in huts. They've got guards but Angelo says they're decent fellas. Still, confinement is confinement, isn't it?"

"It is indeed."

"Angelo says helping out on the farm is one of the best experiences he's ever had."

"I'm sure life in a prison camp must get very tedious," said Tyler.

She nodded. "That's the very word he used. Tedious. The big excitement is on Sunday when they march them to St. Paul's, the Roman Catholic church in Ludlow. I went in there myself last week. Thought I'd see what a mass was all about. I'm chapel-raised so I've never been in a Catholic church before. It's lovely inside, but it all seemed mumbo-jumbo to me. Up down, up down. Now kneel, now stand up. The priest said the whole thing in Latin. Two boys helped him and waved some smoky stuff around, which made me cough, I can tell you." She flicked a quick glance at him. "You're not RC, are you?"

"No, Church of England."

"Whew. Good. I don't want to offend anybody."

"Not at all. The first time I went into a Catholic church I found it strange myself."

"Why did you go? Did you have a sweetheart?"

"No. I thought it was part of my job to know how the other half lives. Do *you* have a sweetheart who is a Catholic?" he asked, although he was being disingenuous. He knew the answer.

She shook her head a bit too emphatically. "No. Not me. I'm fancy-free. I was just curious."

Tyler didn't challenge such a palpable fib, and they drove on in silence again.

"War's stupid, if you ask me," Edie burst out. "All of a sudden somebody up high says, 'We're at war and you've got to go and fight people you've never met, people who haven't done anything to you.' I don't understand it."

Tyler didn't respond. What could he say to that?

"My dad was in the Great War," Edie went on. "He came home at the end of it minus his mind."

Tyler wasn't sure he'd heard her properly. "Did you say *minus his mind*?"

"That's right. Other blokes came back minus an arm or a leg but he left his mind in the trenches somewhere in France. That's what he used to say, anyway. He and my mom were engaged when he left so that's why they got married, but it was hard on her. They only had me. He used to say that was all he could manage. Whatever that means."

Tyler was a little startled by her candour. He could guess what the poor blasted soldier had meant.

"It wasn't that he was a cuss or anything like that. He would just go away in his mind. Didn't seem to hear you. Sometimes he wouldn't get out of bed for days on end. Wouldn't wash or shave his face. He really ponged after one of those bouts, I can tell you. It was hard on my mom, but she loved him. Looked after him until the day he died."

"How long did he live for after the war?" Tyler asked.

"About five years. Not long, really. Truth is, he did himself in. There was a canal near us. One morning he walked down there, put stones in his pockets, and jumped in."

"I'm sorry, Miss Walpole. That must have been very diffi-cult for you and your mother."

"Oh, it was. For her, anyway. I didn't really have much of a relationship with him, to tell the truth. Like I said, he wasn't what you'd call 'present' most of the time. I was just a kiddie. He left a note saying he couldn't take it any more and that she would be better off without him."

"Has she remarried?"

"Not yet. But she's been seeing this nice bloke from down the road. A postman. Never been in the war because he's got bad eyesight so he's more . . . intact, shall we say."

"I wish her well."

Edie beamed. "Thanks for listening. I've been giving you an earful. My mum keeps telling me not to be such a chatterbox but I can't help it sometimes."

"I didn't mind at all."

"Forgive me for being personal, Inspector, but do you have a daughter?"

"Yes. She's a Land Girl too."

"Fancy that. Does she like it?"

"I believe so. We haven't had the opportunity to have a good chinwag yet. She's in Scotland now. I'm hoping I'll get to see her at Christmas."

"What's her name?"

"Janet. She's eighteen."

"Younger than me, then? I'm almost twenty-five. My mum says I'd better hurry up and get myself a bloke or I'll end up being an old maid."

"I'd say you have plenty of time."

"Hope so. You'd think it would be easy to meet a nice bloke these days but they've all been shipped off overseas."

Her words were echoing those of Mrs. Hamilton.

They continued on in silence for a while, and then she said, "I'm going to get four days' leave at Christmas. My mum wants me to come to Manchester, naturally, but by the time I get the train, have a couple of days with her, then come back, it's hardly worth it. Especially now, with what's happened here. I might just stay and save up my leave for later. One thing about a farm is that the animals don't take days off, do they? They still have to be milked and fed, no matter what day it is."

"True."

"Here's St. Paul's," said Edie. "That's where they go."

Tyler could just make out the large church with a domed

cupola. In the midst of this traditional town of Norman and medieval churches, St. Paul's seemed foreign and exotic.

"It was built in '36," she said. "Bloke who designed it is Italian, and he's been interned. He's been sent to the Isle of Man with the other enemy aliens."

"Really. Doesn't seem quite fair, does it? Let's hope he'll be released soon."

"Angelo says it's exactly like the church where he went as a boy. He's from Sardinia. He talks about it a lot. Sounds beautiful. Better weather than we get, that's for sure. Like I said, he wants to study to be a teacher when he goes back. If he does. Go back, I mean. Who knows what the future holds?"

There was no mistaking the wistfulness in her voice but there wasn't much Tyler could say to comfort her.

He pointed. "Turn left at the next road, then right at the top of the hill. I'm just at the end of the lane."

"I wonder how those two Boy Scouts are holding up," said Edie. "They were plucky little nippers, weren't they? And your lady constable was very good with them. She's quite a toff, isn't she?"

"I suppose she is."

"She'd be attractive if she put a bit of meat on her bones."

Tyler didn't comment.

Edie pulled up in front of the police station.

"I hope you don't think I'm unfeeling, Inspector. I know I've been gabbing on, but I'm truly sorry that Mr. Cartwright died."

"I know you are. And you weren't gabbing in the least."

Tyler climbed down out of the lorry.

"Thank you, Miss Walpole. Much appreciated."

"You're welcome. Gave me a chance to get out of the den of misery."

She drove off.

—

When Tyler arrived, as he'd been hoping, Rowell had a meal ready for him.

"It's a Woolton pie, sir. No meat, of course, but I did use a beef gravy. I had mine earlier and it's quite tasty, if I say so myself."

Tyler tucked into the hot pie with gusto. "Delicious, Oliver. I must say, a bit of meat would have been welcome but other than that it's perfect."

"I've got a baked apple and custard for your sweet."

"I'll save it for later. I want to pop down to Mrs. Keogh's to see how the two boys are doing."

"How were they, the tads?"

"Not too bad, all things considered. Shaken up, of course. I put them under the care of Constable Mortimer."

"Good idea. She's a motherly sort underneath it all. She seems the marbles-in-the-mouth type, but she can be very kind."

"True." Tyler remembered the kindness the young constable had shown to the shocked and bereaved victims in his last case.

"What a strange thing, the old man ending up where he did," said Rowell. "You referred to it as a hideout. Who the heck built it?"

Tyler was hesitant. "I'm not supposed to discuss this, but common sense tells me you aren't going to blab to anybody. And you *are* my right-hand man."

"Gosh, thanks, sir. I'm honoured."

Rowell waited expectantly as Tyler used a piece of bread to mop up the last of the gravy on his plate.

"I'd wager it was built by some member of an Auxiliary

Unit," said Tyler. "To be used in case of enemy invasion."

"Auxiliary Unit? I don't really know what that is."

"The Auxiliaries were a big deal in the first year of this bloody war when we feared an invasion was imminent but they're not as active now. Mr. Churchill ordered that they be formed and that the men be trained like the commandos were. Small cells, three or four men each at most, and operating in deepest secrecy – nobody to even know who else was out there beyond their own cell. Ready to kill and sabotage if the Nazis overran us. The hideouts were intended as bolt holes, and they can be provisioned to be lived in for weeks."

"Blimey," said Rowell. "I'd heard the rumours but I thought they were hogwash. Our local men being trained to be killers! I just didn't believe it."

"It's true. When we were all so scared of being invaded after Dunkirk, Churchill thought their role would be vital."

"And Jasper Cartwright was found in one of these hide-outs? You're not telling me this old man was a commando!?"

"It's seems most unlikely, but I'm going to have to find out. And that, Oliver, might be very difficult. When I say this is a deep secret, I mean deep, *deep* secret."

"What was this place like, then?"

"It's several feet underground. They all are. Easier to conceal that way. It's about eight feet long, over six feet high, and six wide. Cold to be sure, but snug. Put a paraffin lantern in there, paraffin stove, and cook yourself a chop. There's even a chemical toilet."

"Blimey. Sounds better than what we've got here."

"Almost. The walls are lined with planks and so is the floor. Originally this one must have been part of a big rabbit warren because three or four holes on the one side look out down the hill slope. They've been glazed in for protection and have blackout shutters. You'd never even know the place existed from that side of the hill. There's a second exit in case of emergencies several feet away, and it's just as well concealed. An old cattle trough stands over the entrance, and when you pull on a latch, a grill drops open onto a chimney just wide enough for a slimmish man to climb into. Jasper Cartwright was lying at the bottom of the ladder."

"How'd the nippers find the bunker if it was supposed to be so well hidden?"

Tyler winced. "Good question. They're keen Boy Scouts, and according to them they decided to look for signs of enemy activity. All the lads are told to do that. Keeps them busy."

"Rotten weather to be out scouting."

"Jan said they were getting some fresh air. He does most of the talking, and according to him his little brother needed something to distract him from the upset of being in a court of law. He talks like that. He's either going to be a successful criminal or a politician, he is. He says they actually investigated what they thought were rabbit holes in case there was a mine buried in the warren."

"You'd think that was a good reason to stay away," said Rowell.

"You would, wouldn't you? But Jan says he noticed the hole was covered with a glass window. Smart lad that he is, he thought that was a bit fishy, rabbits not being big on windows. He and his brother explored all around and realized the trough was in a peculiar place. He could see it had been moved. Remarkably, they found the trigger that released the lid to the entrance. Jan climbed partway down and almost stepped on the old man's body. That's what he told us, anyway."

Rowell whistled through his teeth. "Sounds like a lot of malarkey to me."

"Me too. That hideout is so well hidden it's practically invisible. And it was quite dark when they supposedly came across it."

"What's the truth, then?"

"I don't know as yet. Constable Mortimer also thought the boys weren't coming clean, but what they're hiding she couldn't say."

"Are we to assume the old fellow knew of the hideout and climbed down there to get out of the storm?"

Tyler shrugged. "He must have. A lot of the Auxiliaries were recruited from the Home Guard. However, Jasper Cartwright was a bit long in the tooth to be trained as a commando, not to mention that by all accounts he was starting to lose his marbles."

"Surely there's a list somewhere. Aren't we the police in this region? The chief constable must have some knowledge of the goings-on."

"Presumably he does. He should know who has been recruited and where the hideouts and observation posts were built. But it's highly classified information."

Rowell shook his head. "Lord help us, I can't stand all this rigmarole. If we're not in the know, how the hell – excuse the language, sir – how the heck can we keep law and order?"

"I'm with you, Oliver, but I've been told that the chief had to take a secrecy oath, with a promise to commit suicide if we were invaded so he wouldn't reveal the whereabouts of the cells if he had the misfortune to be tortured."

"Blimey."

"Blimey indeed. Might be a good thing for us we haven't been included in the secret."

"If the chief constable gives you the list of the Auxiliaries, will you have to take that oath too? The one swearing to kill yourself?" Oliver raised his eyebrows.

"God, I never thought of that. I suppose I will."

"Blimey."

"I'll take the train to Shrewsbury headquarters tomorrow. I daren't talk on the telephone. Let's hope the chief will co-operate and not force me to torture him."

He was joking, they both were, but there was something about the topic that cast a dark shadow.

"Do you think there's still a possibility the Krauts will invade us, sir?"

"If we lose the war, they will."

Rowell had splurged and built up the fire, and Tyler watched the flames dancing in the fireplace for a few moments in silence.

"Must have been the devil to get the body out of there," said Rowell.

"You're telling me. He was stiff as a board. Place was dark as hell. Dr. Murnaghan got the job done fast, all things considering." Tyler smiled. "Nimble as a monkey that man. He's past retirement age but he's like an eager kid when it comes to examining bodies."

"How did the Cartwrights take it?"

"John Cartwright took it very hard. His wife not as much. It was obvious there was no love lost between her and her father-in-law. According to Edie Walpole, their Land Girl, Jasper was a righteous old misery to both Susan and her son. He's from her previous marriage, name of Ned Weaver. He hardly said a word, but he certainly wasn't grieved."

"Shame all round, though, isn't it, sir?"

"Certainly is, Oliver."

After his meal, Tyler walked down the hill and through the arch of the old gate into Lower Broad Street. The street was completely dark, no lights showing anywhere. If he hadn't had his torch he would have tripped over the rough, untended patches of pavement. This area of town below the wall seemed like a poor relation, not well cared for.

A rickety gate almost off its hinges guarded the entry to River Close, where Nuala Keogh lived. It creaked abominably when Tyler pushed it open. The row of cottages had originally been built for workers at the gristmill and they all faced the river, which he could hear below but not see. The ground in between had obviously been "dug for victory." Every scrap of land was being used to grow vegetables. This strip was probably lush enough in summer but muddy and barren now, drab and forlorn in the rain.

The cottages were two-storey, narrow-fronted, and seemed shabby and rundown. Only number two, second to the end, showed any evidence of care. The white trim was painted, the brass knocker was polished.

Tyler rapped on the door, which was opened almost immediately by Mrs. Keogh. He was rather gratified by the look of pleasure that came into her eyes. She was wearing a snug plaid dressing gown that fit in all the right places.

He tipped his hat. "Sorry to call on you so late, Mrs. Keogh. You've obviously retired for the night. I just thought I'd do a last check on the boys."

"No, no. That's quite all right. I was reading. They're in bed, though."

"I, er . . ."

"Come in out of the cold, at least."

"I won't stay . . ."

"You can have a cup of tea, surely? I'd be glad of the company."

"Of course. Thank you."

She followed the obligatory blackout regulations and brought him into the dark tiny hallway before closing the front door behind him.

"Here, let me take your hat and coat."

He handed them over, awkward in the confined space and darkness.

"I'm in the kitchen."

She pulled aside a felt curtain and they went inside. Here, the room was lit by only a couple of oil lamps that created deep pools of shadow. It was warm, although the fire in the hearth was low, embers really. Tyler had the impression of worn furniture but, like the front door, everything seemed clean and cared for. There was a smart ormolu clock on the mantelpiece and a couple of framed photos. Wedding pictures, as far as he could tell.

"Here, have yourself a seat," she said, and pulled an armchair closer to the fire. She had clearly been sitting in the other chair, a rocker, and he glimpsed an upturned book. He couldn't see what it was.

"So then would you be for having a cuppa tea?"

"Thanks."

There was a kettle simmering on the hob and she lifted it off and carried it to the sink. While there was obviously no electricity, at least there was an inside pump.

"How are the lads doing now?" he asked her.

"Unusually subdued. As you can imagine, it has been a shocking experience for them." As she poured the hot water into a teapot, her sleeve fell back to reveal her pale forearm.

I truly am love-starved, thought Tyler. *Everything this woman does seems attractive. The way she speaks, moves. Oh, God help us.*

"When she brought them here, your lady constable said you had spoken to the boys, at the farmhouse. I hope we can leave them for the time being. Just so they get a chance to recover. Neither of them wanted to go to bed. I made up a fire in their room to cheer them up a bit and I had to leave a candle lit."

"Of course. That interview about the Woolworth's incident can wait. I just wanted to follow up on today."

Mrs. Keogh brought over a tea tray and placed it on the padded footstool.

"Sorry, I'm all out of biscuits, and you'll have to scrape that bowl to get sugar. I used up my rations too fast this month, and I'm trying to hold back a bit of the sugar for the Christmas."

She poured him a cup of very strong-looking tea and, without asking, added a splash of milk.

"I only moved in here in May, from Dublin. It's hard getting used to having no electricity. We don't even have an indoor toilet here. We have to use the communal privy down the end of the row. Five of us, would you believe. Dreadful."

She dragged the rocking chair in closer.

"This always makes me feel like an old granny but the other chairs are in the parlour. I don't get a lot of company, truth to tell. You know how the English can be with us Irish. Cromwell all over again."

Tyler muttered an apology for his fellow Brits. He took a sip of the tea. It was tepid and very bitter.

She must have seen his expression. "Sorry, it's impossible to get the silly kettle to a boiling point."

"It's fine. Very robust, really."

She burst out laughing. "For a policeman you have excellent manners."

"Hey, come on!" He grinned back at her. "Why shouldn't a policeman have good manners?"

"My apologies. I'm judging you by Irish standards."

Another sip of the dreadful brew.

"You were saying? Your neighbours aren't too friendly?"

"It's not that they're unfriendly exactly, but they don't quite know what to make of us. Me and the boys, that is. It'll take time I'm after thinking. So why am I living here, you're wondering."

"All right. Why are you?"

"I came to be near to my husband. His mother is English and he felt a certain loyalty to her country. He joined up with the 5th Suffolk Battalion. Dublin seemed far away, and there was a position come available at the local library, so I jumped at the chance to be closer to him." She paused. "Nobody knew that the catastrophe of Singapore lay ahead."

Tyler recalled that, according to the magistrates' docket, Mrs. Keogh was a widow. He waited.

"I got word that he was missing in action, believed dead."

"I'm sorry, Mrs. Keogh. That must have been dreadful for you."

She stared into space for a moment. "'Believed dead' leaves one open to hope, doesn't it? Not *confirmed* dead, *believed* dead. I keep hoping he's been taken prisoner. I want him to be alive, but then there are fearful stories coming out about how the Japanese are treating the POWS."

Tyler had heard those stories too, and he felt a sharp pang of sympathy for her.

"I was glad when the town council put out a notice that they still needed homes for evacuees," she went on. "This house is small but I was most happy to have the boys. They give me something to take my mind off Paddy."

A silence fell between them but it was companionable rather than awkward. Tyler found Mrs. Keogh easy to be with.

She spoke first. "Your constable filled me in when she brought the boys home but she couldn't say too much. Even Jan said they had taken an oath on their Scout's honour not to disclose where the body was found. They both seemed so frightened and oppressed by that. The oath, I mean. Was that necessary?"

"I'm afraid it was."

"How did the man die?"

"We don't know exactly. The coroner will do a post-mortem."

"There weren't ghastly wounds or anything like that, were there? I don't want the boys to start having nightmares again. They've only just begun to sleep through the night."

"No. No obvious signs of violence. It's most likely Jasper Cartwright died from exposure."

"And that's all you can tell me?"

"At the moment." Tyler chewed his lip. "One question about the lads. Is it usual for them to go so far afield?"

"Why not? They're used to riding all over the neighbour-hood. Why do you ask?"

"For one thing, the weather was miserable."

"They're hardy. I've bought them macks and boots and they seem to be fine." She winced. "Sorry, I sound defensive even to myself, but I do care for the little rascals, and I've tried to strike a balance between giving them independence and being overly protective."

"And I get the impression you've done a great job," said Tyler. "But when I spoke to the boys about what they were up to, I thought they weren't being entirely truthful."

"Perhaps it's because you're a police officer," she said with a shrug. "Their early encounters with local authorities have not been positive. They've learned to be wary. Not to men-tion the upset of the court experience." She picked up the poker and prodded at the log. The dying fire leaped into flames. "They like being here with me, but school has been difficult. Not all the children are willing to give my two a bit of leeway. They don't understand them." She stared into the fire. "They've said so little. Sometimes I can only guess at what they've already experienced."

Tyler didn't stay much longer, although he would have liked to. Perhaps Mrs. Hamilton had set his mind on a certain track, but he couldn't deny to himself how much he'd enjoyed Nuala Keogh's company. For a few brief moments he'd been able to shove aside his obsessive thoughts about Clare and her letter.

He agreed to return the following day and see how the boys were faring.

He arrived at the house almost breathless after fighting the wind up the hill. Rowell greeted him as soon as he entered.

"A cuppa coming right up, sir. Do you want that baked apple now?"

"Yes, please, but no tea. I just had some."

He followed Rowell into the kitchen. He could smell the apple warming in the oven.

"I didn't get to talk to the boys," said Tyler, sitting down at the table, where Rowell set a plate in front of him. "They were in bed, but according to Mrs. Keogh they're doing all right, all things considered. Bit traumatized, naturally." He ate a piece of the baked apple. "Hmm, scrumptious, Oliver. You have outdone yourself."

"Nothing fancy really, but it is nice to have custard once in a while."

"I almost forgot to ask you. How did it go with the two hooligans? Did they do their work?"

"Pretty good. I think they wanted to make an impression. The floor is spotless, and the wc would do justice to the King and Queen."

"Glad to hear it."

"Oops. I almost forgot something too." Rowell trotted out to the hall and returned carrying an envelope. "Mrs. Hamilton delivered this note for you. Nice woman she is. Very eager to know how I was getting on with Dorothy. I told her we were getting along like a house on fire." He hesitated. "Matter of fact, sir, I was hoping I could ask for a bit of advice."

Tyler raised his eyebrow. "Go ahead."

"As you know, I've been seeing Dorothy for over two months now. She's been hinting that it's time we went a bit further, if you know what I mean . . . I always leave after I've walked her to her door. Sometimes, I'll go in for a cup of tea, but mostly I just get straight back here. Well, like she said just the other day, it's not as if we're kids who don't know what's what. We've both been married before." Again he paused. Tyler nodded encouragingly. "What I was wondering was . . . how long you think we should wait until we . . . well, you know, until we . . ."

"Have sexual relations?"

Rowell laughed. "In a word, yes."

"As you say, Oliver, neither of you are new to the game. And Dorothy is keen. So why not? You've only got yourselves to answer to."

"But that's just it, sir . . ." His voice trailed off.

"What? Why the hesitation?"

"To tell the truth, I feel if I rushed into anything it would be disloyal to Evelyn."

"She's been gone more than two years now, hasn't she?"

"True. But I don't know if she'd want me to take on another woman as yet."

"Are you planning to marry Dorothy?"

"My goodness, I can't say."

"Does she feel the same sense of loyalty to her dead husband?"

"No. But he's been gone for longer than my Evelyn. Five years now."

Tyler rubbed at his own forehead. "These days, time has taken on a different quality. Most people feel they shouldn't wait if they don't have to. Who knows if we'll be around?"

"So you're saying I should take the step. Stay over for the night. When I'm not on duty, of course."

"I can't see any reason why not."

Rowell beamed. "Thank you, sir. I do appreciate you letting me talk like this. I told Dorothy I might drop in on her, if it wasn't too late."

"Sounds splendid, Oliver. I'm sure you will make the right moves."

Rowell spluttered with laughter. "As it were."

Tyler looked at the unopened envelope. He was feeling strangely apprehensive.

"I'll leave you to it, then, sir. If I do come back tonight I won't disturb you. I'll be quiet as a mouse."

"And if you don't come back?"

"In that case, I'll see you for breakfast."

From the gleam in his sergeant's eye, Tyler thought he had a pretty good idea which course of action Rowell was going to follow.

When the door closed behind him, he opened the letter.

Moira Hamilton's handwriting was like her, round, feminine, and distinctive.

Dear Mr. Tyler,

I got in touch with a woman on the top of my list whom I thought would be most suitable. She has agreed to meet you. Now, my philosophy is "strike while the fire is hot." Who knows where we'll be tomorrow? So I have taken the liberty of arranging the first meeting.

    She will be at the Clifton Cinema tomorrow night at half past seven. She has agreed to wear a red beret so you will recognize her. Mention Sincere Introductions so she knows you are bona fide and not just a masher. Her name is Gladys Currie. I'll leave it to the two of you to discover all the relevant details you might need to know about each other.

    If it is absolutely impossible to keep this appointment, I ask you to send word to me immediately and I will cancel it. Otherwise, bonne chance, *and enjoy yourself.*

Yours sincerely,
Moira Hamilton

Tomorrow! God, he'd barely had time to get used to the idea that he'd signed up for an introduction service. He'd vaguely thought it would be a couple of weeks before anything happened. But if he was honest, there was nothing urgently pending at the moment. He was free to go to the pictures with a woman wearing a red beret. And what should he wear? He had only one decent suit other than his daily inspector's outfit. It was grey wool, pinstriped. A little on the itchy side. *Oh hell. Just put on a clean shirt, an unstained tie, and wear the usual brown suit. And polish your shoes.*

His father had always impressed on him the importance of having polished shoes. *Shows a man has self-respect, son. One of the most important things you can do is to shine your shoes.*

Your clothes might be threadbare, but you will always make a good impression with well-polished shoes.

***

The lorry had picked up six other men who, like Angelo, had been forced to stay overnight at the farms where they'd been working. Back in the POW camp, lines of wooden huts connected by wooden walks filled a field. There was the obligatory barbed-wire fence and sentry post, but otherwise security was minimal. These POWs had all been vetted to make sure they posed no risk. Nobody was a rabid fascist. The majority came from rural areas of Italy and had been conscripted into the Italian army before being taken prisoner in North Africa.

With the coming of winter, work on the local farms had slowed down, and a lot of the men now occupied themselves with making toys: wooden tanks, dolls with painted faces, ships. They weren't allowed to sell them but the prisoners liked to give them to the farmers and their families. A quiet thank-you for the kindness they had received. With Christmas coming but severe shortages everywhere, they knew these articles would be welcome.

At the gate, Angelo and the others fell in behind a sentry, who led the way through the camp. It was dark and freezing cold.

"Hope you had a good day, gents," said the sentry cheerily.

For a moment Angelo thought he was mocking them, but then he realized he wasn't. Just a decent man who hadn't lost his humanity.

Angelo and another man, Mario Carella, were both in one of the far huts, and the other men were all dropped off first.

"What's up, Angelo?" asked Mario. "You're limping."

"Cow kicked out at me. I fell and twisted my knee."

"Bad luck. What were you doing to her?"

"Nothing. Should have warmed up my hands, I suppose."

Mario laughed. "I thought you knew how to handle those animals."

"I do," protested Angelo.

"Think of it as practice for when you get yourself a sweetheart. Never, ever touch a female's private parts with cold hands."

Angelo ducked his head in embarrassment. Mario was married, and he might have been able to offer some advice on the intimate issues on Angelo's mind. But Angelo's heart was too tender at the moment. He didn't want to share his experience with anybody else.

Mario had noticed his reaction and he slapped Angelo on the arm.

"What is this, my friend? Have you already done the deed? Did you entice the beautiful Land Girl to your bed?"

"Don't be silly," said Angelo.

Suddenly Mario dropped his banter. "Please be careful. No good can come of this. Only trouble and pain. Don't let anybody find out."

Angelo shrugged. "There is nothing to be careful about."

Mario made no further comment. The sentry halted at the entrance to their hut.

"Here we are. Home sweet home. If you're called out tomorrow, I'll see you here at the usual time."

"Good night. *Ciao*," said Mario.

"*Ciao*," answered the guard, who rather fancied his facility with languages.

Angelo pushed open the door and went inside. Although there was only a small wood stove in the centre, the hut was warm, slightly fetid. Those who hadn't been stranded overnight on nearby farms had stayed inside all day because of the bad weather, playing cards or dice, reading or writing letters. Working on their wood carvings. The things imprisoned men did.

"Hiya, you all," Mario called out. "We're back. Anybody miss us?"

A couple of the men looked up and flapped their hands in their direction.

"Didn't even know you were gone," said one of them.

"Thanks, De Cupo," answered Mario. "See if I'll write your letters for you ever again." He pitched his voice high. "*Now, Adelina, all I can think about day and night is the sweet place between your legs where I long to put my tool. Please tell me you think of me like that as well.*"

The other man jumped to his feet, infuriated. "Cut it out. I don't write that kind of filth."

"Well, perhaps you should before she lets somebody else do it."

De Cupo took a step toward him ready to take a swing, but Angelo grabbed his arm and the other man got in between them.

"Come on, Mario. Stop riding him."

De Cupo shrugged Angelo off. "One of these days, I'm going to get you, Carella."

Mario stuck out his hand. "Sorry, Gino. I'm only joking."

De Cupo turned away, ignoring his proffered hand. Some of the other men who were nearby watched curiously, wondering if this confrontation was going to escalate. Flare-ups among the confined men were commonplace.

Angelo pulled Mario away and the two of them went to their bunks.

"Hey, Mario," called another man from a table in the corner of the hut. "Do you want in? We could handle another player."

"Sure. Give me a minute." Mario dumped his knapsack on his bed and joined the card players. "All right, Matteo. Prepare to lose your britches. Carella is here."

Angelo sat on his bunk. He was only too happy to have his friend distracted. At some point he'd have to tell him about Jasper Cartwright's death, but right now he didn't feel like answering any more probing questions. He'd hardly sorted out in his own mind what had happened.

Swiftly, taking his chance while the others were preoccupied, he lifted the corner of the mattress and slipped the piece of silk underneath.

WEDNESDAY, DECEMBER 9

TYLER WAS AWAKENED BY THE SOUND OF THE TELEPHONE ringing. He waited for a few moments, expecting his sergeant to answer it. *Damn*. He remembered Rowell was off duty and had left with high hopes that he would not spend the night in his own bed.

The room was dark and he had no idea what time it was, but according to his body it had to be early. He swung his legs stiffly out of bed, stuffed his feet into his slippers, and, dragging on his dressing gown, he shuffled downstairs to the hall. The caller was not discouraged and the telephone kept on ringing. He picked up the receiver.

'Tyler here."

"Tom? It's Murnaghan. Sounds like you just got out of bed."

"I did. What time is it?"

A pause while Murnaghan checked his clock or watch or whatever other timepiece he had chosen to ignore.

"Sorry, Tom. I lost track. It's five to six."

"Right."

"Thought you'd like to know preliminary results sooner rather than later."

The hall was freezing and Tyler wasn't sure his brain was capable of functioning at that temperature and that hour. However, what the coroner said next woke him up.

"You need to get over here as soon as you can, Tom. There's something you've got to take a look at."

Tyler had heard Murnaghan utter words like this before, and they didn't bode well for a simple case of death by misadventure.

"Can you give me a hint?"

"Better not. Don't always trust the blower. How soon can you get to Whitchurch?"

"An hour?"

"Good. Come as fast as you can."

"Will do."

What the hell had Murnaghan found? But Tyler knew the coroner wouldn't be persuaded to talk, even if Winston Churchill was asking. He had to do it his way. Tyler said good-bye and rang off.

**

Susan Cartwright was on her hands and knees trying to peer underneath her father-in-law's bed. There were the predictable dustballs, which he'd never allow her to clean away, a dirty handkerchief, and a couple of crumpled sheets of newspaper.

Where would he have put it?

She got to her feet and looked around. The room was desperately untidy, with discarded papers and clothes on the floor, used dishes on the chairs. It made her insides churn. She wasn't going to find anything until they cleared it all out.

The door banged downstairs.

"Susan. Susan? Where are you?" John called.

"Coming," she called back, closing the door quietly behind her.

"What were you doing?" John asked when he saw her on the landing.

"I thought I'd have a look-see in case he really did find treasure."

"For goodness sake, Susan, you know how he was. You've harped on it often enough. He lived in a fantasy world half the time."

"No harm in looking."

John glared up at her, his face furious. "You can't give him any peace even in death, can you?"

Susan flinched as if he had struck her, which he might just as well have.

"Please, John. He tried to destroy us while he was alive. God forbid he should succeed now he's dead."

***

Tyler was heading back upstairs to get dressed when Sergeant Rowell came in. Tyler could hear him whistling as he unlocked the door. Obviously his night had been satisfactory. Lucky man.

He filled him in about the phone call.

"My goodness, is there something suspicious about the old man's death?"

"Knowing Dr. Murnaghan and the thorough way he works, I'm guessing there probably is. He's saving the details until I get there. He doesn't like talking over the phone."

"Shall I make you a quick cuppa and some toast for the road, sir?"

"Much appreciated, Oliver."

"It's chilly in here," said the sergeant. "I should have come over a bit sooner to build up the fire."

"That's all right. I assume the reason you didn't spend the night here was because you resolved your dilemma?"

Rowell actually blushed. "Yes, sir. You might say that. Sorry."

"No need to apologize. I was teasing. It was your time off."

Rowell gave what could only be called an ear-splitting grin. "You were absolutely right. I brought the matter up with Dorothy, about how I felt I might be betraying Evelyn. She was most understanding and said she was happy to wait until

I was ready. Funny thing was, as soon as she said that, I found I *was* ready. More than ready."

The sergeant looked as if he was prepared to go into detail but Tyler cut him off.

"I've got to get over to Whitchurch right away. Is the Austin back from the garage? I'll drive myself."

"Yes. Just ease into the clutch as much as you can, sir. The mechanic says it's a bit precarious."

Tyler turned to go and Rowell called after him. "What are you going to do about seeing the chief constable, sir?"

"I don't know yet. I'll talk to Dr. Murnaghan first. Do me a favour and check on train times to Shrewsbury, will you? See what's still running."

"You could claim taking the car as official business, sir."

"I don't mind going on the train. Besides, it might be more reliable than the car."

Tyler gulped down his tea and toast and headed out the door. Rowell actually stood on the threshold to see him off.

Tyler made the now-familiar trip from Ludlow to Whitchurch in good time. Yesterday's pelting rain had let up, although the sky was grey and lowering. There were no other vehicles on the road. It was getting hard for people to justify unauthorized journeys. Unless they were Sir Edward Spence. Tyler gritted his teeth. He'd bide his time on that one, but he didn't intend to let it drop entirely.

He parked in the hospital car park, declutching carefully. He gave the car a little pat on the dashboard. "Don't let me down, old girl. Think of it as contributing to the war effort."

Tyler headed straight to the basement, where the morgue was. It was too early for the coroner's receptionist to have arrived and the entrance was deserted.

He found Dr. Murnaghan sitting on a chair in the dimly lit room, reading the *Ludlow Ledger*. It was so cold and damp that Tyler could actually see his own breath. Even Queen Victoria, who watched over things from her framed portrait, looked chilled.

The coroner got to his feet. "Ah. Good. I was hoping you'd get here fast. Nothing to do but read depressing news."

"I thought things were looking up for us in North Africa," said Tyler as they shook hands.

"I meant the references to Christmas coming. Always makes me blue."

Feeling much the same way, Tyler rather hoped the coroner would elaborate, but he didn't.

Murnaghan's hand was warm. *He must have good circulation*, thought Tyler. But he was also well dressed for the temperature in his Harris tweed suit and a colourful Fair Isle jersey. Add his lively knitted tie and he might have been at a village fete. The concession to his work was the necessary leather apron.

"Tom, I'm afraid there's more to this business than first met the eye. Come take a look."

He walked over to the gurney where Jasper's body was lying.

"He's still a bit stiff but I was able to do some prelims. First, lividity is all on the anterior side of the body. We can say with certainty that he wasn't moved from where he fell. He died where he was found, or very shortly beforehand."

He pulled back the sheet covering the body.

"It wasn't obvious at first, but when I stripped him I saw this. Look." Murnaghan indicated a dark bruise on Jasper's rib cage. There was a trickle of dried blood below it.

Tyler leaned in closer. "Good heavens, that looks like a stab wound."

"It is. You can hardly see the point of entry because it's only about half an inch wide, but there's no doubt."

"The weapon?"

"A knife for sure. It didn't penetrate very far. His waterproof probably prevented the blade from going deeper. There's a tear in the front of the coat that I didn't see at first."

"Neither of us noticed any blood in the vicinity of the body. I certainly didn't."

Tyler was chagrined that he'd been so unobservant. He was forever going on about the ever-suspicious mind of the copper, but he'd been lulled into complacency in this case. Given the circumstances, he'd simply assumed the old man had succumbed to the cold and the rain and died from exposure.

"It was hard to see much of anything in that Stygian gloom," said Murnaghan. "Besides, there wouldn't have been much blood loss, Tom. As I say, the blade didn't penetrate more than three-quarters of an inch, and it missed any vital organs."

"So it was not the cause of death, then?"

"Hold on. Don't rush me."

"Sorry."

"Given what I've determined so far, I'd say we're faced with two possibilities. One is that the old man was stabbed somewhere outside, got himself to the bunker, went down the ladder, fell to the ground, and lost consciousness."

"So it's medically possible for him to have got there under his own steam? Even with a stab wound?"

"Yes indeed. The tragic thing is that with prompt treatment he most likely would have lived. As I say, there was no significant blood loss. But he was already soaked to the skin and it was freezing in there. Technically, he died from exposure. It wouldn't have taken that long for hypothermia to set in. He might have lasted as little as half an hour."

"Would he have been conscious? Conscious enough to call for help, I mean?"

"Impossible to tell. But I'm placing time of death in the early hours of the morning. Hardly anybody likely to be around at that time. Who knows when his body would have been found if it hadn't been for our Boy Scouts. Of course, the 'own steam' scenario supposes Jasper had a prior knowledge of the hideout." He cocked an eyebrow at Tyler. "From what you told me previously about the Auxiliaries, he doesn't seem a likely candidate for recruitment."

Tyler nodded. "Bit too old. But I'm going into Shrewsbury as soon as possible to talk to the chief constable about who was on the Auxiliary lists."

"I suppose somebody else could have shown Jasper where the place was."

"The location is supposed to be top secret. But then you never know. Somebody could have told him." He looked at the coroner. "You said two possibilities, what's your other one?"

"Ah, yes. The second scenario is that he was stabbed near the hideout and then his attacker carried him there and dumped him down the ladder."

"And?"

"Given all the circumstances, I would say this scenario is the more likely. His position supports the conclusion that he was dropped." Murnaghan lifted up the rigid arm. "There is this, though. Take a look."

There was purple discoloration across the knuckles on Jasper's right hand.

"So he was in a fight? Defending himself, do you think?"

"Impossible to tell. His fist connected with something hard, that's for sure."

Tyler indicated Jasper's hand again. "Somebody would likely have bruises."

Murnaghan nodded. "If it was a fight he was in, I'd say so. But he might have hit anything solid. I can only verify the details of the stabbing wound. The assailant was right-handed, about the same height as Jasper, five-foot-ten. The entry wound was vertical, no evidence that the blow came from above or below. They were facing each other."

The coroner thrust his arm forward to demonstrate a strike.

"Are there any other marks on the body?" Tyler asked.

"Just a few bruises. He's got some fresh scrapes on his knees, which suggests he tripped. And," Murnaghan pointed, "he's got this long scar across his chest, but it's old. He suffered a serious injury when he was younger."

Tyler peered at the pale, scrawny body. The scar was deep and puckered and ran from his upper ribs on the left to his lower ribs on the right. A long slash, by the look of it.

"Apparently he was in the Boer War. That could be a sabre wound."

"Yes, it could be. It has been surgically stitched."

"When I first saw him, his mackintosh was unbuttoned to the waist," said Tyler. "Any theories as to why that was?"

Murnaghan actually chuckled. "I call it the Lear syndrome. As in *King Lear*. You don't commonly see it, but it is a syndrome of exposure. The victim actually experiences a feeling of intense heat as the blood vessels open in a last desperate attempt to live. Although it's the worst possible thing to do, victims will sometimes take off layers of clothing as they try to cool down."

"Why do you refer to it as the Lear syndrome?"

"Remember poor old Lear, wandering around the moor out of his mind? He's suffering from hypothermia. And when he finds his daughter is dead, he cries, 'Unbutton me here.' Critics have explained that as a tender moment but I say it was because he was feeling overheated. Amazing, isn't it, that William Shakespeare knew that?"

"I'll say. He knew a lot of things, that bloke." Tyler bent over Jasper's body. "Anything more you can tell me about the knife that was used?"

"Not a lot, except it was narrow, probably sharp on both sides."

"Domestic knife? Working knife?"

"I can't tell, Tom. Maybe we're dealing with another of those bloody commando knives we saw in your last case. It fits the bill in that respect. Either the coat slowed down the blow or the assailant was faint of heart. Maybe both." Murnaghan walked over to a tray on the counter. "When I checked the pockets of his mackintosh, I found this."

He held out his hand for Tyler to see. In the centre of a handkerchief was a thin coin of some kind, tarnished and slightly irregularly shaped around the edges.

"Looks old."

"It is. About three hundred years. It's a silver shilling from the time of Charles I. The old fellow probably found it in one of the fields. Not surprising, I suppose. The whole area was a hotbed of Civil War skirmishes. Ludlow itself was under siege. Roundheads won the day."

"I thought it was the Royalists."

"Was it? You may be right, Tom. Time blurs them."

Murnaghan rubbed at the coin.

"They're not that rare, but they're not exactly common, either. There was nothing else on his person."

"Do you think it's valuable?"

"Not worth a fortune, but it could bring in enough for the month's rent." He held up the shilling. "There may have been more where that one came from. Maybe Jasper had a whole purse full. Somebody knew of it, and tried to rob him."

"Hmm. Can I have a look at the handkerchief?"

Murnaghan handed it to him. "Nothing distinctive. Plain white cotton. No revealing monograms in the corner."

"Bit on the grubby side, but you're right, nothing distinctive.

I'll hang on to it." Tyler refolded the handkerchief around the coin and placed it in his pocket.

The coroner grimaced. "Given the circumstances of his death I'd call this, at the very least, a case of manslaughter. We'll have an inquest next week and I'll have the complete post-mortem done by then, but that's my opinion at the moment."

Tyler groaned inwardly. It was hard enough for the Cartwright family that Jasper had died so miserably. He didn't relish telling them that a person or persons unknown had assaulted him.

Murnaghan returned to the gurney. "Don't you despair about the world sometimes, Tom? Here we are in the middle of the worst conflagration the world has ever known and even in this little rural backwater there is no respite from a heartless killing." He sighed. "Three centuries ago, men died, spilled other men's blood, and now we can hardly remember what it was all about. Do you think in a hundred years' time posterity will say the same about us?" He put on a posh falsetto. "*I say, pater, why were the Germans and the English fighting?*"

Tyler shook his head. "I hope this war has more at stake than the Roundheads and the Cavaliers disagreeing about whether the King had the right to tax them or not."

The coroner shrugged. "Darn right it does, Tom. Darn right. Don't mind me. It's just my mood today."

Tyler was at a loss as to how to cheer him up.

The coroner stared down at the grey face of the corpse. "Poor old sod. He was in good health for his age. Lived by his muscles all his life. His liver wasn't the greatest – he probably drank too much – but there was no alcohol in his system when he died. Deserved to go peacefully in his bed." He covered Jasper's body again. "I'll put him in the pantry until you can release him to the family. You can take his clothes, if you like. I had to cut them off but they're entitled to have them back."

"It's going to be a shock when I pass this along. But thanks, Doctor. I'll get on to it right away."

"I'll write out my report and have Winnie type it up for you."

He wheeled the gurney into "the pantry," as he called it: a storage area at the far end of the morgue.

"I'd better get on, then," said Tyler.

Dr. Murnaghan returned to the chair he'd been sitting in when Tyler arrived.

"Happy Christmas, Tom." He picked up the newspaper again.

Tyler left him to it.

The wind had picked up but Tyler relished it. He wished it could blow away all troubles. Not possible, of course, and when it almost snatched off his hat, he was irritated and made a dash for the car. After a couple of alarming coughs, the engine started.

"Atta girl."

He depressed the clutch, moved cautiously into first gear, and headed back to Ludlow.

Suddenly, following an impulse he wouldn't allow himself to analyze, he turned off the main road toward the butcher's shop that his former father-in-law owned, where he thought Vera would be working. Why not? He and his ex-wife needed to talk – Christmas was fast approaching.

The bell on the door of the shop tinkled sweetly and the familiar odour of dead meat and sawdust assailed Tyler as he entered. Vera looked up from behind the counter where she was serving a customer. The smile of welcome she was ready to flash at an incoming customer froze.

"I'll be with you in a moment," she said. Ice cold.

"No rush." He stood to one side, trying to appear casual.

Vera's hair was longer than when he'd last seen her, and it suited her. Dark, with a natural wave, her hair had always been one of her best features. She seemed a little trimmer, but that suited her too.

"Thank you, Mrs. Bailey," she said, and she stamped the ration card that the woman handed her. "We're hoping to have some fresh rabbit on Friday. Shall I put you down for one?"

"Yes, please."

The woman picked up her package of meat and dropped it into her shopping bag. "I'm going by Hayden's. He said they might have some onions today. Wouldn't that be grand?"

"It certainly would," answered Vera.

Tyler couldn't help but notice how pleasant she was to her customer. He certainly hadn't been privy to that side of her personality for a long time. He still blamed himself for the unhappiness of their marriage, but Vera was implacably unforgiving.

Mrs. Bailey left with a polite nod in Tyler's direction.

Vera waited until the door closed. Definite drop in temperature.

"So, look what the cat dragged in. You've come about my letter, I presume."

Shite. Tyler had forgotten to even open it. The solicitor's address had been sufficient to make him put it aside.

"No, as a matter of fact. I had to come into Whitchurch and thought I'd drop in for a minute."

"What for? Everything is above board in here."

Tyler made himself swallow an equally sharp response. He knew how deeply he'd hurt her, but he had hoped time might have healed some of the wounds. Especially as he knew she had a new man in her life. Clearly not.

"How've you been, Vera?"

"As well as can be expected."

"You're looking very smart. That a new hairdo?"

Rather than smoothing the waters, his comment seemed to aggravate Vera even more.

"What can I do for you, Tom? I'm too busy to stand here chewing the fat."

"Well, Christmas is coming up . . . and I wondered about our Janet. She says she'll likely get a few days off. I'm not really set up to do much of a Christmas and I'm hoping she'll be able to stay with you and your dad."

Vera scowled. "Of course. She's my daughter too, don't forget. We're her family. She'll stay with us."

"Good. That's good." Tyler hesitated. "I'll write to her, then."

"Do what you like," said Vera with a shrug. "She's a big girl. She can make her own decisions. She knows how to get in touch with me."

The shop was gloomy, only a low light on to show the few cuts of meat in the case. Vera was vigorously wiping the glass countertop.

"I suppose you'll be spending Christmas with your lady friend?" she said.

Tyler forced himself not to react. "I presume you mean Clare? And the answer is probably not. To my knowledge she hasn't returned to England yet."

He wondered how Vera would react if she knew the contents of Clare's last letter.

Vera swiped at the counter. "You'll be alone, then?"

"Well, I've got a good sergeant, we share the house. He's a widower. No family. We'll probably spend the day together."

Tyler was trying desperately to inject some levity into the conversation. To his astonishment, Vera's expression softened.

"Be nice to see Janet, at least."

"It will indeed."

Tyler's anger left abruptly and he felt a wave of sadness sweep over him. He and Vera had been married for nineteen years. They'd had two children together. It was an undissolvable bond.

He spoke quietly. "I understand you've been seeing a new fellow."

Wrong thing to say! Vera's softness vanished.

"So?"

"Nothing. I just wanted to say that I wish you every happiness."

The bell sounded as another customer came in, and Vera's professional smile reappeared immediately.

"Good morning, Mrs. Rowan."

"I'll be going then," said Tyler. "I'm sorry," he added ambiguously, not even sure himself what he was apologizing for. She didn't look up.

Tyler made good time on the drive back to Ludlow, and the car held up, although speed seemed to come at the cost of the heater. As he turned into town he noted that two more black wreaths had appeared on front doors in Mill Street. Two more deaths. He made a mental note to find out who they were so he could visit the families. He was still working at getting to know his new territory. He almost smiled. His former chief constable had described the position of inspector as being a sort of secular vicar. "You should know all your parishioners, so to speak. The good and the not so good. And they should know you. I can't fathom how cops in big cities manage. Here, at least, nobody should be a stranger."

He parked the car, giving the dashboard another little pat of thanks. Maybe the thing needed a name. He'd ask Rowell.

The sergeant was behind the desk.

"Before you tell me what happened, I'm going to bring you a cuppa. You look like you're perishing."

"Thanks, Oliver. Bloody heater gave up the ghost on the way back."

While the sergeant fussed with the kettle and teapot, Tyler removed his hat and coat and went over to the fire to thaw. "By the way, Oliver, I think the car would perform better if we gave it a name. What do you think?"

"I already have, sir," Rowell called. "It's Annabel. I named her after my grandmother. Same cussedness. You never knew which side of her you were going to get, the sweet old lady or the cranky curmudgeon."

"All right. Let's hope she doesn't take after her namesake entirely."

The sergeant came over with the tea tray. "I did bake some scones, sir. I was thinking you could have them later, at tea time, but would you like one now?"

"That would hit the spot all right."

Like a magician pulling a rabbit out of his hat, Rowell plonked a small jar of jam on the tea tray.

"I've been saving it for Christmas, but I think it might be more appreciated today. It's damson."

"Homemade?"

"It is. And the plums are from the tree in my in-laws' garden. Hmm. I'll build up that fire. Be right back."

He picked up the coal scuttle and trotted off downstairs to the cellar.

Tyler sat down in his chair. Recklessly he slathered jam on the scone and stuffed it in his mouth. Scrumptious. Washed down with a cup of strong tea, it was a feast fit for a king. Almost made him forget about rationing, the war, the weather, and the miserable death of an apparently harmless old man.

Rowell poked the fire into doing its job, and for a brief moment it blazed into a gratifying warmth.

"So what did Dr. Murnaghan have to say? Don't tell me – it's a suspicious death! You have that look about you, sir."

"Do I indeed? Well done, Watson. Dr. Murnaghan has determined that Jasper was assaulted. He was stabbed. Died from exposure, but we're looking at manslaughter."

He explained what the coroner had told him. When he'd finished, Rowell shook his head sadly. "Who'd harm a pathetic old fellow like Jasper Cartwright? Off his rocker to boot. I can't fathom it."

"Nor me. But we have the unpleasant task of telling John Cartwright that his father was attacked. And, at the moment, we don't have a clue who did it."

Both men were silent while Tyler sipped his tea.

"I'll need to take a couple of the constables with me. We didn't give the hideout any attention first time around, never thinking we'd be dealing with a situation like this. We should get some photographs, at least."

He removed the handkerchief from his pocket and showed Rowell the coin.

"It was in Jasper's pocket."

"That's an old one for sure."

"Charles I. According to Dr. Murnaghan, not a fortune but a nice little find nevertheless."

"Maybe there's more where that came from."

"Could be. It was the only thing he had on him. I'll see what the family has to say about it."

Tyler noticed that the floor was unusually clean and shiny.

"That's a good job the lads did."

"It is, but that Wickers fellow is so cheeky I could slap him. He is just about to step over the line when he pulls back and becomes all sweetness and light. You can't pin anything on him.

The other one, Oldham, isn't so bad. He's just under Wickers' thumb is the problem."

"What time are they coming in today?"

"They're not. Oldham rang to say they've both come down with terrible bad colds and have to stay indoors. They don't want to spread their germs."

"That's thoughtful of them. Is it a crock?"

"Probably. Oldham sounded like he was all plugged up but that's easy to fake. He just had to hold his nose."

"Where was he calling from?"

"The Mohan place."

"That's the closest farm to the Cartwright one. I'll need to have a chat with our chums." Tyler put down his teacup. "Where's the rest of the crew? Don't tell me they're all off sick too."

"No, sir. Constable Mortimer took it on herself to check on the two evacuee boys."

"And Mady? Biggs?"

"They're both out on the beat."

"When are they due back?"

"In about thirty-five minutes."

"Send them out to Bitterley, soon as they come in. They'll have to bike. It's miserable weather but I'll need them."

"Are you still intending to go into Shrewsbury, sir?"

Tyler bit his lip. "I am, but I think I'll do some preliminary investigation here first.

"Oh, by the way, Oliver, would you check out the latest casualty list? I noticed two new wreaths on Mill Street. I should drop by and offer my condolences."

"I will, sir. One of them must be at Mrs. Dawson's. I know her son was missing in action." He sighed. "Seems like she's heard. Tragic, but at least now she knows for sure. Better that way."

Tyler remembered his visit with Nuala Keogh. It was true what Rowell said: not knowing was the agony.

He headed for his office. "I'll be right back."

There was a toilet for Tyler's personal use beside his office. He opened the door. The tiny room smelled of carbolic and also looked spotlessly clean. It really did seem as if the lads had done a good job.

He used the toilet and pulled the chain to flush. The water filled up in the bowl . . . and overflowed onto the floor.

What the hell?

There was nothing he could do except jump out of the way. The water stopped overflowing but was not draining at all. He went out.

"Oliver. The toilet's blocked. It was perfectly all right yesterday. Why do I have the feeling our chummies might be responsible?"

Rowell shook his head in disbelief. "I shall investigate, sir."

The door opened with a bang and Agnes Mortimer came in. "Good morning, sir."

"Morning, Constable. Leave your coat on. We've got to go out. Can you handle a camera?"

"Yes, sir."

"Why am I not surprised?"

"Beg pardon, sir?"

"You seem proficient at many things, Constable."

"Do I, sir? Er, well, thank you."

"The camera is kept in the storeroom cupboard. Sign it out with Sergeant Rowell. He'll be right back. He's just checking out the plumbing in my toilet."

Rowell came into the room carrying a bucket. He was scowling.

"I found the problem. This was plugging the pipe." He lifted out a wet pair of ladies' underwear. "My apologies, Constable."

"That's all right, Sergeant. Nothing I haven't seen before."

"Oh, er, yes. Of course."

Tyler looked at the offending article. "How the hell did knickers get into my lavatory?" He held up his hand. "Let me guess. Who was last in there doing a spit and polish?"

"Sam Wickers."

"Well, unless he's a ponce and not letting on, he just happened to have a pair of knickers on his person that just happened to fall into the toilet bowl, and he just happened not to notice."

Rowell nodded. "I thought he was being a bit too accommodating. I'll have his hide."

Tyler grimaced. "No you won't. *I* will. He's not going to thumb his nose at me and get away with it. He just added two more weeks to his sentence." He jerked his head at Constable Mortimer. "I'll meet you in the car park. Annabel can take an eternity to warm up. I'll get her started."

"Annabel, sir?"

"Never mind. Oliver and I have christened the bloody car. "

"Yes, sir." She hurried away.

"Where shall I leave the, er, the underwear, sir?" Rowell asked.

"Leave it in the wc for now. It's vital evidence."

"Quite so. We might have to charge those lads with conspiring to obstruct police business."

Tyler laughed. "Good, Oliver. Very good."

He got his hat and coat and went outside into the blustery chill. Rain was coming in the wind. He'd hardly had time to warm up and he had to struggle all over again.

This time, the capricious Annabel started right away. He let it idle for a few moments until Constable Mortimer emerged from the station carrying the camera bag and a tripod.

"Come on, Constable. I daren't stop. She might not start again. Put the stuff in the boot. Hop to it."

She did, and cautiously they crawled out of the car park and turned onto the narrow lane that connected with Broad Street. A handful of women were already queuing in front of the green-grocer's shop. Each carried a basket over her arm. If Hayden did have a new delivery of a fruit or a vegetable, they wanted to be there before he sold out. To Tyler's eyes, these women looked disheartened, already worn down with care. It was hard to witness. He fretted at his own feeling of helplessness.

As they drove, he filled in Constable Mortimer about the new development in the Cartwright case. She looked grave.

"It was sad enough before when it looked like death from misadventure. Now it's dreadful."

"I think our safest bet is to go straight to the hideout. We'll take pictures, see if there are any obvious clues that jump out at us. After that, we'll go and tell the family."

"Do you want me to be present for that, sir?"

"I certainly do. You can take notes, keep your eyes open. Be alert."

"Would any of them be under suspicion, sir?"

"At this point, I'm not ruling anybody out. Who knows? Maybe the old man had a fortune tucked away. Greed can make people do very wicked things."

"We'll have to see if there's a will and who's a beneficiary."

"Farmers like Jasper Cartwright typically don't make wills. If he did leave anything it's more likely to be hard cash and hidden somewhere."

He negotiated the turn at the top of the hill that led to Bitterley. Annabel acted as if the hill might be too much, but with a horrible grinding sound the gear kicked in and they made it.

"I think the transmission might be about to give up the ghost, sir," said Mortimer.

"Cross your fingers it doesn't expire until we've been and come back. I don't want to have to commandeer a tractor." He raised his eyebrows at his constable. "But you're probably as adept at driving a tractor as you are a motorcycle, aren't you?"

"Yes, sir."

"Constable, is there anything you can't do?"

"Of course, sir. Many things."

"For instance?"

She allowed a small smile. "Can't think of anything in particular at the moment, sir. I seem to have an affinity for mechanics."

"Good. When we get back to the station, if we ever do, take a look at this darn machine. See if you can fix it."

"Yes, sir. Be happy to."

It had started to rain heavily. The windshield wipers were doing a feeble job and one of them squeaked horribly. They drove on, Tyler pushing the car as fast as he dared.

Constable Mortimer spoke. "If none of the immediate family was involved, what I was wondering, sir, was who might Mr. Cartwright have encountered? I would think it would have to be someone close by. And was this a planned meeting or a chance one? If chance, why was the assailant out in the early hours of the morning? What was his business? Or her business, for that matter?"

"Excellent questions, Constable Mortimer. For which I currently have no answers."

Tyler parked the car in a lay-by off the side of the road. From there the ground sloped upward to the crest of the hill and the road curved sharply right. He could see the cattle trough, looking innocent enough, at the western end of the north field.

"Keep your eyes peeled, Constable. We'll flag any spot where there might be evidence of activity. As you say, at this point we don't know if Jasper met anybody, either with intention or accidentally. Neither do we know whether he entered the hideout of his own free will or was dumped down there. Although Dr. Murnaghan said there wasn't a lot of bleeding from the stab wound, there may be minute traces of blood that we failed to notice before."

"We had no reason to suspect foul play originally, sir."

"I realize that, Constable," said Tyler. "However, I'm a policeman. I shouldn't have been asleep at the helm."

"If I may say so, sir, you are being unnecessarily hard on yourself."

Her voice was so earnest, Tyler actually smiled. "Thank you, Constable. I'll keep that in mind."

"And you didn't seem quite yourself that day, sir. I thought perhaps you hadn't slept well."

"Good grief, Constable. Drop it, will you?"

"Yes, sir. Sorry. I didn't mean to intrude."

Tyler sighed. "And I apologize for snapping."

They got out of the car and Constable Mortimer hoisted the bag of wooden flags over her shoulder. Rain was lashing the fields, stirred periodically by violent gusts of wind.

"I can't imagine anybody trying to push through that hedge unless they had to," said Tyler. "They would likely have entered by the gate at the lower end of the field. Let's do the same."

They proceeded slowly to the gate, pausing to examine it thoroughly, but there was no sign of anything out of the ordinary. If there had once been traces of blood on the gate or the ground, the rain had already washed them away.

They continued on to the trough.

Tyler stared down. The bottom was covered with layers of sodden leaves. He certainly would not have guessed there was a hidden entrance if he hadn't already seen it. He moved aside the debris to reveal the grill.

"Take a photograph, please, Constable Mortimer. I want views of the entire trough, inside and out."

"Yes, sir."

He waited while she set up the tripod and camera. Then he pulled on the lever and lifted the grill, revealing the entrance. Here again, he examined the area carefully but saw no sign of blood.

"I'll go down first and you can hand me the camera."

There was some light coming from the peepholes but it was too dim to see anything clearly. He flashed his torch on the floor where Jasper had been lying. Even here there were no blood stains. The plank flooring didn't show any clear footprints either, only a few small clumps of mud that had likely come from the coroner's shoes. They didn't tell him anything.

Constable Mortimer lowered the camera to him and then climbed down. There were two narrow cots, one on each side, leaving an aisle just wide enough for Tyler and Mortimer to stand next to each other. The ceiling was quite high and they were both able to stand without stooping. At the head of one cot was a shelf on which perched a paraffin lamp. Across from it on an identical shelf was a heater, also paraffin. Tyler sniffed at them. Neither had been lit recently.

"Will we need to take fingerprints, sir?"

"Not sure if we'll get much from these surfaces but we'll give it a try. Who's our fingerprint man these days?"

"Well, since Eaves got called up, sir, I think it has devolved onto Constables Mady and Biggs."

"The ladder might yield something. Possibly the lamp and the heater. Keep your gloves on when you touch anything."

"Yes, sir. I was intending to do that."

There was a drawer underneath one of the cots and Tyler pulled it open. It contained a couple of neatly folded blankets and a pillow.

Agnes pointed to one of the planks that was shoring up the wall. "I think there's a compartment behind here, sir. You can see that the wood doesn't quite align."

"Good observation, Constable. Let's take a look."

He tugged at the join in the wood with his fingernails and, sure enough, it opened.

Agnes Mortimer is turning into a first-rate copper, he thought. *I could do with more like her.*

There was a shallow cupboard built into the wall. It was crudely lined with tin. Tyler flashed his light on the interior. Inside was a wooden box stamped "ISSUED BY SPECIAL ORDER OF THE WAR OFFICE. NOT FOR PUBLIC CONSUMPTION." He moved it out a little. It was sealed, but there was a printed list of the contents pasted on the side. Tyler read: "*Quarter pound of tea; tin of condensed milk; tin of pudding; tin of dried eggs; tin of sardines. Bar of chocolate. Bar of soap. Tin of tooth powder. 50 Cigarettes.* That would keep you going for a while. Maybe as much as a week."

"You talked about the Auxiliary Units, sir. Would these be standard rations for one of the hideouts?"

"I'd say so. The box hasn't been opened so I assume it was part of the furnishings when the hideout was built." Tyler turned around. "Where there's one cupboard, there's bound to be another. Ah. There we are."

Next to the other cot there was the same slight misalignment in the planking.

"Shall I try, sir?"

Mortimer opened the door to the compartment easily. Inside was a Peek Freans biscuit tin. Tyler took it out and removed the lid.

The tin contained several rather furry-looking boiled sweets and a couple of paltry Cadbury's Ration chocolate bars. They were untouched, but there was an empty wrapper from a Kit Kat bar indicating that a tastier treat had been devoured.

There was also a rather tattered newspaper clipping. He directed the beam of the torch on the paper and read out loud.

QUEEN WILHELMINA ADDRESSES
HER SUBJECTS ON BBC

The indomitable queen of the Netherlands has expressed her determination to never be defeated. She assured her loyal subjects that she has not nor will she ever abandon them. "We will support our Allies until this Nazi scourge has been driven from our land. Do not lose heart. Your queen is with you at every moment."

Tyler aimed his torch back inside the cupboard. "What else have we got?" He slid out a little bundle of comics. "Two *Beano*s, two *Wizard*s, a *Rover*, and a *Hotspur*." The dates ranged from August to just three weeks ago.

"Hello, what's this?"

Tucked inside the *Wizard* were two small pieces of cardboard. On one was written the number 2204, on the other 2206.

"They look like the identification tags that evacuee children have pinned on them when they first arrive here," said Mortimer. "Necessary but sad, I think. As if they're parcels."

"Well, no prizes for guessing who numbers 2204 and 2206 might be." He turned the tags over. Sure enough, the names printed on the back were Jan Bakker and Pim Bakker. Tyler sighed. "Our lads were not telling us the truth, were they, Constable? It's not likely you're riding all over the countryside in bad weather with your precious tin of sweets and your favourite comics clutched to your bosom and then, by sheer chance, you discover a secret hideout which turns out to be the final resting place of a very dead body. In the midst of all that you have the presence of mind to locate a hidden compartment where you stash your treasures. All before going off for help."

"They'd been here before, sir."

"This is probably what you sensed they were hiding when you talked to them at the farmhouse."

"I hope there aren't other things they've been lying about. I must say, I'm becoming quite fond of the little rascals." Mortimer's expression was woebegone.

"Don't let your personal feelings cloud your judgment, Constable."

"Don't worry, sir. I won't."

The Cartwright household, together with Edie, were in the kitchen seated around the table. John had the Bible open in front of him. He had a wide black band on his sleeve. Susan Cartwright was dressed entirely in black, and the plainness of her frock made Tyler think of a housekeeper. She looked drawn and haggard.

Mortimer discreetly took a position by the door while Tyler delivered his news concerning Dr. Murnaghan's findings.

John was the first to break the silence that fell upon the room.

"Stabbed!" he whispered. "By who? Who'd do that to Pa?"

"I don't know as yet," said Tyler. "But I am declaring his death an indictable offence."

"What does that mean?" asked Susan.

"Let's put it this way," answered Tyler. "The coroner is sure that Mr. Cartwright was wounded shortly before he ended up in the hideout, although the stabbing wasn't what killed him directly. He likely died soon after from exposure. Somebody was culpable, though, and I must determine who that person was."

Tyler paused. John Cartwright stared down at the floor; his stepson wasn't looking up either. Almost reflexively, Susan started to brush invisible crumbs from the table. Only Edie continued to focus on Tyler. Her eyes were wide.

"When we spoke before, you all said you heard nothing to indicate Mr. Cartwright had gone outside. I assume you all stand by that?"

One by one they nodded.

"I didn't ask this question before because it didn't seem necessary, but now it does," he continued. "After you had all retired for the night, did anyone leave the premises? At any time? For any reason?"

He didn't miss the flood of colour that came into Edie's cheeks.

But it was John who had the strongest reaction to the question. He actually slammed his fist on the table. "What! Am I being thick, here? Are you suggesting one of *us* may have stabbed my father?"

Susan reached over and touched his arm. "Don't be foolish, John, of course the inspector doesn't mean that."

"I'm simply trying to get a picture of what went on Monday night and early Tuesday morning, Mr. Cartwright," answered Tyler.

Ned Weaver glared at him, his eyelid twitching wildly. "If it's drawing a picture you're after, you should speak to the POW. He'd probably jump at the chance to get back at an Englishman."

"How can you say that?" said Edie. "He had nothing against Mr. Cartwright."

"You can't know that for sure," Ned shot back. "In Jasper's mind the Itie was the enemy."

"Mr. Cartwright didn't die anywhere near the barn," Edie replied. "Regardless, Angelo was locked in. You know he was." Tyler noticed the utter dismay on Edie's face.

John shoved his chair back. "Not when I went to call him for breakfast he wasn't. The bolt was not shot from the outside the way it should have been." He held up his hand to stop Susan's recrimination. "It didn't seem important to mention. Angelo hadn't run away. He was in the barn where he was supposed to be. I thought Ned might have forgotten about bolting the door. Maybe he'd had one of his nervous collapses."

Ned spluttered, "Whoa. You can't pin that on me. I walked the Itie over to the barn after we had our supper. I let him in and bolted the door behind him. I did exactly what I was supposed to do."

"Are you certain?" Tyler asked. "It might not be something you'd pay a lot of attention to. In a hurry to get in out of the rain, that sort of thing."

"Course I'm certain. I wouldn't let an Itie have the chance to roam around the countryside. Never."

Tyler addressed John. "Mr. Cartwright, if you found the door was not barred in the morning, and Mr. Weaver says it was barred the previous night, who might have unlocked it?"

It was Susan's turn to jump in. "Perhaps Jasper did. He might have gone to the barn looking to get into a fight with the Itie. You know how he could be."

"That's utter nonsense," said Edie sharply.

"But how would he have got into that hideout?" said John. "Like Edie said, it's nowhere near the barn."

"Maybe Mum's right," said Ned, speaking very quickly. "Jasper could've attacked the Itie, and he was the one carried him out and dumped him there."

Edie glared at him. "Don't be silly. Of course he didn't."

"The Itie's problem is he could hardly lock the door behind himself, could he? If it wasn't fastened this morning, who knows what he'd been doing? He could have been wandering all over the countryside for all we know. All he had to do was return to the barn and then act all innocent when somebody came to get him."

Tyler thought there was some credibility to what Ned was saying.

John shook his head. "No, no. I can't believe that young fellow would harm Pa."

"We hardly know him," said Susan. "Who knows what he's capable of?"

John continued, "Besides, how would the Itie know the whereabouts of the hideout?"

Ned shrugged. "Why not? Those kids found it, why couldn't he have?"

"Wait a minute," interjected Edie. "Hold on. Even *I* didn't know the place existed and I've been working here all summer."

Ned winked. "Never underestimate the cunning of a POW." He leaned toward Edie. "Face it, Edie. It's not out of the question that he's the one responsible. Jasper was delusional half the time. Saw ghosts. He could have been the one on the attack."

Edie's lips tightened. "No. I simply don't believe Angelo is capable of such a thing, even in self-defence."

Ned's eye was flickering nonstop. "Why not? He's a trained soldier and he's in a foreign land. Last time I looked we were at war with Italy."

"No. I can't accept that." Edie looked as if she was ready to jump up and run out of the room. Mortimer moved slightly so she was blocking the doorway.

"All right, everybody," said Tyler. "Let's calm down for a minute. I know what I've had to tell you is shocking but, as I said, I am now making a full investigation."

"I knew we should have locked Jasper's bedroom door," said Susan. "None of this would have happened if we'd done that, but John was dead set against the idea."

"I couldn't stand to make his own home a prison," said John.

Susan was weeping openly now, tears trickling down her cheeks. Edie quietly handed her a handkerchief. John ignored her.

"Any opinions as to what he was up to when he went out?" Tyler asked.

"I can't claim to know what was going on in Pa's mind," said John, "but he took his treasure box with him. It's not in his room, and it was usually under his bed. I saw him put it there on Sunday."

"His treasure box? What was that?"

Susan answered the question. "He liked to collect all his 'special treasures,' as he called them. Nothing of any real monetary value. The kind of things a child might keep. You know, his old dog's collar, photographs of his dead wife, her wedding ring."

"What did it look like, this case?" asked Tyler.

"Metal. About the size of a small suitcase," said John. "It used to be a typesetter's case. He's had it for ages. Meant a lot to him. I'm guessing he went to stash it somewhere."

Susan straightened her back. "What John isn't saying is that his pa became convinced I was going to destroy his precious things." She dabbed her eyes. "I'm not a monster, Inspector. I would never have done that. My lord, I have souvenirs of my own. Isn't that true, John?"

Her husband didn't reply.

"If he did intend to hide the box," said Tyler, "was there a special place he might have used?"

"Not in the house, for sure. I might've found it." Susan's voice was bitter.

"Not that I know of," answered John.

"Miss Walpole? Mr. Weaver? Any ideas?"

"None. I haven't seen it," said Edie.

"Could have been anywhere," said Ned. "No shortage of places around here."

This seemed like a good time to show them the old coin. Tyler took out the handkerchief that Murnaghan had given him and opened it on the table.

"This was in Mr. Cartwright's pocket. It's an old coin. I wonder if you know anything about it."

John picked it up and examined it. "Charles I."

"Did Mr. Cartwright show any of you this coin or talk about other coins he'd found?"

John answered, "I've never seen it before. But Sunday night Pa did say he'd found treasure. I didn't take him seriously."

"It wasn't the first time he'd got excited about something he found," interjected Susan. "Usually it turned out to be junk. He dug up an old watch once. Didn't work, but he was as excited as if it was worth hundreds of pounds. So there was no reason this so-called treasure was any different."

Edie touched the coin. "It's three hundred years old. Maybe it could communicate with us about those past times. Give us some help."

"Ha. I doubt it," said Ned. "They was at each other's throats just as much as we are. Worse, really. That coin comes from Civil War time. Same kind of people fighting each other. Not as if your neighbour was a foreigner, like the Krauts or Ities are to us. Fighting them is understandable."

Tyler thought this was a rather more perspicacious comment than the young man had offered to date.

"Well, I don't care what you say," said Edie. "This coin would reveal something wise if it could."

Tyler thought the shilling might give them a lecture on the futility of war, but it wasn't communicating at the moment. Perhaps they needed a clairvoyant.

He rewrapped the coin in the handkerchief and returned it to his pocket. "I'll give this back to you after the investigation is concluded, Mr. Cartwright. I will also return his clothes, of course."

"Do you think the coin has anything to do with why he was attacked?" John asked.

"I don't know, Mr. Cartwright, but the more gaps I can close the better. Speaking of which, I must repeat my original question. Did any of you leave the house at any time between Monday night and early Tuesday morning?" This time he addressed each of them directly. "Mr. Cartwright? Mrs. Cartwright?"

They both shook their heads.

"Mr. Weaver?"

"Not me. It was too miserable a day to go anywhere. I stayed tucked up in bed until six thirty."

"Miss Walpole?"

Edie muttered a quiet "No."

"Very well. Is there anybody at all who you think might have encountered Mr. Cartwright?"

Ned answered. "You'd better talk to the two blokes who board at the Mohan farm, Sam Wickers and Tim Oldham. I suspect they're poachers, them lads. I'll bet they go out early to get their rabbits."

Do they indeed? thought Tyler. *Is that why they were out on their bikes the other night?* "I'll have a word with them," he said.

There was a tap at the door. Mortimer opened it to take a look.

"Biggs and Mady are here, sir."

"Good." He turned back to the little group. "I'll keep you informed as to any further developments. We'll have to take fingerprint samples so we can rule out those that should be there and those that shouldn't. One of my constables will do that shortly."

"Are you going to talk to Angelo?" burst out Edie.

"If we can. Is he back working here today?" Tyler asked.

"Yes, he's been busy all day in the barn. Can I come with you? I might be of help in interpreting. My Italian is basic but passable."

"Thank you, Miss Walpole. I'll take you up on that."

She got up immediately and put on her coat. Ned began to light a cigarette. Susan was watching her husband anxiously. John stayed where he was. He appeared to be lost in his own unhappy thoughts.

Tyler followed his constable and the Land Girl out the door.

Edie hurried ahead through the gate and turned in the direction of the barn.

Mortimer whispered quietly to Tyler. "I myself am quite conversant in Italian, sir. Finishing school days. Shall I speak to the POW?"

"No, let's leave it as is. Don't let on you know the lingo. People are apt to reveal more if they think you don't understand what they're saying."

"My thoughts exactly, sir."

"Glean anything from our little meeting?"

"Quite a lot actually, sir."

"Good. You can fill me in later."

Tyler and Mortimer caught up with Edie as she opened the door to the barn.

Angelo was sweeping out a stall, but he stopped when he saw them.

"*Ciao*, Angelo," said Edie. "The police want to talk to you about Mr. Cartwright's death. He didn't just die from exposure he was – "

Tyler interrupted her. "Let me tell him, Miss Walpole."

Angelo said something in Italian to Edie, who nodded at him and replied also in Italian.

"Let's speak English, if you don't mind," said Tyler.

"He simply asked me why I was here as well, and I said I'd help interpret."

Tyler caught an almost imperceptible shake of the head from Agnes. That was not what the exchange had been about.

"Why don't we sit down, take the weight off our feet," said Tyler, and he walked over and sat on one of the hay bales. Mortimer took the one next to him. Slowly Angelo went to a bale facing them and perched on the edge. Edie hesitated, then walked over and sat beside him. She left a distance between them, but her deliberate casualness was a dead giveaway.

Lord help us. I'll bet they've slept together. And that could create a huge problem for both of them.

There was a lantern hanging on a beam close to where the Italian was sitting. Tyler could see him clearly, and it was obvious the young man was extremely apprehensive.

"The reason I have come to speak to you again, Private Iaquinta, is because there has been a new development in the case of Mr. Cartwright's death." Tyler paused. "All right so far? Do you understand what I'm saying?"

Angelo nodded. "*Si. Capisco.*"

"The coroner, er, the doctor, has discovered that Mr. Cartwright was in fact stabbed . . ."

Angelo was looking bewildered.

Edie interrupted. "You're speaking too quickly, Inspector. His English is good but you have to speak slowly."

"Miss Walpole, please. I shall have to ask you to leave if you interrupt again," said Tyler. "Angelo seems to understand quite well."

She subsided but it was obviously difficult for her. Tyler turned back to the Italian and mimed plunging a knife into a body.

"Stabbed. Mr. Cartwright was *stabio.*"

Tyler thought the young man was genuinely shocked.

"That is truthfully a very bad thing. What was the occurrence?"

"That is what I intend to find out. You told me yesterday that you didn't see Mr. Cartwright, senior, after you came in here for the night."

"*Si.* Er, I mean, no." He put his hands together against his cheek. "I sleep."

Tyler paused. "According to Mr. John Cartwright, when he came to fetch you for breakfast the door to this barn was not barred. Can you explain why that was the case?"

Angelo stiffened. "No, I cannot."

"Did you by any chance have a visitor during the night?"

"Visitor? No, of course not. I sleep." He repeated the hand gesture. "I have the sleep of the justified."

Out of the corner of his eye, Tyler could see that Edie was clutching so hard at the side of the hay bale her knuckles were white.

"Right. I wondered if old Mr. Cartwright himself might have come in here. Perhaps you had an argument? He could get confused. Perhaps he attacked you? You defended yourself. He left –"

"No. No. No fight. Never with man with no weapon."

Angelo slumped forward. He uttered something in Italian. Edie responded immediately, speaking in the same language. Her Italian was stumbling but she seemed able to make herself understood. Angelo shook his head at her.

"Miss Walpole," said Tyler, "I would like Private Iaquinta himself to respond." He turned to the Italian. "Did you understand what I said?"

"*Si.*"

"I'll ask you again. Did you have anything to do with Mr. Cartwright's death?"

His face full of misery, Angelo looked up at Tyler. "No, sir. I did not. I swear to my honour, I did not."

"Do you own a knife?"

"No. Not allowed to us."

"Did Mr. Cartwright come into the barn during the night?"

Angelo didn't respond.

"Answer, please."

Angelo stared back at the ground. Edie's expression was agonized.

"Private Iaquinta! Did Jasper Cartwright enter the barn yesterday?"

"Yes, sir," the Italian said in a low voice. "Yes, he did."

Tyler let that revelation sink in. Edie had turned her face away and he could see she was trembling. He stood up and took a few paces from the young man, then turned to him.

"At what time did Mr. Cartwright enter the barn?"

"I am not sure of it but it was very early in the morning. Not yet dawn."

"Why didn't you admit that right away?"

"I was afraid I be blamed for something. I am the bad one, the enemy, after all."

"I promise you won't be blamed for anything you didn't do. Please tell me what happened when Mr. Cartwright came into the barn."

"Nothing . . . I swear, nothing. He was most confused. He came in. I was awakened and I called out to him. He did not answer to me. He simply turned around and left."

"No attack?"

"None."

"Did he say anything at all?"

"No. Nothing."

"Perhaps he was frightened? Mistook you for an enemy?"

"No."

"If he had mistaken you and attacked, you would have had to defend yourself. Nobody would blame you for that."

Angelo shook his head.

"I notice you have been limping, Private Iaquinta. Is that because you were in a struggle – a fight – with Mr. Cartwright?"

"Please, *signor*. I told you, no fight. It was the pesky cow I was milking."

Tyler let a pause drop between them. Angelo shifted on the hay bale. Edie was still staring at the placidly munching cows.

Finally, Tyler said, "Why should I believe you? It's not that hard to come across a knife on a farm. Somebody stabbed Mr. Cartwright. I only have your word that it wasn't you. There are no witnesses."

"I am sorry, Inspector. It is utter truth. I not touch him."

Again Edie interceded. "I can vouch for Angelo in this matter, Inspector – "

The Italian caught her by the arm. "No. I will answer."

Their eyes met, something was communicated, and he let her go. She turned to Tyler. "What I was going to say is that I myself was present when Clover kicked him. I was here. I saw it happen."

"And when was this, Miss Walpole?"

"Monday. It happened during the afternoon milking."

Tyler regarded Angelo. "Did you report it to your medical officer at the camp?"

"No, no. I am very well. It is nothing of importance."

"You understand that I will have to come to the camp and give a report about what has occurred."

"*Si.*"

"One more thing. Did you notice if Mr. Cartwright had anything with him when he paid this unexpected visit?"

"What mean you?"

"Was he carrying anything? Did he leave anything behind?"

"I see nothing. It was dark. I just hear the door open I and came up from my bed to see who. I recognized it was Mr. Cartwright."

"How did you know it was him?" Tyler interjected. "You said it was dark."

"He was carrying a lantern, but as I have said recently, he turned around and left. It was only moments."

"Thank you, Private Iaquinta." Tyler stood up. "I shall drive you back to camp later. In the meantime, you'll have to come over to the farmhouse with me."

"*Sì.*"

"Does he have to go there?" Edie burst out. "They'll all be ready to pounce on him."

"We don't have much choice at the moment, Miss Walpole. I'll have him remain in the parlour for now."

"That's worse. He'll be stuck by himself, wondering what's happening."

"No matter what he'd be stuck by himself, as you put it."

Suddenly the girl burst into noisy sobs. "It's so stupid. It's all so stupid."

Tyler waited a moment or two to let her cry.

"What is stupid, Miss Walpole?"

"War," cried Edie. "This horrible war."

"In many ways I agree with you. Regardless, I'm the representative of the law. Until Private Iaquinta is cleared of causing the death of Jasper Cartwright, he will have to be under surveillance."

Angelo was regarding the young woman with obvious dismay. He went to reach out to her again, thought better of it, and let his hand drop to his side. Tyler could feel in his own body the young man's ache to touch the woman he was so clearly in love with.

Tyler installed Angelo in the parlour across from the sitting room. There was no lock on the door but the Italian had no way of getting out without being seen.

"Do you want something to read?" Tyler asked. "You'll be here for a while, most likely. Call if you need to use the toilet."

"Thank you, that would be super. I would like this *Boy's Own Annual*, if you please. I was given a copy and it is teaching me super English."

Could be worse, thought Tyler. You got language *and* very British attitudes in the *Annual*. He left the young man to peruse the pages featuring the derring-do of clever, plucky English boys.

Susan Cartwright gave him permission to take over the small "best" sitting room. John was upstairs, "paying his respects to his father," as Susan put it. Her eyes were red from weeping. Ned Weaver was fiddling with the wireless. Crackling noises came from the set. He had stared at Angelo as Tyler led him through to the parlour but hadn't said anything.

Edie went directly to the sink. "I'll help you with the dinner, Mrs. Cartwright. Perhaps we had better make more stew, just in case."

"That's the last of the carrots. You'll have to add more potatoes."

Tyler left them to it and went across to the front sitting room with Constable Mortimer.

"Let's light the heater," he said. "I'll have them put in a requisition for compensation if they need to. This is police business, and I'll be darned if I can work in subarctic conditions."

There were folding doors that partitioned off the sitting room from the kitchen, and he left them open a crack so he could keep an eye out for any activity. He didn't want anybody else in this family going wandering.

"Did you catch what Miss Walpole was saying to Angelo?"

"She was telling him not to worry. Everything would be all right."

"Ah, the optimism of youth. Was that all?"

"Yes, sir. Her Italian is imperfect but that was the gist of it." She frowned. "Do you think they are having relations even though he's a prisoner of war?"

Tyler had thought it was as obvious as a newspaper headline but he had to give his young constable some leeway. She probably wasn't as experienced as he was in covert love.

"Sir?"

"What? Oh yes, of course they're having relations. I am pretty sure she was with him on Monday night. It's likely she was the one who unbarred the door. She may have forgotten to bar it again when she left."

"Oh dear, that could put them into a lot of trouble, couldn't it?"

"Certainly could. At the very least, they'd be separated for the duration. A veritable Romeo and Juliet, those two."

"Angelo has admitted Jasper Cartwright entered the barn. If she was there he might have seen them together?"

"He might have."

"She seems so nice. He does too. Do you think it's likely that fear of being found out might have compelled them to silence Mr. Cartwright?"

"That's not what my gut says, Constable, but we'll keep an open mind."

"Your gut, sir?"

"Yep. One of a policeman's most effective tools."

She pursed her lips while she considered this. "Is that the same as a woman's intuition, sir?"

Tyler chuckled. "Probably."

"But didn't you tell me not to let feelings cloud my judgment?"

"That's quite different. But tell me quick. What were your impressions of the meeting with the Cartwrights and company?"

Mortimer paused. "Mrs. Cartwright strikes me as a woman with a strong sense of duty. I believe she blames herself for not locking the old man in his room. If you will forgive me for being personal, sir, her marital relationship is reminiscent of that between my own parents."

"Indeed? How so?"

"The wife wants more from the husband than he is willing or able to provide. As a result she is harbouring a lot of resentment."

Tyler peered at her. "Very good, Constable. You're wasted on the police force with observations like that."

Mortimer looked pleased and shy at the same time.

As for Tyler, he felt a big pinch of guilt. Mortimer might have been describing his marriage to Vera.

"What else?"

"Ned Weaver seemed anxious to direct blame toward the POW. Miss Walpole was equally determined to declare him above suspicion. Perhaps she needed to convince herself."

"Very good, Mortimer, very good. I concur with your observations. Of course, if one of them was responsible for Jasper's death, he or she is a good actor."

Mortimer gazed at him in dismay. "Oh, surely none of them is a suspect, sir? I find that hard to believe."

"Remember what I said, Constable. Being a successful copper is finding a balance of feeling and fact. Now, chop-chop. Let's concentrate on facts. I want you and Constable Mady to go to the barn and do as thorough a search as you can."

"Is there anything in particular I should be on the lookout for?"

"Anything untoward. Angelo says Mr. Cartwright came in and left immediately. That may or may not be the truth. He was so awkward it was hard to tell what he was dissembling about other than his relationship with Miss Walpole. But if, in fact, there was a struggle between them, you might see some evidence of it."

"It sort of makes sense, doesn't it, sir, if Jasper went down to the barn to stash his treasure box?"

"Finding it would certainly be helpful to our investigation. Off you go then. As soon as we can, I'll have Biggs start on taking fingerprints."

—

There was a telephone extension on the upstairs landing and Tyler went up there so he could call the camp commandant in private. Captain Beattie was abrupt. Army business was army business and police business was something else entirely. Tyler had encountered this attitude before so he wasn't surprised, but it irritated him nevertheless. As far as he was concerned, a person or persons unknown had brought about the death of a fragile old man. Anybody in the vicinity had to be questioned, POW rules or not.

"I'm hardly going to slap him in the glasshouse on the mere *possibility* of his having committed a crime, Inspector," said Beattie. "All you're telling me is that the young man was not secured as he should have been. Not his fault."

"He has acknowledged that Jasper entered the barn in the early hours."

"But the old man left immediately?"

"That's what he claims."

"If you discover Iaquinta has done something against the law, then we'll have to follow due process. But we don't know that he left the barn. Isn't that right?"

"He says he didn't, sir. He was there in the morning when John Cartwright went to get him."

"So you see – "

"I do need to pursue every possibility."

Suddenly, Beattie changed his tune. "Of course you do, Inspector. Of course. You are a police officer, after all. And I will give you all the help I can. It's just that I don't want unsubstantiated accusations being flung at my POWs."

"Neither do I, Captain. I can bring him back to the camp this afternoon. Perhaps we could have a meeting, the three of us, and go over what has transpired."

Tyler didn't think it was relevant to the case at this point to inform the captain that Angelo was more than likely having a liaison with a Land Army girl. And that was definitely against the rules.

"I know this fellow," said Beattie. "He took part in a little entertainment the priest arranged for the men. He has a rather fine singing voice. Not in the least a troublemaker."

"Glad to hear that, sir. But in order to rule him out, I'll need to take his fingerprints. Exclusion principle. Shall we have that done here, or would you rather I do it at the camp?"

There was a rather long pause, then Beattie said, "I think it'll be all right to do it there. I presume it will be simpler that way?"

"Indeed it will, sir."

"Good. Er, by the way, Inspector, sorry about what has happened. Any ideas as to what and so forth?"

"None at the moment, Captain."

"Right! Well, keep up the good work."

"Thank you, I will, sir."

They hung up. Tyler leaned back in his chair and stared at the ceiling. The captain had been overly protective of his prisoners, but Tyler supposed that was better than being hell-bent on using them as whipping boys.

He was about to go and see what his constables were up to when there was a knock at the door and Constable Mortimer came in. She was carrying a small grey metal case.

"I thought you'd want to see this right away, sir. We found it on a shelf in the barn. It was underneath some sacking."

"Put it on the chair and let's have a look."

She did so, being careful not to touch too much of the surface.

"John Cartwright was sure it was in his father's room on Sunday. Even if Jasper took it to the barn the next day and hid it himself, it's not a very good hiding place. It was where the cleaning supplies for milking are kept. There are various people who go into the barn, including the POWs."

Tyler lifted the lid. There wasn't a lot inside: a dog collar, a broken pocket watch, three photographs of the same woman, taken at different ages. A Sunday school medal, engraved "To Jasper Cartwright, for perfect attendance." The kinds of things that are of sentimental value to the owner but likely worth nothing to anyone else. However, there was also a thin, tarnished coin.

Tyler picked it up carefully. Like the one found in Jasper's pocket, this was stamped with the head of Charles I. He took the handkerchief from his pocket and removed the other coin.

"They look the same, don't they, sir?" said Mortimer.

"Indeed they do."

Tyler returned to the case. There was a torn piece of lined paper tucked into the corner, which he removed. A pencilled notation was scrawled across it.

"*Clee Hill at north. Forty paces east to west, then twenty. Go South Ten feet.*"

"Make any sense of this, Constable Mortimer?"

She studied the paper for a minute. "Directions of some kind by the look. We've got two coins now. Are we talking in fact about buried treasure?"

"God. It's beginning to sound like a tale right out of *The Boy's Own Annual.*"

"We have no way of knowing when this was written, or how long Mr. Cartwright had it in the box, do we, sir? Or even if he was the one who wrote it."

"The paper looks fresh enough. School notebook, I'd say."

He turned over one of the photographs in the case: "*Grace at a church picnic.*"

"Looks like the same handwriting, wouldn't you say?"

Mortimer nodded. "Definitely. The curly *G*s and the *C*s are identical."

She reached into her pocket. "We also found this, sir." She held out a tortoiseshell hair comb.

"Where was it?"

"Near the cot. It was underneath the rug."

Tyler put the comb in his pocket and returned the piece of paper to the case. "Let's go and see what our Romeo has to say about this."

***

Angelo sat unmoving. *The Boy's Own Annual* was open in his lap, but he was looking out the window. The wind was becoming even more ferocious, shaking the very house itself as if it wanted to destroy it. He knew he couldn't run. There was nowhere to go. He began to murmur softly to himself, *"Ave Maria, gratia plena, Dominus tecum."*

Saying the prayer took him straight back to his childhood. And of course straight back to his grandmother, so full of prayers and sayings. Now that he was grown up, he could better understand how difficult her life had been. Widowed at a young age, she had struggled to raise four children. Poverty had blighted her. Perhaps she had loved her husband and missed him but she said little, and what she did say wasn't particularly loving. His mother was her daughter, and she hadn't been happy about her marriage to a young man from the village. Had Nonna wanted more for her children? He didn't know. There had been so little of praise and encouragement, so much of carping and criticism.

For as long as Angelo could remember, he'd feared his grandmother and the malevolent expressions that flitted across her face. She was dark-skinned, hairy-chinned, and bony. She'd made no secret of disliking his fair hair and blue eyes, which set him apart from the other children in his family. They were dark-eyed, and dark-haired, like her. She insinuated that their mother had stepped outside the bounds, had lifted her tail to the wrong man. *The passing stranger.* His mother had been enraged when Angelo asked innocently one day what Nonna meant, but even after that row, nothing changed. The old lady still minded them for long dreary hours, and she still trotted out her meagre store of sayings. *Money is the root of all evil. The Devil makes work for idle hands.* And, for Angelo the most pernicious: *Crying comes after laughter.*

He took a deep breath and began to recite his poem as if it were a prayer. He'd written it in English.

Across a chasm we call to each other,
Will our love be the bridge or will it be our death?

The door swung open and the red-headed policeman came in. The tall, thin female constable was with him. The inspector was carrying the metal case.

"Amen," said Angelo.

***

Tyler put the case on the table in front of the settee.

"Have you seen this before?"

"No, *signor.*"

"It was on a shelf in the barn. How did it end up there?" He spoke slowly and deliberately, not wanting to leave any room for misunderstanding, real or feigned.

"I do not know, *signor.*"

"It belonged to Mr. Cartwright. His son says it was in his father's possession on Sunday. So unless it walked, it must have been brought to the barn sometime that night or sometime on Monday."

"Pardon?"

Tyler repeated what he'd just said.

Angelo frowned. "I was working in tool shed most of day, Inspector. I could not know if Mr. Cartwright brought it to the barn or not."

"You admitted earlier that, in fact, Mr. Cartwright did enter the barn in the early hours of the morning. Was he carrying it then?"

"No, sir. He was not."

"This kind of case is fairly heavy. If Mr. Cartwright did bring it with him into the barn that night, perhaps he dropped it, and you picked it up and put it on the shelf until you could give it back . . . In all the excitement you forgot to mention it. Is that what happened?"

Angelo was looking very uncomfortable. "No, sir. It did not."

Tyler held out the tortoiseshell comb. "Do you recognize this?"

"Er . . . it looks like a lady's hair pin. I might have seen such in the hair of Miss Walpole."

"Why would it have been underneath your cot?"

Angelo lowered his eyes. "I do not know, *signor*. She is in here often. To milk cows. She must have dropped it."

"Underneath your bed?"

"Perhaps she was cleaning."

"Let's put it this way. It would help your situation if there was a witness. Somebody who could verify your account of Mr. Cartwright's comings and goings in the early hours of Monday morning."

The Italian looked at him in alarm. "A witness? No, nobody. I was alone. Just myself."

All right. He wasn't going to get much from him on that score. For now, anyway.

"And you have not touched this case or seen it before?"

"No, *signor*. I have not."

Tyler tried another tack. He opened the case, took out the torn piece of paper, and held it in front of the Italian.

"Does this look familiar to you?"

"No, *signor*. Not at all."

"They seem to be directions of some kind. Do you know what they refer to?"

"No. No clue."

Angelo's confusion seemed genuine. Tyler returned the paper to the case.

"I'm going to ask you to give a sample of your fingerprints. We are asking all the members of the household to do the same. Understand so far?"

"Yes."

"I have spoken to Captain Beattie and he has given permission for us to do that here at the farmhouse. Do you have any objection?"

Angelo shrugged and his expression was full of despair. "Would it matter if I did? I am prisoner of war. You can do what you like."

"Maybe in your country and your allies', but not here. You are indeed a prisoner of war and that means you have certain rights. I cannot force this upon you."

"And if you decide I am guilty of a bad crime, what then? A firing squad? Hanging?"

"We will follow the laws of the land. It is not for me to decide. It is my job to present evidence only. If you are charged with a crime of any kind, you will be tried in a court of law. You will be no different from anyone else so accused."

But even as he said the words, Tyler wondered if they were true. Revenge and the justice system often blended together in a way that made them impossible to differentiate.

"So, Private Iaquinta, do I have your permission to take fingerprints?"

In answer, Angelo held out his hands.

"One more thing," said Tyler. "I will have to conduct a search of your person. I'll ask you to remove your clothes and put them on the chair."

Angelo actually summoned up a rather impish grin. "Will your constable be embarrassed if I strip down to my underwear?"

"To avoid any such possibility, I will ask her to step outside."

He nodded at Mortimer, who was looking decidedly embarrassed.

"Shall I have Constable Biggs examine the case, sir?"

"Good idea. See what he can bring up. Handle it carefully."

"Yes, sir. I had every intention of doing that."

She picked the case up by the handle, using her handkerchief, turned around, and left quickly.

Angelo began to unbutton his coverall. He put it on the chair as directed and Tyler checked the pockets. He removed a folded piece of paper, which he opened.

> _To my love: My America_
> _Lost in your land,_
> _Your strange territories,_
> _I search your face for messages,_
> _Try to trace a path there._

The words were written neatly in pencil.

"Nice poem," said Tyler. "I'm not familiar with it."

Angelo lowered his head. "It is mine. I wrote it. It's not yet finished."

"Is it for anybody in particular?"

"No, no. It is what you say . . . 'general'?"

Tyler put it on the chair also. Under the coverall, Angelo was wearing his regular army uniform. He took off the trousers and brown jacket with the telltale yellow patches signifying he was a prisoner of war. At Tyler's nod, he also turned out these pockets. They were empty.

"Do you want I go to completely bare?" Angelo asked. He'd removed his shirt and was standing in his underwear. His arms and legs were muscular.

"That's good enough, thank you, Private Iaquinta. Get dressed before you catch a chill. My constable will be here shortly to get your fingerprints. Why don't you work on your poem while you wait."

Angelo blinked. "I regret that under the circumstances I am not inspired to write a poem about love."

***

Jan emptied the contents of his piggy bank into a handkerchief. He added the old silver coin, tied up the corners, and stuffed the handkerchief into his pocket.

"Are you sure the Queen w-will meet us?" Pim asked.

"Of course she will. She is a very noble and kind woman. And we will present her with the silver coin, like ambassadors do. Now come on, let's get cracking."

His brother peered into the knapsack. "We shouldn't take t-too much," he said. "We don't want Mrs. K. to have n-nothing left."

"We've got one tin of beans, a quarter pound of tea, condensed milk, powdered eggs, and the tin of salmon."

"Oh, that's precious."

"We'll pay her back when we can. And we'll take half the loaf of bread. That should do us."

"You c-cut it, then. I always m-make a m-mess of it."

"You can fill the water bottles."

Pim went to the sink. "Jan, I had a b-bad dream last night."

"I thought you did. You were whimpering like a puppy without its mother."

Jan had intended his remark to be a joke, sort of, but his brother stopped what he was doing and stood stock-still. His scrawny shoulders began to tremble. Jan put down the knife he'd been using to slice off thick pieces of bread and went over to him immediately, pulling him close into a hug.

"Don't be a silly goose. I was teasing. I'm not surprised you had a bad dream. I'm not ever going to forget seeing the old man like that. I thought I'd be having nightmares myself, but for some reason I didn't."

Pim moved away slightly, not mollified. "You're lucky, then. Mamma used to s-say you'd sleep through the second c-coming."

Jan squeezed the back of his brother's neck. "All right, all right. I'm sorry. What was your dream? Tell your big *broer*. Come on."

Pim swallowed hard. "We were b-back at home. I think we were doing our homework at the t-table like we used to. I was getting hungry, I could even feel a p-pain in my stomach. I looked out of the window and there was Mamma. She was walking p-past the house with her b-basket on her arm as if she was going to the shops. I knocked on the window and started to c-call to her. I don't know where you were, you seemed to have v-vanished. But Mamma didn't hear me. She just kept on walking away. You know how she sort of b-bobbed her head when she was in a hurry? Well, she was doing that just the same way. But I didn't understand why she wasn't c-coming in." Pim choked back a sob. "Oh, Jan, do you think my dream m-meant we won't see her ever again? Is that what it means?"

"No, no. It's just a bad dream. We'll see both Mamma and Pappa. The Queen will help us bring them here."

"But the war isn't over. How c-can they get out of Holland?"

"It's going to be over soon. Everybody says so. Better we be in London when it is."

"Mrs. K. will be upset when she f-finds we've run away."

"We're not running away, Pim. We're Scouts. Scouts don't run away. We're on a mission. Scouts take action when it's called for. We're assessing our position."

The younger boy looked doubtful. "All right. Do we have to g-go to the hideout to assess our p-position?"

"Just for tonight. Scouts have to learn to live off the land if necessary."

"Well, I'm not going to the one in the f-field. What if the old man's g-ghost is in there?"

Jan frowned. "There's no such things as ghosts."

"You don't know that for certain. There c-could be. Let's go to the other one instead."

"It gets damp."

"I don't c-care. I'd rather be in there if it's only one n-night."

"All right. We'd better bring a blanket."

"That's stealing. We won't be able to t-take it with us. We'll have to l-leave it in the hideout."

"For goodness' sakes, Pim. You're such a sissy. We'll write to Mrs. K. from London and tell her."

His brother stared at him in horror. "We can't do that. We swore in blood we wouldn't reveal where the hideouts are. What if C-Captain thinks we've told? We could be executed for t-treason. We could be hung or shot."

"All right, all right. Stop mithering. We won't take a blanket. I think there's one there anyway."

"What if Captain's there and he gets c-cross?"

"I'm sure he'll understand. Besides, I don't think he uses it regularly. Not the woods one anyway."

"Shall we leave Mrs. K. a note saying what we're d-doing?"

Jan thought for a moment. "I don't know. We don't want her going to the police."

"But what if she thinks we've been k-kidnapped and goes to the police anyway? Captain said we must never involve the police, they're not to be trusted."

"I thought the lady officer was decent."

"Yes, but the inspector k-kept giving us the evil eye. He didn't b-believe us."

"All right," said Jan in a burst of impatience. "Have it your way. Write her a letter."

Pim pulled open the drawer where Nuala kept scrap paper and pencils.

"What shall I say?"

"Just tell her not to worry. We are going – no, *relocating* to London to see Queen Wilhelmina and we'll write to her from there."

"How do you spell *relocating*?"

***

Tyler decided to visit the Mohan farm while Biggs was collecting fingerprints. He instructed Mortimer to hang around the Cartwrights' kitchen.

"Just like you did before. Watch their reactions to getting their fingerprints taken. Take note of what they say to each other. Be discreet. Act like wallpaper."

"Yes, sir. Spy on them, you mean?"

Tyler smiled. "You can call it that if you like. It's just ordinary police work."

He left his constables to it and set out for the other farm. A sleety rain had set in, the trees dripped wet. They bent and swayed in the wind. He walked as briskly as he could to keep warm.

He wondered what Clare was doing now. Shortly before she'd left, they had walked together along the deserted country roads outside of town. It had been unseasonably cold and windy then too, and she'd drawn his arm in tightly against her body for warmth. She was skinny. Needed some meat on her bones, as Edie would have said. But he had felt her warmth, her sympathy for his terrible grief when Jimmy was killed. He would have kept her there beside him forever if he could have. But she had to be obedient to the dictates of war, and she'd left for Switzerland soon afterwards. Her country needed her, Grey had said. *But so do I*, Tyler had wanted to cry out. *So do I.*

Another gust of icy wind slapped his face. He stopped abruptly in the middle of the road and shook himself like an irritated dog. He couldn't just lie down and roll over because she said so. He needed to talk to her. Surely there was some way to reach her even in these wartime conditions. He'd have to go and see Mr. Grey in Whitchurch. The chief intelligence officer would surely know the truth of what she was up to and where she was. He'd go as soon as he could.

He made a fist and shook it in the air. "I'll find you, Clare Somerville," he shouted. Nobody was around to hear him except a few bedraggled blackbirds huddled together on a nearby tree. He felt sort of foolish. But he also felt warmer.

The Mohans' farm was just around the bend of the road at the top of the hill. On his left was a thick stand of trees but the farmhouse was plopped in the middle of bare muddy fields, unprotected from the elements. A thin wisp of smoke came from the chimney and there was a lamp shining from the front room. As he got closer, he could see an elderly woman sitting by the fire, knitting. Perhaps on a different day the indoor scene would have appeared cozy and welcoming, but today her solitary task seemed lonely.

Tyler opened the garden gate and walked up the path to the front door. The old-fashioned iron door knocker was in the shape of a lion's head and he lifted the ring in its mouth and thumped a few times. Nobody came. He stepped to the right and peered into the front window. The elderly woman – Mrs. Mohan, he supposed – looked up, and he waved to her. She didn't move, whether from fear or incomprehension he didn't know. He gestured again and this time fished in his coat pocket to find his identity badge. He smiled as disarmingly as he could. Finally, she got to her feet, stiff and arthritic, and began to shuffle to the door. Tyler returned to the front step and finally the door opened.

How old was Mrs. Mohan? It was impossible to tell. Her hair was iron-grey and tucked into a roll at the nape of her neck. Her clothes were sober. Out of date. She moved so stiffly she gave the impression of being truly ancient. But when she looked at him, her blue eyes were clear and shrewd enough.

"You've come about Jasper Cartwright, I presume," she said before he could even introduce himself.

"Yes, I have. Am I speaking to Mrs. Mohan?"

"You are. You'd better come in out of the cold." She indicated the front room. "I'm in here. I built a fire. Blow rationing, I couldn't stand the chill."

Her voice was loud and rather harsh, the way it often is with people who are hard of hearing. She went ahead of him into the room. "I was prepared to burn the chairs," she said with unexpected humour. "Fortunately for me, my lodgers brought me a bucket of coal. Good lads." She sat down in the chair by the blazing fire. "I probably shouldn't tell you things like that. You're a police officer. You might feel compelled to investigate where they got it."

"It is my job after all, madam," said Tyler.

"Well don't expect me to testify against them because I won't." She reached for her knitting, a multicoloured scarf by the look of it. "Anyway, that's not what you've come about. Go ahead. Speak up. I'm going a bit deaf."

Tyler raised his voice. "As I believe you already know, Mr. Jasper Cartwright's body was found yesterday."

She stopped the racing of her knitting needles and her shoulders sagged. "Tragic that was. I've known him for many years. He and my husband were good friends when Albert was alive. We saw a lot of them. Then Jasper's wife, Grace, died about three years ago." She tapped at her own head. "He started to lose his marbles, sad to say. I believe it was Grace kept him together. She was Non-Conformist. Devout but good with it. She took care of Jasper like he was her child. I thought he'd be lost without her, and he was, poor man. I'd meet him going out to the fields sometimes and he seemed so confused. The only reason he could plough at all was because his horse knew what to do. Sad. Very sad. I thank God every day I've still got my faculties. You need them when you get old."

The spate of words slowed down and Tyler could see her eyes were filled with tears. She wiped them away with a handkerchief, stuffed it back up her sleeve, then fished in the knitting bag at her feet and took out a fresh skein of red wool. "I've unravelled an old Fair Isle jersey of my late husband's. I'm making a scarf for one of the boys. Sam. He doesn't have much and said he'd like something colourful. I'll do something else for the other boy when I've finished."

"Very distinctive," said Tyler.

Mrs. Mohan began her knitting again, weaving in the new skein. "Jasper took a real scunner against John's wife. Made no bones about it. She's all right is Susan, but she's not from here. She didn't know a steer from a heifer when she first arrived. Nor that son of hers. Sad sack if ever I saw one, all that twitching and blinking. You'd think he had St. Vitus's Dance. Not much help around the farm either. Too nervous, apparently." She halted her knitting for a moment. "I'm rattling on, I know. Jasper was an old friend, but I didn't like the way he was with Ned, nor Susan. He kept comparing her to Grace. Well, you can't do that, can you? It's not fair. The dead always come off better." Her knitting needles started to click again. "Susan used to be in service, you see, and it made her, shall we say, a little inflexible. Meals served on the dot, tidiness throughout. Jasper complained. John should have stood up for her but he never did. Too much under his father's thumb." Mrs. Mohan sighed. "I suppose it's an ill wind blows nobody any good. Now that he's gone, those two might have some happiness."

Tyler was wondering how he could politely bring the conversation back to the matter at hand when Mrs. Mohan helped him.

"You've got a particular expression on your face, Inspector. You're the bearer of more bad news, aren't you? Spit it out. I won't have the vapours. At least I hope I won't. Can't be any worse than news I've had before."

Tyler plunged in. Mrs. Mohan did not have the vapours, but she did look very shocked when Tyler informed her that they were treating Jasper's death as suspicious.

"Who'd do that?" she whispered. "He was an old man. Harmless, really, for all he could be bad-tempered some of the time. Salt of the earth you'd call him. What do you think happened?"

"Well, we think he might have got into an altercation with somebody."

She gaped at him. "Jasper Cartwright was seventy-five if he was a day. Who'd he fight with?"

Tyler hesitated. "I don't know as yet. I'm trying to talk to everybody in the vicinity. Determine if anybody heard anything. As I understand it, you have two lodgers living here."

"Yes." Her glance was sharp. "Sam and Tim. Good lads, both of them."

"Sam Wickers and Tim Oldham. I've already met them."

"You've already met them? How so?"

"They had to appear in court yesterday. They were charged with riding bicycles without proper lights and using bad language to an officer of the law."

She actually laughed. "Not exactly serious, wouldn't you say, Inspector? These days everybody uses bad language. I feel tempted myself some days when I hear the news."

"Perhaps *those* charges aren't serious, but I've heard these young men might be involved in poaching." He held up a hand to stop her from protesting. "That's not so much the point as the likelihood they'd be out very early. As far as we can determine, Mr. Cartwright died in the wee hours of the morning."

She looked alarmed, her knitting completely at a standstill. "Oh dear."

"Indeed," said Tyler. "Where might the young men be now, Mrs. Mohan?"

"I'm . . . I'm not sure. Usually they go out to the woods after the chores are done and gather firewood for me. They're probably over there. To the east side of the fields, not the west."

Tyler got to his feet. "I'll go and see if I can find them. Thank you, Mrs. Mohan. Sorry to be the bearer of bad news."

Those were the words she had used, but what else could you call it?

"I'll let myself out," he added.

She nodded. "They're good lads, Inspector. Even if they can be wild sometimes, especially Sam, they've got kind hearts. I don't know what I'd do without them, I really don't."

There was nothing he could say to that, and he left the warmth of the parlour and returned to the *blasted heath*, as the countryside was beginning to define itself in his mind.

***

The bicycle ride out to Bitterley seemed even harder than it had the day before, the wind fiercer. Icy sleet was starting to fall. Pim was on the saddle again and Jan puffed as he pedalled.

"That's the policeman's car," cried Pim as they went past the Cartwright farm.

"He can't be looking for us," said Jan. "We haven't been gone long enough. If he sees us, we'll keep on going."

They rounded the bend in the road and the farmhouse was out of sight; the woods where they were heading were on their left. Jan slowed down and stopped the bike abruptly.

"This is it. We'll have to walk from here."

Pim dismounted and they turned off the road, Jan wheeling the bicycle and Pim trotting behind. The narrow path wasn't easily seen but Jan knew where it was. He kicked aside branches that had been snapped off by the wind. They walked like this for five minutes until they came to a crumbling stone wall. Behind it were the remains of a small stone hut that had probably been used once upon a time by shepherds.

Jan pushed the bike inside the ruined hut and the two of them dragged branches over it until it was completely hidden. Then Jan bent down and lifted what appeared to be a short piece of plank from the ground. It was actually attached to a wooden trapdoor which rose up, revealing a narrow entrance.

Like the other bunker, this one was reached by way of a metal ladder. Jan snapped on his torch.

"I'll go first."

He clambered down into the darkness.

"All clear. Come on. Close the door behind you."

His brother obeyed.

**

The heavy soil sucked at Tyler's boots and he was briefly and unpleasantly reminded of the mud of Flanders. Another world war within living memory, and this one promising to be even more devastating. Not for the first time, he wondered what they had been fighting for last time. *The war to end all wars* hadn't.

He plodded on to the edge of the woods, where he stopped to listen. The wind was shaking the branches of the trees but he heard a voice.

"Over here, Tim. Hurry up."

Tyler moved in cautiously, hoping to catch the men unawares.

As he had suspected, they weren't collecting wood. Neatly stacked at the edge of a clearing was a pile of dead rabbits. Wickers and Oldham were hovering over a rabbit hole, and even as Tyler watched, a terrified rabbit shot out, entangling itself in the covering net. Tim caught it immediately, extracted it from the net, and with a swift, sure twist broke its neck across his leg. Sam reached into the hole and lifted out a white ferret. Tim dropped the dead rabbit on the ground.

Tyler stepped forward out of the protection of the trees and both young men turned.

"Can't get away from you, can we, Inspector?" said Sam. "You've come a long way to give us a mark for our good work at the station."

"If I was intending to do that, which I wasn't," said Tyler, "you just lost it for poaching. I take it you don't have a permit to catch rabbits here."

Tim looked nervously at his mate. "I, er . . ."

"Our mistake, Inspector," said Sam. "We're just doing our bit for the war effort. People need the meat these days. We thought this was all common land past the field."

"Don't give me that malarkey," said Tyler. "You live here, and you didn't know you're on the Desmond property? Pull the other why don't you."

"Funny thing is, Inspector, we took up a brace of rabbits to Sir Arthur just last week and he didn't object. Only too glad to get them. You can ask him."

"You're being cheeky, Wickers. I'm getting fed up with it. Get your stuff together right now. I'm going back to the farmhouse. I'll see you there in ten minutes. If you're not standing in front of me by then, I'll charge you with black marketing, poaching, and obstructing police business. If I think of anything else I'll add it to the list."

Oldham hobbled to collect the nets that they'd placed over the rabbit holes. Wickers put the twittering ferret into its box.

"We'll come as quick as we can, Inspector. Wouldn't consider giving us a hand, would you? Move things along faster? Tim don't move too swift right now."

"No, I won't. Get on with it. Ten minutes!"

He turned and pushed his way back through the undergrowth.

***

Jan had lit the oil lamp and the heater but the hideout was still cold and dark. The smell of the paraffin was strong in the air.

"Are you hungry?" he asked his brother.

Pim snuffled. "I d-don't like it in here, Jan. I can't breathe. Can't we g-go somewhere else?"

"There isn't anywhere else. You're afraid of the other place. Look, we'll only stay here for tonight, I promise. I'll turn up the heater and it'll get warm in a jiffy." He fished in his knapsack. "Here, I brought my *Wizard*. I haven't even read it myself yet. Why don't you lie on the bunk and have a look at it."

"All right," said Pim with a sigh. "But I hope we d-don't get into trouble."

"We won't. Captain said we could use the hideouts whenever we wanted. We've just got to keep them tidy." Taking a bar of chocolate from the knapsack, he broke off a piece and handed it to his brother.

Pim stuffed it in his mouth, then stretched out on the cot and pulled a blanket over himself. "I still d-don't understand how the old m-man ended up in the other hideout. He was t-too old to be a Scout. Do you think he w-was a f-fifth columnist?"

Jan furrowed his brow. "Probably. He wouldn't be dead otherwise, would he? Captain said we always had to be on the lookout for traitors. And if you found one it was only your duty to dispose of him."

"Do you think C-Captain killed him?"

"He might have. He's a brave man."

***

Tyler had got Mrs. Mohan to agree to remain in her sitting room while he questioned her two lodgers. She protested vociferously about their innocence of any crime other than high spirits and reluctantly closed the door behind her. Wickers and Oldham arrived within the allotted ten minutes and took their places at the kitchen table. Tyler remained standing.

"I'll come straight to the point, gents. Put you out of your misery. Forget the rabbits and forget the bit of mischief at the police station. No, don't pretend you don't know what I'm talking about, Wickers."

Sam had been about to do the ostentatious protest of innocence.

"Like I said," continued Tyler, "I'm putting that aside for the time being. The reason I'm so eager to have a chinwag with you two blokes is because we have new information from the coroner about Jasper Cartwright's death."

That got their attention.

"Dr. Murnaghan has determined that the old man did not die from purely natural causes."

Tyler paused to see the effect his words had on the lads. Wickers' expression was inscrutable; Oldham looked alarmed.

"Can you expand on that a little, Inspector?" said Wickers. "I thought he'd died from exposure. Maybe had a stroke or something like that. That's natural, ain't it?"

"No stroke. Somebody attacked him. They stuck a knife in his ribs."

Wickers dropped his mask. "Bloody hell. What are you talking about, Inspector? *Who* stuck a knife in his ribs?"

"That's what I'm trying to find out. The wound was not in itself enough to kill him, but that and the cold and damp were probably too much for his system. Put it this way. If he'd received proper medical help he might have survived – but he didn't."

"Weeping Jesus," said Oldham. "Why'd that happen?"

"Don't know yet. I said 'somebody' attacked him but it could have been more than one. Accomplices. A couple of mates or something like that."

Wickers threw up his hands. His eyes were angry. "Oi. Don't look at us. We had nothing to do with it. Did we, Tim?"

Oldham shook his head. "Christ, no. Nothing."

"We didn't stir from this house that night or the next morning till you saw us in the court," said Wickers. "Ask Mrs. Mohan. She cooked us supper *and* breakfast."

Tyler clicked his tongue. "You know as well as I do that she's as deaf as a post. You could have come and gone in the night with a brass band two times over and she wouldn't have heard you. The fact that you were present at breakfast proves nothing."

The two men exchanged glances with each other. Oldham was pale.

"I swear we had nothing to do with any killing."

"When do you usually go out to snare the rabbits?" Tyler asked.

They both hesitated, and Oldham left it to Wickers to answer.

"Varies. Depending on what other kind of farm work we've got going on."

"Early mornings?"

"Sometimes. Not in this weather, though. Even the bunnies want to stay in bed."

Tyler placed his hands on the table, leaning in close to them. "Let's put it this way, lads. It would help me a lot to get a fix on Mr. Cartwright's whereabouts after he left his house. I'll overlook any little misdemeanour you might have been up to if it means you tell me the truth. Now, I'll repeat the question. Did you encounter the old man at any time between Monday after ten o'clock at night and the early hours of Tuesday morning?"

Wickers nudged his pal. "Tim. You tell him. I went out to check on the nets Tuesday morning, but I came right back in. I told you the weather was too bad. So we didn't go out. We got a bit of extra kip until breakfast. Tell the inspector."

Oldham gulped. "That's right, sir. Just what Sam says."

"Would you consider yourself a sound sleeper, Tim?"

"Er . . . I suppose so, Inspector."

"Now I can see that you yourself aren't up to much action at the moment, but what I also see is all kinds of possibility for your mate to get into trouble."

"Hey . . . what are you getting at?" Wickers said.

"Let him talk for once." Tyler faced Oldham. "Did Sam wake up first or did you?"

"Me."

"Was he in bed when you woke up?"

"Come on, Tyler," protested Wickers. "You're not going to pin this on me."

"It's Inspector Tyler to you, lad. And if you interrupt again I'm going to slap a charge on you for interfering with the progress of justice."

He turned back to the nervous Oldham. "So, Tim. When you came to consciousness was your mate still in bed or not?"

"Er, no. He was up."

"Dressed?"

"Yes, I think so. I don't really remember."

"Did he talk to you?"

"How'd you mean?"

"Did he say, 'Rise and shine, Tim. Lovely day out. Time to get us some rabbits'?"

"I don't remember."

"What time was it when you got yourself out of bed?"

"I dunno. Close on seven, I think."

"But you didn't go out to the warren because Sam said the weather was too bad."

"That's right."

Tyler could see that Oldham was virtually squirming in his chair as he tried to work out what was going on. Wickers didn't move. He started to pick his teeth with his fingernail.

"All right," continued Tyler. "Let me get this clear in my noggin. Tim, you woke up to see your mate was already dressed.

You naturally assumed you were going to go out and catch rabbits like you usually do . . ."

"Yes, er, I mean, no."

"But he said you weren't going out because the weather was too bad."

"That's right. And my ankle was hurting."

"Of course. And he's a considerate pal, isn't he?"

"Yeah."

"And if he told you the weather was too bad to go out, we might suppose he had been outside himself. That's how he knew."

Wickers was still.

Tim paused. "Not necessarily. He could have looked out of the window."

"It was pitch-black at that hour, how could he tell?"

Tim glanced desperately at his pal. Sam took pity on him. He rocked back in his chair.

"You've no need to ride Tim, Inspector. I did get up and get dressed 'cause I wanted to see if we could go rabbitting. When it was obvious the weather was too foul, I woke up Tim. Previous to that I was fast asleep. All night. Didn't stir."

Tyler looked at Oldham. "Do you verify that?"

"Certainly do."

"Even though you were asleep?"

"Well, I did wake up once or twice because of the gale. Sam was right there sleeping, like he said."

"All right. I'll be going back to the station shortly. Do what you have to do here then get yourselves into town. You haven't fulfilled the conditions of your remand yet."

Wickers frowned. "I thought we'd cleaned up pretty good."

"Not good enough. The toilet somehow or other got blocked. Made a mess. You're going to have to scrub it down."

—

He left the two men to the ministrations of Mrs. Mohan, who came into the kitchen and fussed over them as if they were schoolboys who'd been victims of a bully. Perhaps they were. He'd been a bit hard on them, he supposed. Simple farming lads getting by in wartime. But he couldn't shake the image of Tim Oldham so casually and skilfully breaking the neck of a struggling rabbit. Killing didn't seem to faze him. However, so far Tyler had not discovered any reason why either man would harm Jasper Cartwright. Even if he'd caught them poaching, it wasn't a reason to connect them with a brutal assault.

Tyler put his head down into the wind and walked back to the Cartwright farm as fast as he could. Sleet was thickening. Biggs was coming through the garden gate as he approached. He was so excited he had a little bubble of spittle at the corner of his mouth.

"I was just coming to get you, sir. I've made a discovery."

"Can it wait until we get inside? I'm freezing."

"Sorry, sir. I thought it better to tell you in private."

"Go on, then. Let's at least step out of the wind."

They moved closer to the house and the protection of the eaves. There was a droplet of moisture at the end of the constable's nose and he wiped it away with his hand.

"Right. Out with it, lad," said Tyler. "You've got fingerprints, I presume?"

"Yes, sir. I took the prints of the POW as directed."

Biggs had to take a deep breath.

Tyler waited. "And?"

"He has a tiny scar on his thumb. And lo and behold there was an intact thumbprint on the metal box. Exact same scar."

"Any others?"

"Not as clear, and there's lots of overlapping, but they all look identical so I assume they belong to Mr. Cartwright senior."

"What about the ladder in the bunker?"

"Couldn't get anything good at all. We had the coroner and his crew and the boy going up and down so there was mud and dirt on the rungs. People were probably wearing gloves as well."

"Mr. Cartwright wasn't. But you didn't see anything that could be his? Anything that matched the prints on the metal box?"

"No, sir. Nothing at all."

"And the rest of the hideout?"

"Nothing, I'm afraid, sir. The surfaces were intractable."

"Intractable, were they? All right. Let's go inside. I'll need to talk to Iaquinta again."

The sitting room felt crammed. Angelo was on the couch, Tyler seated in front of him. Mortimer was standing next to the chair, Biggs was inside the door, Mady outside.

Tyler leaned forward.

"Private Iaquinta, you haven't been telling the truth, have you?"

"Sir? I know not what you meant."

Tyler pointed to the metal case that Biggs had placed on a cleared table. "This belonged to Mr. Jasper Cartwright. You said you didn't know it was in the barn and that you hadn't touched it."

"That is correct."

"Can you explain why we have found your fingerprints on the lid?"

Angelo drew in a deep breath. "There must be a mistake."

"May I have a look at your right hand?"

Reluctantly, the Italian held out his hand.

"You have a scar on the tip of your thumb."

Angelo stared at his own hand in a poor imitation of surprise, as if the small, jagged scar had suddenly appeared.

"Ah, yes. I received it when I went fishing one day with my *padre*. The hook got caught there when the fish jumped."

"It must have been a deep cut."

"Yes, it was. Two stitches of necessity."

"I can show you the fingerprint impression my constable took from the case. The scar is quite obvious. It's your fingerprint. How did it get there?"

"I have no explanation, Inspector. Surely I am not the only man in the world who has scars?"

"You are the only person on this farm who might have handled Mr. Cartwright's case who has such a scar on his right thumb."

"That is all I can say."

"All right. I'll have to take you back to the camp and we'll continue this investigation in front of the commandant."

"Am I being charged?"

"Not at the moment, but you are part of the ongoing investigation. Do you understand what I am saying?"

"Yes, I do."

Tyler turned to his constable. "Biggs, stand by while Private Iaquinta puts on his outdoor things and then escort him to the car. You will sit in the back with him."

Young Biggs looked decidedly queasy for a minute, and Tyler realized the poor bloke had probably never had to be in such close contact with a suspect in a violent crime case.

Tyler nodded at Mortimer. "Constable, you will assist Constable Biggs as necessary."

"Yes, sir."

Angelo shifted. "Would it be possible to say goodbye to the members of the family, Inspector?"

"'Fraid not." Tyler ignored the expression of distress on the Italian's face.

"Constable Mortimer, I'd like you to move the car out of sight onto the road and wait there."

Tyler didn't quite spell out to himself what he wanted to avoid, but he knew it was seeing a pretty young woman demonstrate that her heart was broken.

Tyler went to tell the Cartwrights he was returning to Ludlow. Susan was dealing with something at the sink. Edie was setting the table, where John and Ned were sitting.

"Excuse me, folks. Just wanted to let you know I'm going back to Ludlow. I'll drop off Angelo Iaquinta at the camp on the way."

"Any developments?" Ned asked.

"We have located the metal box that belonged to Jasper. It was in the barn. It was underneath some sacking on one of the shelves."

Ned frowned. "You're telling us the Itie stole it?"

"He didn't say that," protested Edie. "That's an unwarranted assumption."

"Is it? Inspector, did the Itie steal Jasper's treasure box?" John asked.

"We don't know yet."

"If he did, what's to say he didn't stab him into the bargain?" Ned winked.

"Don't say that," Edie cried.

Susan went to her husband and put her hands on his shoulders. "Don't fret, John. The inspector will get to the truth."

Tyler wished he had as much confidence as she was expressing. At the moment, he didn't really have a clue as to what had happened.

"By the way, Mr. Cartwright, Mrs. Cartwright, I'd appreciate it if you could give me a list of what you think was in the box. I'll ring you as soon as I know anything further."

The last thing he saw as he closed the door behind him was the pale, stricken face of Edie Walpole.

—

Tyler sent Constable Mady back to Ludlow, riding one bicycle, wheeling the other. He himself joined the others in the car, and, after a couple of coughs, Annabel started up.

Nobody spoke for the entire trip into Ludlow. Angelo sat ramrod straight, his eyes closed. Tyler could only guess what was going through his mind. It was hard to believe he was capable of stabbing an old, unarmed man, but who knew, maybe he'd done it in the heat of the moment. Wouldn't be the first time a crime had been committed in that way. But there was still the thorny question of how Jasper had ended up in the hideout, a place known to so few.

As Mortimer turned into the camp a soldier stepped out of his sentry hut and came over to the car. Tyler showed his identity card.

"I'm bringing Private Iaquinta back from the Cartwright farm."

The soldier peered into the car. "Hello, Angelo. How come you're getting a lift from the police? Not in trouble, I hope."

Angelo shrugged. "Better ask the inspector, not me."

Tyler ignored the curiosity in the sentry's face. "Where will I find the commandant?"

"Keep right for about one hundred yards. He's in the hut at the end of the road."

He lifted the barrier and they drove on through.

"Charlie is a nice chap," said Angelo. "All the guards are good fellows."

The grounds were utterly deserted, with only a couple of soldiers parading the area. They looked wet and cold.

"I'll just check in with Captain Beattie," Tyler said to Mortimer. "I'll be quick as I can. You can wait in the car."

He got out, and another sentry stepped forward who was guarding the hut.

"Inspector Tyler to see Captain Beattie."

"Righty-o," said the guard in a cheery voice. "I'll see what he's up to."

Was it something in the drinking water that was making these soldiers so very pleasant? Tyler wondered. Not that he wanted them to be officious and surly, but the two he'd met so far seemed to be going out of their way to appear un-military. Did this mean they were too lax? It could happen to anybody whose only job was to keep an eye out for trouble that nobody was in the slightest bit interested in creating. He felt he might well be in a stage play instead of a brutal war. And the story was a modern version of *Romeo and Juliet*. Or maybe it was *King Lear*? What was his role, then? *Come on, Shakespeare, don't let me down. Give me some words of wisdom to hold on to.* But before he could commune with the Bard, the guard reappeared.

"Captain can see you, sir. Come right in."

Tyler entered not Prospero's lair but a warm hut, furnished in an unexpectedly cozy way. He glimpsed cushions on chairs, a wool rug on the floor. There was a smell of fresh coffee in the air. Captain Beattie had made himself at home. The man himself was behind a long table that was unencumbered by papers or files. He stood, hand outstretched to Tyler.

"Good afternoon, Inspector. I'm Jim Beattie. Can I offer you a cup of coffee? Just made a pot. It's courtesy of a Canadian aunt. Bit strong for British tastes, perhaps, but I've acquired a liking for it."

"Thank you, not for me."

"Tea? Won't take a minute."

"Thanks, but no. I've got my constables waiting in the car . . . we brought the POW in with us."

"Ah, yes. Young Iaquinta."

"I should tell you, Captain, that matters seem a little more serious than when we first spoke. We've found an exact match of his thumbprint on a metal case that belonged to the deceased man."

"Prisoners aren't supposed to handle any of the farmers' personal items. Hard to avoid sometimes, I suppose. What does he say about it?"

"He denies any knowledge of the case."

"Where was it, exactly?"

"Underneath some sacking on a shelf in the barn where Iaquinta spent the night."

"Was it deliberately hidden?"

"Possibly."

Beattie poured himself a cup of coffee from a carafe on a hot plate by his desk.

"Question is, then, how did his fingerprint get on there? There's no doubt it is his, I suppose?"

"None. I can show you the cards. He has a scar on his thumb that is quite distinctive."

"So he must have handled the case at one time or another."

"Which he emphatically denies. However, he has admitted that Mr. Cartwright did come into the barn in the early hours of the morning. I have reason to believe he was likely carrying the case at that time."

"Oh, lord. That doesn't look too good, does it?"

"Iaquinta claims Cartwright just turned around and went right out again. He can offer no explanation for the presence of the case on the shelf."

The captain took a sip of his coffee. "Hmm, good."

Tyler understood him to mean the drink and didn't respond.

"I would like to conduct a search of the prisoner's quarters, if that's all right with you, sir."

"I don't know that you'll find much. The boys get inspected every two or three days. No place to hide anything. They're allowed a locker but that has to be opened for inspection as well. What would you be looking for?"

"Can't say as I know exactly. We haven't found the weapon yet. The coroner believes it was a short double-edged knife."

"Oh no, no weapons allowed in the camp. We are strict about that. Some of the men like to do wood carving, especially now that Christmas is coming up – and very good they are, I must say – but they have to do it in a special workshop, and all tools must be accounted for. No, Angelo couldn't have concealed a knife, I guarantee that. And that description doesn't fit the regular cutlery, which is also counted after every meal."

Tyler thought the captain was being ridiculously trusting, but maybe it was he who had become too cynical. In his experience, prisoners of any kind could create whatever they wanted to if they were ingenious enough.

Beattie put down his coffee cup. "I'll come with you to the hut. Most of them are inside today because of the bad weather." He smiled. "They're probably all having a singsong. They like to sing do our POWs. Opera, mostly. It's in their blood I suppose."

Beattie instructed a sentry to escort them to the hut. Tyler told Biggs and Mortimer to remain in the car, and he walked beside Angelo and Beattie across the compound. He didn't know if the captain was right about music and heredity but he was right about the POWs having a singsong. When the sentry opened the door, a blast of sound hit them. Not operatic though. Very much British. "It's a Long Way to Tipperary" – the naughty version, which was creating a lot of laughter.

The men stopped in mid-note at the sight of their compatriot with the commandant and a stranger.

"Attention!" yelled the sentry, in best sergeant major manner. More quickly than Tyler would have expected, the POWs scrambled to get to the foot of each bed and stand straight.

"At ease," said Beattie.

They obeyed.

"Gentlemen, this is Inspector Tyler from the Shropshire constabulary. He is here to make a search of Private Angelo Iaquinta's bed and locker. I will ask you not to interfere with this search, or to comment on what he is doing. I ask you especially not to comment in your own language." He gave a disarming smile. "You know our grasp of Italian isn't the greatest. I assure you Private Iaquinta's rights will be protected at all times. This is not a military matter but one that concerns the local police. Those of you who can translate must wait until we are finished here. I shall make a full report to you at the evening meal." He turned to Tyler. "Go ahead, Inspector. Angelo has the bottom bunk."

There was a small locker beside the bunk bed and Tyler opened it. The only thing inside was a dog-eared Italian-English dictionary. He riffled through the pages but there was nothing there. He turned his attention to the bunk.

The hut was silent, all the occupants intent on watching his every move. Even if they hadn't understood every word the commandant had said, they could tell something serious was going on.

Tyler removed the pillow and pulled back the covers. Nothing.

Angelo was standing behind him but he could feel the man's tension. It was like the children's game of "Hotter, Colder."

As he lifted a corner of the mattress, he almost expected the POW to call out, *Hot!*

For it clearly was.

Tucked into the canvas webbing underneath the mattress was a tiny piece of blue silk. Tyler removed it. Wrapped inside was a thin gold wedding ring.

"Where did you get this, Private Iaquinta?"

Angelo ducked his head. "I found it."

"Where?"

"Outside the barn somewhere."

"You should have turned it in," said Captain Beattie.

"I am knowing that, sir. I'm sorry."

"*When* did you find it?" Tyler asked.

"Sometime on Sunday afternoon."

"And the piece of silk?"

"It was lying in the kitchen."

Captain Beattie came forward. "Private Iaquinta, I will have to put you on a charge. The rules are strict about found property where you are working. You are not allowed, ever, to keep anything you find on English soil."

The POW was looking suitably chastised. The watching men were silent.

"You will be held in the detention hut for the next few days while we sort this out. After that, you will be confined to quarters until the end of the month, with extra KP duty. Sergeant Pullham, please take note and write this up. Inspector, perhaps we can reconvene in my office."

Together with the sergeant and Angelo, Tyler followed Beattie out of the hut. He had to admit to a twinge of sympathy for the young Italian. No, make that several twinges. He wasn't likely to be seeing his Juliet in the near future.

The captain made a fresh pot of coffee and this time Tyler accepted. Beattie was right, it was strong. Tyler loved it.

"I will be continuing my investigation as I would with any civilian," Tyler said. "If I do determine the fellow has committed a felony, how do you want me to proceed?"

Beattie gazed at Tyler over the top of his cup. "Frankly, Inspector, I don't know. No such situation has arisen under my command before that crosses into the province of non-military law. I'd better look it up. Of course, denying that he'd kept property he shouldn't have doesn't necessarily mean he assaulted the old man, does it?"

"No. But according to Susan Cartwright the wedding ring that belonged to his deceased wife was among the objects her father-in-law always kept in the case. The same case that Iaquinta says he didn't touch."

"I see." Beattie leaned back in his chair and made a tent of his fingers. "You said that the old man may have been dumped in that hideout?"

"It's hard to tell for sure. The entrance is by way of a metal ladder. It is very narrow. Mr. Cartwright would have to have been unconscious to get him there against his will without a struggle, and there is no sign that one took place. On the other hand, Dr. Murnaghan says he could have remained mobile for a little time after he was stabbed, so he might have climbed into the hideout himself. For shelter, perhaps."

"The first case presupposes somebody other than the victim himself knowing the whereabouts of the hideout as well as having the freedom to move about the countryside. Surely neither is applicable to Private Iaquinta?"

"As I told you earlier, he was not in fact secured during the night. The two boys claim to have come across it by accident. Private Iaquinta has worked on the farm since harvest. He could have run across it too."

"But you said it was well hidden."

"It is. I'm going to pursue that line of enquiry. I'm going to get the list of the members of the Auxiliary Units who would know it was there. They have to be local men."

Beattie nodded. "Sounds like a good plan. I'd say that the hideout is the key to the whole tragedy."

Tyler was inclined to agree with him. It was certainly a place to start.

On the way back to the police station, Tyler told his constables what he'd found underneath Angelo's mattress.

"I find it hard to believe the ring just happened to fall conveniently out of the case, which seems to fasten quite securely. Angelo must have taken it. Ergo, his thumbprint."

"We still don't know when, do we, sir?" said Mortimer.

"He might have found it, like he claims," said Biggs from the back seat. "My cousin found a Viking helmet once. He thought it was some old bucket. It was in a pond on his farm. He took it home, but my auntie thought it might be special and they called in a local archaeologist. Sure enough, it was a rare and very valuable museum piece. Auntie Pauline kept the compensation money but she did give my cousin Vic a pound. He became totally obsessed with finding more treasure after that, and spent the entire summer holidays searching the fields. He was like a dog looking for a bone."

This was a long speech for Biggs. He fell silent.

Tyler said, "And? Is this relevant to our investigation, Constable?"

"Not exactly. Sorry, sir."

"No, that's all right. It is interesting."

"Yes, sir."

Tyler was sorry he'd caused his constable to clam up like that.

"Did your cousin ever find anything else?" he asked.

Biggs brightened. "Oh yes, sir. Not as valuable as the helmet, but he dug up a Roman die made from bone. And a couple of coins from George II's time. For a while he was going to be an archaeologist but he lost interest when he found out how much extra schooling it involved."

"When did all this happen?" asked Tyler, glancing over his shoulder.

"Three years ago. He's in the army now." Biggs actually grinned. "Would you believe he's a sapper? His job is mine-detecting."

"That's dangerous work."

"I know. Auntie Pauline nearly had a fit when she heard what he was doing. But he says he likes it."

I hope the lad eventually comes back to search for treasure, not death, Tyler thought.

They drove on quietly for a while, then Mortimer said, "The big treasure in our family is the head of one of my ancestors."

"What?" exclaimed Tyler. "Lost it, did he?"

"In a manner of speaking. He was implicated in a rebellion against Henry I. He was executed, head chopped off, but, as was the custom in those days with so-called traitors, the body was buried in one place and the head in an unmarked spot. We know it was near the house but not exactly where. We keep expecting it will surface one of these days and we can reunite it with the rest of his body."

"And where is that?"

"In the family crypt in St. Laurence's Church."

Ah yes, those Mortimers.

Tyler had no idea where his distant ancestors were buried. His grandparents on his mother's side had been laid to rest in Whitchurch in the parish church. His mum had taken him to replace the flowers on the grave on a regular basis when he was in school. As for his father's side, he'd come from the south and they were buried down there as far as he knew. Family lore had it that they were descendants of the rebellious Wat Tyler, "leader of a lot of revolting peasants," as his father was fond of saying. His mother said that Tom got his red hair and his restless nature from that long-ago man, but maybe that was a convenient myth.

They turned into Corve Street. Not many people were out and about in town, and the pavements were slick with rain. It was the time of year when all you could do was long for a bit of blue sky, "enough to make a sailor's trousers," his mother would say. So much for "this green and pleasant land." He'd take the North African desert any day. *Brilliant blue cloudless sky, white sand, exotic palm trees where coconuts containing cool delicious milk dropped into your hand . . . Even if it was sown with land mines; even if the sand storms were cruel; even if the irritation of the sand caused sores that wouldn't heal; even if you could go blind from the sun . . . Even if . . . oh, forget it.*

Mortimer guided Annabel into the car park beside the police station.

"I've got to go into Shrewsbury this afternoon," Tyler said to the constables. "You can report to Sergeant Rowell. You've both done good work today. I'll tell the sergeant you can leave an hour early."

Biggs' face lit up.

"Thank you, sir," said Mortimer. "That won't be necessary. We were just doing our job."

Briggs grimaced.

As it turned out, Tyler's offer had to be immediately rescinded. Hurrying toward him across the car park was Nuala Keogh.

***

"I'm just going to get a start on the milking," said Edie.

"All right. Good idea. I thought we'd have an early supper, all things considering," said Susan.

Ned was huddled close to the wireless, apparently listening intently to the organ recital being broadcast at that moment.

"Do you want some help?" he asked.

"You, with the cows?" His mother scoffed. "You know how you are. They'd let down sour milk more than likely. I'd sooner you help me with the supper and let Edie get on with her job."

He ignored her. "Edie?"

"I'll be fine, thanks, Ned. Better you give your mum a hand." She touched Susan's arm gently. "How is Mr. Cartwright bearing up?"

"I haven't seen him since the police left. He's very upset, I realize that, but Jasper was old. He'd lived his life. Death happens to us all sooner or later."

Edie almost gasped at the words. Surely the point was that Jasper's death hadn't just *happened*. Somebody had caused it. Susan seemed to have wiped that completely out of her consciousness.

"I shouldn't be too long," Edie said and escaped.

As always the warm smell of the cows and the straw was comforting. Edie hung up her raincoat and hat and lit one of the oil lamps.

Clover, already uncomfortable with her full udder, bellowed.

"I'll be right there, girls," Edie called.

Carrying the lamp, she walked around the half-wall that partitioned off the area set aside for the POWs. At the sight of the cot, she felt a glow of pleasure. This was where she and Angelo had lain together. What phenomenal luck that the weather had turned so bad and John had decided Angelo should stay overnight and not have to bike back to the camp. As soon as she knew that, Edie had made her decision. Who knew when or if ever they would have the chance again?

Feigning nonchalance she had spoken to Angelo in Italian. Both John and Ned were mucking out the barn, but she'd been clever. First she'd said, "Don't look surprised." Then, as if she were instructing him where to sweep, she'd pointed and said, "I'll come to you tonight." She could see his fair skin redden but the others weren't close enough. He didn't speak immediately, and for a minute she was afraid she'd overstepped the mark. That he was offended by her boldness. But that was not the case. He fell just as easily as she had into subterfuge. He replied in Italian, "That would be good."

At which point Ned called out, "Oi. English only, if you don't mind. What are you talking about?"

"Nothing," said Edie. "I was just telling him he'd missed a spot in the corner."

They finished the chores and all of them returned to the farmhouse for the evening meal. Edie thought it would never end. John turned on the wireless and they listened to the news. It wasn't as dire that night as it often was. Another thing she was grateful for. Bad war news was very likely to set Jasper off on one of his tirades.

She made herself pick up the darning she was doing. She thought her hands might even be shaking.

"Are you feeling all right, Edie?" Ned asked. "You look flushed. Hope you're not coming down with anything."

"You know, I am feeling a bit seedy. I think I'll have an early night."

Susan didn't react, and John as usual seemed oblivious, concentrating on his Bible. Surely he knew it by heart by now, thought Edie. But she was grateful he was preoccupied. Thank goodness Jasper Cartwright was in one of his withdrawn moods rather than the belligerent, rude state that he could fall into. Tonight had been blessedly peaceful.

Edie put away her darning. "I'm off to bed, then. Nightie-night. See you in the morning."

Somehow she forced herself not to look at Angelo, although she wanted desperately to meet his eyes. To know that he was as eager as she was.

She went to the parlour that doubled as her bedroom. Her cubbyhole, really. She didn't undress but lay under the blankets. Not too long afterwards, she heard the creaking of floorboards. Angelo called out "Good night," and she knew Ned was escorting him over to the barn.

Stiff with tension, she waited until she heard the door again signalling Ned's return. Jasper had already gone upstairs, with John and Susan close behind. Ned went straight to his room.

She had to wait until she was sure they were all asleep. The two hours until her clock showed midnight dragged by. She felt like Cinderella going to her first ball. She listened, but the only sound was the soughing of the wind in the trees. She slipped out of bed, collected her outdoor things, and tiptoed to the front door. Lifting the latch, she slipped out into the cold night.

Edie ran to the barn. The night was pitch-black and the wind was vicious but she didn't care. The thin beam from her torch danced in front of her. Her desire kept her warm. She thrust up the bar on the barn door and stepped inside.

"Angelo?"

"I am here," he replied, and there he was, standing by the partition. She ran to him and he lifted her up.

"My love," he whispered into her hair. He started to carry her to the cot.

It was all so darn romantic, except that he tripped over one of his shoes and they both crashed to the ground. Edie tried desperately to suppress her laughter.

"Shush," whispered Angelo. "Somebody will hear us."

"Just the cows, and they won't mind."

He got to his feet and pulled her up into his arms.

"Perhaps I'd better walk," she said.

"No. I carry you. I will carry you across the threshold as if we are man and wife."

"Shouldn't we have a ceremony first?" she said.

He took both her hands in his. "Do you, Edith, take me, Angelo, to be your lover and husband in the eyes of God, forever and eternally till death us do part?"

"I do."

Perfectly on cue, Clover bellowed.

"I think she approves," said Edie.

Angelo swung her up and carried her over to the cot, laid her down gently, and stretched out beside her.

"I have a poem I have made for you."

"Say it to me."

His finger moved along her chin. "*Lost in your land, Your strange territories, I search your face for messages, Try to trace a path there.*"

"Sounds like you're talking about a spy," said Edie.

"No. No. It is that I am in wonder and bewilderment at how strange and wonderful you are to me. I wish to know you as well as . . . as well as I know my own mother."

She giggled. "Your mother! That is about as romantic as a cold cup of tea."

He looked hurt. "I am sorry. My English is bad. I simply wished to convey to you that I have come to love you. You have come to my bed. I have dreamed this for weeks and now you are here."

"We'd better get on with it then. I can't stay too long."

"I wish to do everything properly."

"I'll help you if you like," said Edie.

But it turned out she didn't have to.

***

Nuala was holding a piece of paper in her hand and she showed it to him. "Inspector. The boys have taken off. They left this note. I just got home but I think they left some time ago. I went straight to the school and Miss Lindsay said they hadn't been there all day."

Tyler unfolded the paper. The handwriting was neat, childishly round. "*Dear Mrs. Keogh. We are relokating to London. We want to speak to Queen Wilhelmina about Mamma and Pappa. We hope she will help us find them. Do not worry. We will write as soon as we have settalled ourselves. Your obediant servants, Jan and Pim.*"

"How the heck were they going to get themselves to London?"

"I don't know. I asked myself the same question. They each had a piggy bank and I encouraged them to save money when they could. Both banks have been opened and the money is gone. But as far as I know the most they could have is about five or six shillings between them. Not exactly enough to get them to London on the train."

Tyler tried to reassure her. "I'm sure when they realize that they'll come home."

"I hope so. It's just that the weather is so bad and they've had this awful experience. I couldn't bear it if anything happened to them."

"Look, why don't you walk down to the train station?" He turned to Mortimer. "Will you go with Mrs. Keogh? Ask the station master if he's seen the boys. Report back to me."

"Yes, sir."

Nuala Keogh managed to pull out a smile. "Thank you, Inspector. And if they haven't been at the station, what then?"

"Did they take the bike?"

She bit her lip. "I don't know. It's usually kept in the shed. I was so upset, I didn't think to look."

"All right. If there's no word at the train station, check on the bike. We'll take it one step at a time."

The two women set off across the car park to the street.

Tyler beckoned to Biggs. "You'd better stick around after all, Constable. Little monkeys. I'll give them a piece of my mind when we find them. Poor woman is worried sick."

"They probably need a father, sir."

Tyler winced. "Good point, Biggs."

But these days, fathers were becoming as scarce a commodity as pork chops.

***

The paraffin heater didn't seem to be making much headway with warming up the hideout. Jan wished he'd hadn't given in to his brother and that they'd brought a blanket with them.

"Are you hungry?" he asked Pim. "I could open the beans and heat them up. There's a saucepan here. We can have them with some dried eggs."

Pim sneezed violently. Then again. And again.

"I'm getting a c-cold," he muttered.

"No, you're not, it's just the mildew. It'll be better soon. So, do you want me to make your tea or not?"

"I want to go h-home, Jan. I d-don't like it here."

The tip of his nose was red and his eyes were swimming. Perhaps he *was* getting a cold. But Pim was right. The dark hideout was damp and smelly, as if an animal had done its business there. Jan had lit the oil lamp but it was flickering and dim. Soldiers sometimes had to give up on a mission. He knew that. They'd talked about it at a Scout meeting. No shame in that. Better to get out and live to fight another day.

"All right. Have it your way. We'll go home for tonight and leave in – "

He was interrupted by a loud crash overhead. A rain of dust and dirt fell from the ceiling.

"What the hell was that?" cried Jan.

He clambered up the ladder as fast as he could. But when he tried to lift the trap door it wouldn't budge. He shoved again, hard, and opened it up just a crack.

"Weeping Jesus. There's a bloody tree fallen across the entry."

Pim let out a wail.

"Come and help me," yelled Jan.

Pim squeezed himself up beside his brother and they both pushed at the trap door.

In vain. It wouldn't budge.

"Shall we shout f-for somebody?" Pim asked.

"You know there's nobody anywhere close," snapped Jan. "That's why the hideout was built here."

"What shall we do?" Pim whimpered.

Jan didn't answer. He had no idea how they were going to get out.

***

Nuala and Mortimer returned after about half an hour. Both of them were wet and cold, and Tyler could tell by the expression on Nuala's face that they'd had no luck.

"The station master is definite that they didn't try to get on a train. We came back by way of my house and the bike is missing."

"Anything else?"

Nuala nodded. "Constable Mortimer suggested I check their room and see if they had taken anything."

"And?"

"They took their latest comic. They also took some bread from the pantry – half a loaf, I believe – along with a tin of beans, a tin of condensed milk, a tin of salmon, and some powdered eggs. Won't sustain them for long but clearly they intend to camp out for a while. Where on earth could they be?"

Tyler grimaced. "Mrs. Keogh, what I have to tell you must be kept secret."

She nodded solemnly.

As succinctly as he could, Tyler explained about the Auxiliary Units and the hideouts that they had built.

"It looks like the boys have been using at least one of these hideouts on a regular basis."

She absorbed the information for a few moments, then she said, "Please, let's check them."

"We only know of one at the moment. That's where they discovered Mr. Cartwright's body."

"But there might be more?"

"Probably. I'm going to Shrewsbury this afternoon to see if the chief constable will release information to me. It's still top secret."

Nuala clenched her jaw. "All this skulduggery is more than I can stand. What if my boys have got into some trouble? I tell you, Inspector, I'm frightened. They're no match for men trained to kill."

"I'll move as fast as I can," said Tyler. He addressed Mortimer. "I want you and Biggs to go to the bunker where

Mr. Cartwright died, just in case the boys have gone back there. Mrs. Keogh, do you want to go with them?"

"Of course."

"Constable, you can take the Austin. I'm catching the four o'clock train to Shrewsbury. I'd like you to telephone the police station there as soon as you get back from Bitterley and let me know what's happened, if anything."

A gust of wind rattled the windows. Nuala shuddered.

"Silly, silly boys. They're going to be so cold out there."

***

Jan had finally agreed they should at least try to call for help. He opened the trap door as far as it would go and the two of them shouted at the top of their voices. Nothing came back to them except the rush of the wind in the trees and the splatter of the rain.

"There'll be people out in the morning," said Jan. "Let's have something to eat. That'll make us feel better."

But his brother went over to the cot and dropped on to it, face down.

"What if nobody f-finds us, Jan?"

"Course they will. We have to think like Scouts. They can survive for months on end on almost nothing."

"I have to pee."

Jan looked around the tiny space. "There's no bucket in here. Just go over to the corner and do it there."

"What if I need to do number two?"

"You can't. You'll have to hold it."

The paraffin heater didn't seem to be giving out much heat. Jan touched the side. It was lukewarm. Quickly he unscrewed the lid on the oil reservoir. There was about a quarter of a tank left. Enough for now. He didn't know what was wrong with the damn thing.

"Come on, Pimmie. We'll have our tea. We've got bread. We can have some salmon."

"I thought we were going to have some b-beans and eggs."

Jan forced himself to be patient. He was the leader, and a leader didn't lose their temper with the pack. Besides, making himself be calm kept some of the terror at bay.

"The heater is on the fritz. Salmon is better cold." He opened the tin of salmon and scooped some out onto the bread. "Here," he said to his brother.

Pim took the slice of bread and ate it quickly. "Can I have another p-piece?"

Jan shook his head. "No, we've got to ration it. Have a drink of water."

Pim howled suddenly like a feral creature. "I f-forgot to fill the bottles. We don't have any water."

***

For once the train was on time. The platform was crowded; most of the passengers were soldiers in uniform, going who knew where. Home on leave? To another posting? A scattering of women in the uniforms of their various armed services mixed in with the crowd. Several women in civilian clothes were there to say goodbye to the men.

Tyler headed for a carriage, squeezing himself past a couple locked in an ardent embrace. The woman was young, dark-haired. She reminded him of Janet. In a reversal of the typical scene, she was the one in military uniform, the Auxiliary Territorial Service. The young man was in civvies.

Tyler took his seat by the window in a compartment that

was almost full. The guard blew the warning whistle and the couple broke away from each other. The young woman hurriedly got into Tyler's carriage and the guard slammed the door shut. She immediately turned, lowered the window, and leaned out so she could touch her sweetheart's hand. She was weeping openly; he looked teary himself.

The whistle sounded again and, with a shrill blast of steam, the train wheels began to turn and the train started to pull away.

"Bye. Bye. Write to me," called the young woman.

Tyler was afraid she might fall out of the window, she was leaning out so far. All along the platform people were waving goodbye, many of them keeping pace with the train as it gathered speed. The man in civvies was one of them, and he continued until the train pulled out of the station completely and the platform ended. The girl waved and waved until the track curved away with much shaking and swaying so that she lost her balance. She virtually fell into Tyler's lap.

"I'm so sorry," she said.

He raised his hat politely. "That's quite all right."

However, the middle-aged man seated directly across from him scowled. He had a thin, pale face that looked as if it hadn't seen the sun, or any joy, for a long, long time.

"I recommend you take your seat, young lady. You're going to do somebody some damage if you're not careful."

"I'm sorry," she said again, and she sat down at once next to Tyler.

With palpable irritation, the pale man stood and pulled the window closed.

"We should try to conserve what little bit of heat they allow us, don't you think?" he muttered.

The other occupants had observed this exchange with great interest, but now they reverted to English good manners and pretended to ignore it. The two soldiers in the far corners both took out letters and began to peruse them studiously. Next to the younger of the two was a grandmotherly woman who reached into her knitting bag and took out her needles. As far as Tyler could determine, she was knitting a pair of socks.

The situation reminded Tyler of the time he'd been caught in a bombing raid in Birmingham and had to go into a bomb shelter. He'd been with those people, those strangers, for eleven hours. They'd sung and told stories, and it had ended up actually being an enjoyable night, even with bombs exploding all around them. However, the occupants of this carriage didn't seem inclined to relate to each other at all.

The young ATS woman pulled a compact out of her handbag and snapped it open. She examined her reflection carefully in the mirror.

"I look a mess," she said to nobody in particular as she straightened her cap.

Tyler felt impelled to answer. "You look just fine," he said, in what he hoped was an avuncular tone of voice. She was indeed very pretty, with a fresh complexion and blue eyes, only slightly dimmed by tears.

She gave him a brief smile. "I hate goodbyes, don't you?" she said.

"I do indeed. But I hope you will see your young man very soon."

She slumped against the back of the seat. "That's the problem, though, isn't it? You never know these days what can happen. I mean, I'm safe. I don't work in a combat zone or anywhere we're likely to get bombed. I'm in ciphers. But

Simon is engaged in dangerous war work." Her fingers flew to her mouth and she flashed Tyler an anxious look. "Oh dear, I didn't say anything I shouldn't have, did I?"

The po-faced man across the aisle frowned over at her.

"I wouldn't worry," said Tyler. "Your statement was very general. Besides, I'm not a spy, I'm a police officer."

"That's a relief. I guessed you were in the government in some way. You have a sort of, well, a sort of air of authority about you."

Tyler was absurdly pleased with this remark. It was a characteristic he aspired to.

The other man said, in a voice that was too loud for the circumstances, "You were indiscreet, young lady. This man could easily be a trained actor for all you know. I've heard that the special services have men who go up and down the rail routes seeing if they can trick people into revealing information about the country's defences. They get into what seem like friendly little chats and, before you know it, young women like yourself are spilling the beans. Then, when you arrive at the next station, there are two military police officers waiting for you."

The other members of the compartment were now looking nervously at Tyler.

He addressed the sourpuss. "I assure you, sir, I am a police officer. I can show you my identification card. There have been no indiscretions in this conversation."

He took a card from his jacket and offered it to the man, who examined it carefully.

"All right. You're genuine. But you could just as easily not have been."

This was a man on a mission. as far as Tyler could see. He took back his ID card. The young ATS girl had inched away from him, and she went back to looking out of the window. The others resumed their previous activities. Nobody said a word. There was just the sound of the knitting needles click-ing busily.

As for Tyler, he watched the rain-lashed fields flash past, huge old trees swaying in the force of the wind. His thoughts drifted toward Christmas and the presents he would buy. He had missed the last two Christmases with Clare. The first time, 1940, hoping she'd be able to return to England, he had pur-chased an expensive lambswool cardigan for her, but she hadn't come, and the gift was still wrapped and sitting in a drawer. He'd bought nothing for the Christmas of 1941, not for rea-sons of economy but because he felt almost superstitiously that, if he didn't buy her anything, she would be there. She wasn't. That year, he'd handed out presents that hadn't required a lot of shopping – pound notes in envelopes for every member of his family, including his parents. Not that there were a lot of ways to spend the money right now. Non-essential items were getting more and more scarce. However, his dad had been able to buy a new spade, and that seemed to please him greatly. Janet had been delighted with her five-pound note. As far as he could tell, she had turned around and used some of the money to buy him a pair of leather gloves. Much to his chagrin, he'd lost one of them almost immediately. He supposed he'd have to fess up when he saw her. He shifted restlessly. *I suppose I'll do the same thing again this Christmas. Money is easier.*

He closed his eyes, hoping to doze off, but his thoughts wouldn't let him go. For the past two years, he'd held up the relationship with Clare as hope and inspiration, not really questioning that they would be together eventually. But the dictates of the war had postponed that. She was working for Special Operations Executive, essentially as a secret agent. She had to go where she was needed. No choice in the matter.

All right, then. If you're going to daydream about her, direct it. Don't be at the mercy of sweet memories and images. Go on.

What if she comes back soon and we set up house as man and wife? Life goes on. The war ends favourably for the Allies. The years slide away. We grow old together.

He smiled to himself as a vivid memory came suddenly back to him. It was the summer when they consummated their love. Intense and all-consuming, nothing else had mattered. In a moment of sentimentality, he'd bought a book of Yeats poems. He liked one particular poem and he'd memorized it. With the interruptions of his job, it took him most of the week until he'd got it down cold, but he did. That night, they'd been able to go to their favourite hotel. They made love first, but when they were both lying in bed side by side, skin of arms and legs touching, he'd started to recite it to her.

"*When you are old and gray and full of sleep, And nodding by the fire, take –* "

He didn't get any further.

She sat bolt upright. "What? What do you mean, *full of sleep?* I will never, ever be the kind of old lady who dozes off in front of the fire."

He was hurt by her rejection of what he thought was a romantic gesture on his part. He'd taken great pains to learn the poem, after all.

"It's a poem about loving the woman when she's no longer young. When she's lost her beauty. Yeats wrote it to the woman he loved."

"Should I be grateful for that? Is that what you're saying? That love is based on physical attractiveness? That men don't have to worry but women should be thankful if their husbands stick around long enough to wipe off their drool for them?"

"Clare. Don't be ridiculous. Of course that's not what I'm saying. I thought it was very tender and loving."

"Yes, but they didn't grow old together, did they? Maud Gonne turned him down several times. She married somebody else."

"I didn't know that. Besides, whatever his actual life was like, Yeats still wrote a bloody good poem." Tyler tried to bring the focus back to what he'd been trying to say. "I want to grow old with you, Clare."

"Hmm. Are you likely to nod by the fire?"

"I don't know. Probably. Will you still love me in spite of the fact that by then I'll have a fat gut and jowls?"

At that she burst out laughing. "I can't imagine you with a fat gut. But yes, I suppose it wouldn't stop me from loving you." She rolled over and caressed his face. "I'm sorry, Tom. You took me by surprise. The truth is I don't want to ever grow old."

"What's the alternative?"

She laughed at that. "Good point."

"Besides," he continued, "everybody goes through a phase when they think they're going to die young. The world would end if it all came true."

She paused. "I can always depend on you to be practical." She went back to tracing his lips with her finger. "Finish the poem, please, Tom. Please. I promise I won't interrupt."

So he had. And he still remembered it.

"And one man loved the pilgrim soul in you, And loved the sorrows of your changing face."

Tyler felt a wave of desperation sweep over him. He had to find out where she was and how she was. He had to.

***

The camp didn't have a proper place of detention. So far, there had been no need to punish anybody for anything more than minor infractions: not keeping their bunks and lockers tidy; being insolent to the guards (very rare); quarrelling among themselves (more frequent now as Christmas approached and bad weather kept them confined). Usually the punishment was being confined to barracks, with extra KP duty added in some cases. However, if Captain Beattie thought one of the POWs needed a cooling-off period, as he put it, a small hut near the guardhouse had been set up to hold a couple of men for a short period of time.

The sergeant unlocked the door and directed Angelo to step inside. There were two bunk beds, a small table, and a chair. Functional not fancy.

"You'll be by your lonesome," said the sergeant. He scowled at Angelo. "You were a silly laddie, weren't you? You know you shouldn't have kept that ring. Not your property. Why'd you do it?"

Angelo shrugged. "Weak moment. It was there lying in mud. I pick it up."

"Do you now see the error of your ways?"

"Indeed I do, indeed I do."

He wasn't going to confide in the sergeant how the delicate ring had been intended for his love. His wife in Christ.

Angelo put his knapsack on the lower of the two bunks. "I might as well take this one."

The sergeant removed a little booklet from his pocket. "I'm obliged to read you the Geneva Convention rules for the treatment of prisoners of war who, for reasons later specified, are held in detention. First. You will be served three meals a day, same as the others, but you will have them here, not in the mess hut. Second. You get two periods of exercise a day, half an hour in the morning and half an hour in the afternoon. You have the right to refuse these periods if you so desire." He looked at Angelo over the top of his glasses. "I recommend you take them. It can get mighty tedious in here after a while. Especially as you don't have company at the moment. Third. You can request a pastoral visit. In your case that is probably the local padre. Good fellow. Name's Father Keegan. He don't speak Italian but I don't suppose that matters. I recommend that as well. Breaks up the solitude. Four. You are entitled to receive writing materials, that is, paper and pencil. Five. You are expected to keep your sleeping quarters clean and tidy. There is a bucket for the necessaries. I recommend you hold on until you get to the latrines, which you can ask to do. Keeps the room a bit sweeter that way. You have an oil lamp over there but it must be extinguished by ten o'clock. Any questions?"

"No, Sergeant. Thank you."

"Good. You might find it chilly in here but you have some coal for the heater. I recommend you don't overdo it with the coal. It's rationed. Wear your overcoat if you get too cold."

"Thank you, Sergeant," said Angelo. It was indeed very chilly in the hut.

The sergeant smiled kindly. "Don't look so down in the dumps. You'll only be here for a week. You'll survive. Besides, the captain's heart is softer than a baby's bottom. He'll probably show you mercy and let you out sooner. It's not as if you've done something so terrible." He reached into his pocket. "Do you want your ciggie ration?" He held out three cigarettes.

"I'll take two, and I'd be obliged if you would have the third one."

The sergeant chuckled. "If you insist. They're worse than smoking rope but better than nowt, I suppose." He put one of the cigarettes into his jacket pocket.

Angelo took the other two and placed them on the bed beside him. The sergeant left and Angelo heard the sound of the key in the lock. He sat on the edge of the bunk and put his head in his hands.

***

"All change. All change," the guard called as he walked up and down the platform. The train engine gasped and steam rose from its sides like an overworked horse. Passengers were spewing out of the carriages. Most seemed to know where they were going and immediately headed away from the train, threading their way through the dense crowds of other travellers. Mr. Misery had jumped out at once and was swallowed up, but Tyler paused and offered his hand to the ATS woman as she stepped down.

"Thank you. Nice to have met you."

He would have liked to have utter words of comfort that would bring a smile back to that young face, but he didn't have any. "Good luck" was all he could manage.

She hurried away in the direction of another platform where a train was waiting. At least she had been completely discreet as to her final destination. It obviously wasn't Shrewsbury.

He headed for the exit.

He'd been to Shrewsbury many times but he never failed to be impressed by the strange and wonderful architecture of the station. A castle? A grand manor? Could have been either. Not to mention the carved heads around the windows. The prison on the hill was visible across the platform, although a high wall now screened off the special platform that was used for incoming prisoners. He knew that those who were considered more reliable were offered the chance to shorten their sentences by enlisting. Apparently a lot of them were doing just that. Tyler wasn't completely in favour of this new practice. As far as he was concerned, the seriously criminal characters weren't going to change that much if they were soldiers. Perhaps the opposite would happen. The army would give them an opportunity to act out.

He headed for the police station. The crowds on the platforms had dissipated like the blowing leaves and the streets were empty, the pavements wet and black with rain. It wasn't yet five o'clock but the dreary weather made it seem later.

Darkness was pressing in fast. He hoped he could finish his business with the chief constable quickly.

Slightly to his surprise the reception desk at the police station was in the charge of a female auxiliary police officer. She looked to be a lot older than Agnes Mortimer but seemed just as competent and efficient. Tyler gave her his name and reason for being there.

She smiled at him. "Lieutenant Colonel Golden is ready for you, Inspector. I'll show you to his office."

She opened the connecting door into a narrow hall and he followed her. She tapped discreetly on a door farther down and he heard, "Come."

"I'll bring you some tea," she said as she opened the door, and he stepped inside.

Tyler knew the chief constable of the Shropshire constabulary was a long-serving military man, as all those in the upper echelons were. He also knew Golden was about his own age, but he wasn't prepared for how young his chief looked. His complexion was ruddy, his eyes clear, his moustache neat and trim. He exuded the aura of a man who was fit and vigorous. For some reason he made Tyler feel flabby, and he sucked in his stomach without quite realizing he was doing so.

Golden got to his feet and came around the desk with his hand outstretched.

"Inspector Tyler. Welcome. I'm glad to meet you finally. I've heard a lot about you."

The obvious rejoinder was "All good, I hope," but Tyler didn't feel like engaging in superficial jollity. He didn't think the lieutenant colonel was the kind of man who tolerated coy rejoinders. If he said, "I've heard a lot about you," that's what he meant, no more, no less. Handshake (firm) over, he gestured for Tyler to take a seat and returned to his chair behind the desk.

"What can I do for you, Inspector? I must admit, your telephone call was most mysterious. You said you could not talk about your business unless we had a face-to-face meeting."

Tyler nodded. "It involves the Official Secrets Act, sir."

"Does it indeed?"

There was a tap on the door and the female officer entered carrying a tea tray. Tyler thought he'd relay this to Mortimer.

"Thank you, Miss Blandford," said the chief. "You can put it on the desk. Ah, I see you've managed to dig out some biscuits. How clever of you. And my favourite digestives too." Miss Blandford slipped away unobtrusively. Golden held up the teapot, which was protected by a knitted tea cozy. "Inspector? Allow me to pour you a cup. You must be parched after your journey."

For a moment, Tyler thought the chief had him confused with somebody else who had come in from the wilds of London or Scotland. His journey, after all, had lasted only half an hour. Nevertheless, he smiled politely and accepted the cup of tea the chief offered him.

"You can doctor it as you like," said Golden.

Tyler helped himself liberally to milk and sugar. Why not? This was the seat of the county constabulary, after all. They probably had more generous rations than Ludlow.

All that ritual taken care of, Golden put his cup and saucer on his desk.

"Now then. Do continue. Official Secrets Act, you said."

Tyler related what had happened to Jasper Cartwright and where they'd found him. Golden listened attentively.

"Poor bugger. What a rotten way to die. And the coroner thought he could have been saved if he'd got medical attention soon enough?"

"That's right. I will press for a second-degree murder charge."

Golden drummed his fingers on his desk. "I can see how it would be most important to find out who would know the whereabouts of the hideout." He bit his lip. "Bit of a problem. We've eased up somewhat from '40, when it was all most hush-hush – directives from Churchill himself. He thought it was only by keeping the cells small and absolutely tight-lipped that we could protect the wider network in the event of capture by the enemy. It's the principle foreign Resistance organizations should operate on and don't always."

"You said it was a bit of a problem, sir. I assume you *do* have a list of Auxiliaries?"

"It's locked in my safe. Thank God we haven't been invaded to date and I haven't been coerced into revealing the combination."

Tyler had the impression Golden wasn't the kind of man who would be susceptible to coercion, as he termed it, but who knows? He'd been told every man had his breaking point.

The chief constable tossed back the dregs of his tea, stood, crossed the room, and locked the door.

"Miss Blandford is totally trustworthy but this is standard procedure."

He walked to the wall behind his desk, where there hung a rather insipid framed portrait of King George. He removed the print, revealing what looked like a small safe recessed into the wall.

"Not too imaginative a concealment, but this safe is supposed to be completely bombproof." He began to turn the combination lock. "I've memorized this . . . or at least I hope so."

Whatever he did must have been right because the safe opened at a tug. He reached inside and took out a manila envelope. It was sealed with a red wax seal that looked very official. The words "TOP SECRET" were stamped across the front. Using a letter opener he quickly slit the wax seal and removed a single sheet of paper from the envelope.

"Let's see, the only ones you are interested in are the members of the Bitterley cell. There are two agents in that area. This county isn't considered high priority so all of the cells are small." He scanned the paper. "Now here it gets a mite complicated. What I have are the code names. Their real names are somewhere else." He looked at Tyler with a rather embarrassed expression. "Makes things awkward but obviously much safer. If this did fall into Boche hands, they still wouldn't know who the men were."

The chief handed him the sheet of paper. There were only two names: EZEKIEL and ZECHARIAH.

"The Auxiliaries favour biblical names," said Golden.

"How can I get the real names, sir?"

"Those are in the possession of the chief inspector for Shrewsbury." He drummed his fingers again. "Deuced bad timing for you, but McDavitt is this moment undergoing an emergency appendectomy in hospital. Oh, he's not in danger, apparently, but he won't be *compos mentis* until tomorrow. However, I shall visit him first thing and get the combination to his safe. I'll get the real names you're looking for. We won't be able to ring you, can't risk being compromised. Do you want to stay here overnight? Or would you rather get back? Won't make things move any faster if you do stay."

"I'll get back then, sir."

"All right. I'll have one of my constables catch the first train into Ludlow and deliver the information personally."

Tyler exhaled. Damn. He didn't think there was any way they could speed up the process but he didn't want to let anything – make that *anybody* – slip through his fingers.

"I'll have that paper back, if you don't mind," said Golden. "Have you memorized the information?"

Tyler nodded. Two names weren't exactly taxing to his brain.

He stood up. "Thank you, sir. I wonder if I mightn't make a telephone call to my sergeant before I leave."

"Of course, ask Miss Blandford to connect you. And next time you come to Shrewsbury, Inspector, let's make sure we get in a luncheon or even a dinner. I have the feeling we have a lot in common."

Tyler was rather flattered by the comment, although he wasn't sure what the chief could be referring to. They came from totally different backgrounds. *Perhaps he's was suffering from a heartache as well.*

Golden walked him to the door, his hand on Tyler's shoulder.

"I hope you nab the culprit quickly. We've got enough savagery happening on the front. Last thing we need is to bring it here." He lowered his voice. "Tell you the truth, in confidence, Inspector, I'm thinking of re-enlisting in the army. I've been a military man for so much of my life, I can't get used to sitting behind a desk while the fight goes on elsewhere. I believe my experience might be put to better use on the front lines than pushing paper around here."

"Good luck, sir. I wish you well."

They shook hands again, and Tyler went out to the reception desk to make his request to the efficient Miss Blandford. She put him through to the Ludlow police station immediately and Rowell came on the line.

"Any word on the boys, Oliver?"

"I'm afraid not, sir. It's so blasted dark now that I don't know what else we can do. I told the search party to come back. They've been out there for two hours at least. With the blackout in operation we can't show much light as it is."

"Nothing from the hideout?"

"Not a jot. We went there right away but there's no sign they've been there."

Damn. Tyler had been hoping the boys would be found in the hideout.

"How is Mrs. Keogh holding up?"

"She's blaming herself, but I don't know what she could have done differently. She was at work, and obviously the nippers were determined to take off."

"Surely they can't have gone that far, Oliver."

"There is some traffic on the high road, sir. Perhaps they hitched a ride. Although, God knows, you'd think a driver would question two kids off on their own."

"I wouldn't put it past Jan to have cooked up a plausible story."

"I can send off a general telegram to all Shropshire stations. Tell them the boys are considered missing."

"Good."

"How did your meeting go, sir?"

"I can't talk about it over the telephone. I'll fill you in when I see you. I'm catching the next train in half an hour. I should be home by seven – "

Rowell gave a little cough. "Excuse me, sir. If you won't be back until seven, will you be able to make your appointment with Mrs. Hamilton's client?"

Tyler gasped. "Oh my God, I completely forgot. I was supposed to meet her at the pictures."

"That's right, sir. Half past seven I believe you said was the time."

"Oliver, I won't make it. Even if I did get back by seven, I'm in no mood to romance a strange woman."

The cough again. "I don't think you have to romance, exactly, but I do agree you might not be able to give the appointment your full attention."

"What shall I do?"

"I was about to take my tea break. I'll run down to Mrs. Hamilton's and tell her. Hopefully, she'll be able to head her client off at the pass."

"Thank you, thank you, Oliver. You are my saviour. I'll make it up to you, I promise. Tea at De Grey's as soon as we can arrange it."

"Not necessary, but thank you, sir. I won't say no. I do enjoy their Eccles cakes in particular."

"Get me out of this mess and it's a week of Eccles cakes for you."

***

"Jan, I'm going to be sick."

Pim was as good as his word and he vomited before he could even get his head over the side of the cot.

"Weeping Jesus," said his brother.

"I'm sorry. I couldn't hold it b-back."

Jan grabbed his handkerchief and tried to wipe up the mess.

"I have a b-bad headache," whimpered Pim.

"Get up the ladder and stick your nose through the crack. You probably need fresh air."

"I don't know if I can. My legs feel wobbly."

Jan made himself speak calmly. His head was hurting too, and he felt queasy, but he had to set an example.

"Lie down, then. I'll see if I can force open the trap door a bit more. It'll make us colder but we'll get a bit of air."

He started to climb the ladder but his legs didn't feel as strong as normal either. He made himself get to the top and shoved hard on the trap door. It didn't budge. He did what he'd told his brother to do and shoved his face against the narrow gap. The chill damp air felt wonderful. He tried again to push the trap door open and for a moment there was some movement, but then the tree branch moved and fell farther across the trap door, closing it even more tightly with a clang. His blessed air hole was almost gone. Outside he could see nothing but pitch-dark. No sound except the wind howling in the trees. The rain was lashing at the branches.

He knew calling for help would do no good. He shouted anyway.

"Help! Help! Is anybody there? Please help us!"

***

The return journey to Ludlow took double the time. The train stopped twice so the engineer could clear debris off the tracks. It was a corridor train, and all the seats in the compartments were taken up by weary factory women already half asleep. The men, Tyler included, had to make do with sitting or leaning outside in the corridor. Nobody talked much, they were too tired. Other than sharing a cigarette with a bloke, Tyler didn't engage anybody in conversation.

His legs were aching by the time they pulled into Ludlow Station and he climbed stiffly down to the platform. There was the usual muted light of torches as the passengers made their way across the bridge toward home.

Suddenly a shadowy figure appeared at his elbow. "Hello, sir. I've come to give you a lift."

"Good lord, Oliver. Are you real or are you an angel?"

"Quite real, sir. I thought, seeing that it has been such a long journey, you'd appreciate a lift to the station."

"*Appreciate*, Oliver? If I weren't your boss, I'd kiss you."

Rowell chuckled. "Not necessary, sir. That hill can seem like Everest when you're tired." He swung his torch. "The car's out front."

Tyler walked with him across the bridge. All the other tiny lights bobbed away from them like fireflies as the passengers departed.

"This is a terrible extravagance, Oliver. I don't know how I can justify it."

"Don't worry, sir. I applied a bit of ingenuity, as it were."

He flashed his light on the solitary car parked in the tiny car park.

"Am I hallucinating, Sergeant? Do you have a magic wand? You seem to have turned Annabel into a Rolls-Royce!"

Rowell beamed. "Like I said, I applied a little ingenuity. When I rang the station master to check on your arrival time, he said the train was delayed as much as an hour. I know how tedious that can be so off I trotted to see Sir Edward Spence. I told him that I needed to requisition his motorcar for important police business."

"My God."

"In my view, picking you up on a night like this was at least as important as Sir Edward driving off to see a man in Wem about some bloody birds."

"Did he agree willingly?"

"Fairly willingly. I did say he could have some of our petrol ration to compensate him."

Tyler whistled through his teeth. "You rogue. I had no idea such a devious nature was lurking under that law-abiding exterior."

Rowell opened the rear door of the Rolls but Tyler shook his head. "I'm not going to sit in the back. Passenger seat for me."

"Very well, sir."

He opened the other door and Tyler climbed in.

The interior of the car was leather, the dashboard mahogany. It reeked of cigars but Tyler didn't mind. When Rowell started up the engine, it immediately sprang into life and purred like some tame exotic cat. He sat back.

"Drive on, James, and don't spare the horses."

In fact, the journey up the hill to their house was a short one. Tyler would have been happy to go farther in this unaccustomed luxury.

"You're probably famished, sir," said the sergeant. "I have a nice hot supper waiting for you. Hope that's all right."

"Another proof that I have truly died and gone to heaven," replied Tyler.

"By the way, sir, I managed to get hold of Mrs. Hamilton and she said her client only lived around the corner so she was able to get in touch with her at once."

"Thank goodness for that. I couldn't stand the thought of some poor woman in a red beret waiting all forlorn on the steps of the Grand. The boys haven't turned up, I presume."

"Alas, no."

"Damn. Damn. Where are they? As soon as it's light, we'll continue the search. If you don't mind, I'll tell you what I found out from the chief over supper. Right now my stomach is grumbling so loudly I can't hear myself think."

"Of course."

Rowell manoeuvred the Rolls into the narrow lane that led to the house and brought it to a velvet-soft halt.

"I told Sir Edward we might not be able to return his car until tomorrow. We can use it in the morning if we need to."

Tyler paused for a moment, bracing himself to make the dash from the car to the house in the pounding rain. Before he could do so, Rowell reached into the back seat and pulled up a large umbrella.

"Don't tell me – you requisitioned this as well?" said Tyler.

"I did, sir. For some reason the umbrellas of the gentry run bigger than those of us common folk."

"That's because they consider everything about themselves is bigger . . . head . . . the nether parts . . ." He made a rather vulgar gesture and Rowell laughed.

"Stay there, sir. I'll play valet."

Together, Rowell holding the umbrella, they dashed to the door. Once inside, Tyler inhaled deeply.

"Good lord, Oliver. Are those onions I smell?"

"Yes, sir. I made you a mixed grill."

"Marvellous."

"I have it on good authority that it is Saint Peter's favourite food."

***

When Angelo realized how easy it would be for him to escape, he almost laughed.

The guards, all of them over conscription age, had learned to trust the POWs. After all, the prisoners were all "whites" and considered a very low escape risk. Over the months, nobody had given any trouble. And now, nobody was out looking for it.

After he had eaten the meal brought to him on a tray, Angelo lay back on his bunk and waited. In the evenings after supper, many of the men congregated in the mess hut to play cards, chat, sing. At half past nine they had to return to their huts for lights out, which was at ten o'clock sharp. It was the job of the guards to settle them down, get a final count in each hut, make sure the blackout was observed properly, and shut off the light. The mood was relaxed and friendly.

The detention hut had been built closer to the gate than the others, and was directly across from the guard hut, where presumably it would easier to keep an eye on it. However, during the half hour when the prisoners were returning to their huts for the night, all guards on duty would be occupied.

At twenty to ten Angelo got off the bed, went over to the window high up on the wall, and opened it. The chatting and laughter of the men was subsiding. He had to go now.

First, he stuffed the pillow underneath the covers to look like a sleeping body. He was counting on not being missed for a long time. The 2:00 a.m. check was perfunctory; the guard just peeked through a tiny window in the door. They wouldn't realize he was gone until the guard brought his breakfast at 7:00 a.m. That was plenty of time for him to get to the farm. After that? Angelo didn't dare think any further.

He shoved the chair underneath the window. He squeezed through the small opening and dropped to the ground, panting from the exertion and from fear. He stayed there for a few moments until he was sure nobody had seen him.

He scuttled across the soaked grass to the bike shed, which was a few feet away on the east side. There he took one of the bikes out of the rack and wheeled it towards the gate. The rain was driving into his body and the fear of being detected made his legs shake. He could hardly see his hand in front of him but he knew where the gate was, and he made for it as fast as he could.

There was no barbed wire on top of the gate so it was easy to climb over. With a prodigious effort he hauled the bike up after him and lowered it to the other side. He mounted and, keeping close to the edge of the road, he shot off.

***

Over dinner, Tyler filled his sergeant in on his meeting with the chief constable.

"Ezekiel? Zechariah? I'd think I'd choose Job if I had to pick a code name," said Rowell. "I've always felt a certain sympathy for him."

"Let's hope the inspector survives his surgery and can tell us the real names. If I were a praying man, I'd send up a prayer for those two kiddies. God knows where they are."

"You're thinking they might be in one of the other hideouts are you, sir?"

"I'm hoping so. At least they have been set up for men to survive in them, for days if necessary."

Rowell started to gather up their dishes and carry them to the sink.

"I'll do the washing up, sir."

"Thanks, Oliver. I need to make a telephone call."

He went out to the hall telephone and rang Mr. Grey, the chief intelligence officer in Whitchurch. To his dismay, the phone rang and rang but nobody answered.

He hung up and redialled, in case he'd made a mistake the first time. Same result. The phone simply rang on and on. He almost felt like banging his head against the wall in frustration.

Where is Clare? Will I ever see her again?

There was nothing more to be done. He'd have to wait until tomorrow.

He rejoined Rowell in the living room. "Was that meal my ration allowance for the next month, Oliver?"

"Almost, sir. I'll probably be able to get some more sausage but no more eggs for a fortnight."

"It was worth it. Sausage, fried egg, fried bread, and fried onion. I'm awash in fat but I don't care."

The clock on the mantel began to chime the hour.

"I'm going down to see Mrs. Keogh," said Tyler. "You don't think it's too late, do you?"

"Not if you go right away. I bet she'll be happy for the company."

Tyler headed for the door.

"Do you want to take the Rolls?" Rowell asked. "It's ours for the next while. Police business and all that."

Tyler grinned. "No, thanks. I'd better walk off the extra piece of fried bread you insisted I eat. I'll take that great brolly, though."

The sergeant yawned discreetly behind his hand. "I'm knackered. I think I'll turn in early."

"Good night, then," said Tyler. He couldn't help but muse that Oliver had a very good reason for being tired – a late night with your lover would do that to you. Lucky bloke.

Tyler knocked a few times and was starting to think it was too late after all when the door opened and Nuala Keogh stood in front of him. She was hardly more than a silhouette on the dark threshold. He flashed his torch briefly on his own face.

"Good evening, Mrs. Keogh. Tyler here."

Her hand flew to her heart. "Any news?"

"I'm afraid not. I thought I'd just come to tell you that, at least. And maybe talk over some more possibilities."

She stepped to one side. "Do come in. You'll have to come forward a bit so I can close the door behind you before I give us some light."

He did so, which brought them into close proximity. She smelled like soap and her hair seemed damp. Tyler suddenly felt like a sixteen-year-old lad tripping over his big feet and his desire.

"Wretched blackout. So many things to think about."

"True."

They were still standing very close together but she managed to squeeze past him without touching.

"I've just made some Horlicks, would you like a cup?"

"No, nothing for me, thank you."

Tyler hated Horlicks, which made him queasy. Besides, he didn't know if he'd trust himself to hold a cup without trembling.

"Do sit yourself down," she said, and he took the armchair opposite hers. "Please excuse my appearance. I wasn't expecting company."

She was in her dressing gown, the snug green wool plaid she'd been wearing the night before when he'd come to check on Jan and Pim. Her dark hair was loose about her shoulders. Tyler found her very hominess overwhelmingly attractive.

"You look fine," he said, and she smiled rather shyly back at him.

"For a minute there, I thought you had some good news for me. That they'd been found."

"I'm sorry. Unfortunately, they seem to have vanished into thin air. We've sent out telegrams to all other police stations in the near vicinity asking them to keep their eyes open. So far no response."

"But where would they go? It's a dreadful night. Weather like this can be deadly. Look what happened to Mr. Cartwright."

"He was elderly. The boys are resilient, and I don't think they're foolhardy. If they had nowhere to find shelter I'm sure they would have come right back."

Her eyes met his. "Nobody would want to harm them, would they, Inspector? Perhaps they discovered something they weren't supposed to."

Tyler himself was worried about just that possibility, but he didn't want to add to her anxiety by saying so.

"I have been to see the chief constable in Shrewsbury. Unfortunately he couldn't give me the names of the original users of that hideout but I should know first thing tomorrow. At least I'll be able to question them."

Suddenly she bit her lip. "Jan and Pim are orphans. Or as good as. I know they haven't been with me for that long but they feel like my own children." She turned to look into the fire and the shadow of the flames danced across her face. "I tell you frankly, Inspector, I would like to have children. I don't suppose that will happen now."

"You're still a young woman. You could remarry," said Tyler softly.

She didn't turn her head. "Could I? What if Paddy is not dead? What if he did come back and I was married to somebody else? What would happen then? There have been too many situations like that. There was one reported in Ludlow a couple of months ago. The family had even given the missing man a funeral service. Then they heard he was alive. He was in a hospital in Canada. God knows how he got there. He was badly injured, apparently, couldn't talk, and the papers got all mixed up." She began to fish for a handkerchief but couldn't find one. She sniffed. "Sorry."

"Here, take mine," said Tyler, and he tugged his out of his pocket and offered it to her. "It's clean."

She rubbed at her eyes rather harshly and he caught her hand. "Don't. You'll hurt yourself."

His face was very close to hers. Inches away. Without thinking, he reached up and brushed aside a strand of hair from across her forehead. She moved her head back but her eyes were fixed on his.

"What is your first name? I can't keep calling you Inspector. Not when I'm sitting here with our knees touching and I'm in my night clothes."

It was his turn to move back. "Sorry. I do apologize. I didn't mean to overstep the line."

She shook her head. "You didn't. Overstep, I mean. It's just that you're comforting me so tenderly I feel as if I'm going to melt."

All he could manage was, "Oh."

She put her hand on his. "I actually do know what your name is. You said it in court. It's Tom."

"That's right."

If he was breathing it would have taken a doctor to detect it. "Are you married?" she asked him.

"Not any more. I've just got divorced."

"Are you still in love with your ex-wife?" Her question uncannily echoed that of Mrs. Hamilton, and he gave the same answer.

"I don't think I ever was."

"I loved my husband."

She shifted and leaned her head into the crook of Tyler's neck. Her breath was warm on his skin and he could feel the wet of her tears.

"I am so lonely, Inspector Tom, I sometimes feel as if I am going to die from it."

He pulled her closer.

"Do you think it would be possible for you to bed me this night?" she whispered. "Or would that be against all regulations?"

Tyler began to stroke her hair. "The answer to the first question is yes. To the second, no."

"That is most reassuring to hear," she said, and her body folded into his.

The plaid wool dressing gown was soft under his hands. The flesh underneath even softer.

***

Jan and Pim were curled up together on the cot. Jan had turned down the wick of the lamp to conserve the fuel. The darkness pressed in on them. Pim appeared to have fallen asleep but he moved slightly and muttered through dry lips.

"Mamma. Mamma. My head hurts so." He spoke in Dutch.

"Go to sleep, there's a good fellow," whispered Jan. "We'll be all right in the morning."

"Mamma?"

"Mamma isn't here. It's Jan."

"Will Mamma be coming soon?"

"I think so. Just try to go to sleep and you can have a dream about her. A nice dream. Dream that we're back at home and we're drifting down the canal on our boat. The sun is shining and Pappa is steering. He's taken off his jacket. He's having a fine old time. We're going to Mr. Benne's for tea."

"I'm so cold, Jan. Will you cover me up?"

There were no blankets to cover him with but Jan pressed harder against his back to warm him.

"Will you sing to me?" Pim asked.

"If you like. What shall I sing?"

"Anything. But not too loud. My head hurts so."

Jan began to hum an old song that their mother used to sing when she was working around the house.

The only other sound was the hiss of the paraffin heater.

EDIE DIDN'T NEED THE ALARM TO WAKE HER UP. SHE had been lying in bed wide awake for the past hour unable to go back to sleep. She hadn't cried much since last night. It was almost as if tears would break her in two. All she could think about was Angelo and what would happen to him, to the two of them. Would she even see him again? There was every possibility that she wouldn't. He could be sent anywhere.

She'd said Angelo would never harm an old man, but how well did she know him, really? Not at all, truth be told. She loved his skin, his mouth, the way he caressed her, but how much did that count? Unbidden, her mother's voice came back to her. "*You're too soft by half, my girl. You can't go through life with stardust in your eyes. The devil himself could come up to you and offer you an apple and I swear you'd take it. Feel sorry for him, most like.*" Why had her ma said that? Edie couldn't remember, but it had something to do with some encounter in the park with an older boy. Her dad had come along "just in time," according to her mother, although what the boy would have done Edie didn't understand. Not then.

But look at her now. She'd been the one to initiate the liaison with Angelo. She hadn't waited for him to offer the apple, she'd snatched it herself.

When John Cartwright had said the barn door was not barred, Edie had doubted herself for a moment. Had she dropped the bar when she left? She was certain she had. She had stayed with Angelo as long as she'd dared. They'd exchanged kiss after kiss, so passionate they had made love again.

"I must go," she'd whispered in his ear. "I can't risk anybody discovering I'm not in bed." Finally, he'd let her leave, and she'd hurried back to the house, the wind pushing her backward, the rain soaking her. It must have been two o'clock by then and all was dark and silent. She'd undressed and climbed into bed, shivering in the chilly air. She was so happy she half expected she wouldn't be able to sleep, but she did. A deep sleep that nothing disturbed.

She reached for her dressing gown now. It was too big for her, an old blue flannel affair that had belonged to her granny. Edie allowed herself a small giggle. Good thing Angelo hadn't seen her wearing that – a passion-killer if ever there was one. But it was warm, and she was grateful for that as she scurried across the linoleum-covered floor and headed for the toilet. No dawn yet. Nobody else seemed to be up.

She didn't even wait to make herself a cup of tea. She could breakfast later. Right now she was so anxious she had to keep on the move. She could start by milking the cows. They wouldn't mind if she was a bit earlier than usual.

She shrugged into her overcoat, grabbed her torch, and, fast as she could, she ran down to the cow barn.

She opened the door. "Morning, girls," she called out.

She took one of the lanterns from the hook by the door and lit it.

A figure rose out of the shadows. She gasped.

"Don't be scared, Edie. It's me," said Angelo.

***

Tyler let himself into the house. He moved quietly, not wanting to wake Rowell. However, he had barely removed his hat and coat when he heard a creak on the stairs and his sergeant came down.

"Good morning, sir."

"God, Oliver, you gave me a fright."

"Sorry, sir. I didn't know if you were you, if you know what I mean."

"Right. I could have been a parachutist."

"Precisely."

They stood awkwardly, looking at each other. What was not being said was screaming for attention.

"I stayed the night with Mrs. Keogh," Tyler said.

"Ah."

Another silence.

"Is that all you're going to say, Oliver?"

"I didn't think it was my place to comment, sir."

"Comment away. I give you permission. After all, you were the one who set the example."

"Me, sir?"

"Yes, you, Sergeant," said Tyler in exasperation. "And you sent me to Mrs. Hamilton, don't forget."

"But Mrs. Keogh isn't one of Mrs. Hamilton's clients, sir."

"Does that matter?"

To say he had enjoyed having intimacy with a willing and attractive partner after so long was putting it mildly.

"I only bring it up because Mrs. Hamilton is quite rigorous about only accepting clients who are what she would call 'ready for romance.'"

"Mrs. Keogh seemed very willing to, er, to be romantic."

"It wasn't her I was thinking of so much as you, sir. The lady in question has a husband who is presumed dead. Her feelings around love are probably quite, shall we say, cloudy. Timing is important in these matters."

"I know what you're saying, Oliver. I'll be careful. Both of the feelings of the lady in question and my own."

"Of course, sir. Shall I put the kettle on for some tea, sir?"

***

Edie extricated herself from Angelo's arms.

"What are you doing here? I didn't think they'd release you so soon."

"They didn't. I have escaped."

"Escaped! Oh my God, Angelo. You can't. You must go back."

"I won't. I'll hide here. The war with Italy will be over soon, I know it. I'll hide until I am no longer considered the enemy. Then we can get married and make lots of babies until we are too old."

Edie didn't laugh. "That's mad. It could be months, years even before the war's over. You can't hide in here for months."

"Why not? People have. I'll live on cow's milk and what you bring me."

"What *I* bring you? Angelo, for God's sake. You would be discovered in a minute."

"Ah. You don't love me after all. You gave me your body, your strange territory, but you won't take the risk so we can be together." His words were angry but his tone was almost playful and teasing.

It was Edie who was angry. "Love has nothing to do with it. What you are proposing is insane. Not practical. Fraternizing is not allowed. We'll both go to jail. I will be seen as a traitor. What good would that do us?"

Suddenly serious, he caught her face between his hands. "Then let us run away together. We'll be like cunning foxes."

"We don't stand a chance. We'll be caught right away."

He turned her head toward him and kissed her. "Any time with you, however short, is better than no time at all."

Before he could continue, the barn door banged open and Ned Weaver burst inside. He hesitated for only a moment, then raised the revolver he was holding and pointed it at them.

"Step away, Edie. He's a dangerous man. Step away from him."

Edie had been standing in Angelo's arms, her back to the door. She turned at once so that she was shielding her lover.

"No. No. Ned, please, put down that gun."

"I'm taking him back where he belongs."

In a split second, Angelo responded. He pushed Edie away from him and leaped toward Ned.

Before he could reach him, Ned fired.

***

Tyler was just about to leave for the police station when the telephone rang.

"I'll get it," he said to Rowell, who was still tidying up in the kitchen.

Captain Beattie was on the other end.

"Tyler, something serious has happened here. Angelo Iaquinta has apparently gone missing."

"What!"

"His absence was detected this morning at roll call. It looks as if he got out of the window at the back of the hut and escaped that way."

"Have you started a search, sir?"

"I was about to do just that, but I want to keep it under wraps as long as possible. I don't want to scare the bejesus out of the civilian population. You know how jumpy everybody is about enemy parachutists and so on. I don't consider the fellow to be dangerous, do you?"

"Hard to say, sir. If he's desperate enough, he might do anything."

"Bloody stupid to run like that. Where does he think he's going? He took one of the bikes. He has no currency he can use.

No identification, unless you count his uniform. Where's he heading?"

Tyler thought he could take a good guess.

"I'll get over to the Cartwrights' right away. Angelo knows the farm, he might be going there."

"All right. Good thinking. Call me at once if you get a lead. I'll see what I come up with this end."

Tyler hung up, but before he even moved from the telephone it rang again. This time it was John Cartwright.

"Inspector! You had better come at once. There's been an accident here. A terrible accident."

His voice was so choked, Tyler could hardly understand him.

"What's happened?"

"Edie's dead," John whispered.

***

Angelo could barely manoeuvre the bicycle. The wind was fierce and the wound in his right arm was bleeding freely where the bullet had sliced off a piece of flesh. He could hardly breathe with the effort and the force of his feelings. He had to get away. Rationally he knew he couldn't get far under these conditions, but he was like a wounded animal that has to go to ground – the instinct to run and hide, to stay alive as long as possible, was a powerful one.

He pedalled as hard as he could up to the crest of the hill. The trees were tossing and heaving in the wind. Suddenly he remembered there were the remains of a shepherd's hut deep in the woods. He'd come across it in the summer when he was foraging for firewood. He might be able to make himself some kind of shelter. He could hole up there until he made a plan of what to do.

He turned the bicycle off the road onto the narrow dirt path that led into the woods. There was some respite from the wind there, but in the deep shadow of the trees it was hard to see where he was going. He dismounted. The ground was so rough and uneven that it was easier to walk and push the bike. The tumbledown hut was just ahead.

What was that?

There seemed to be a pinprick of light coming from among the loose bricks at the base of one ruined wall. He moved closer. Was it a dropped torch? He held his head up, almost sniffing the air like a dog. Was there somebody else in the woods? The only sound was the creaking of branches. He pulled out the gun that he'd taken from Ned Weaver and cocked the hammer, aiming the barrel toward the dot of light. Nothing moved.

He risked bending closer. He put the gun carefully on the ground and unhooked the lamp from the bicycle. He flashed it over the wall of the hut. There was a narrow opening at the base, perhaps the size of a postbox slot. Impossible for anybody to get through. But then he realized that a heavy branch had fallen across the lower bricks. He could see that the tiny light was coming from some kind of underground space.

Quickly, he returned to the bike. He had to get away before anybody saw him.

***

The silence on the other end of the line was so profound that, for a moment, Tyler thought they might have been disconnected.

"Mr. Cartwright? Mr. Cartwright? What happened? Please talk to me."

"It was the Italian," whispered the voice on the other end of the phone. "He was in the barn hiding out. Ned must have heard something because he went in with his revolver. He was afraid for Edie. He was trying to protect her. The Itie shot both of them. And . . ." John stopped. Then he said, "Ned is seriously hurt."

"Is the POW still there?"

"No. He seems to have taken off."

"I'll send for medical help and I'll come as fast as I can."

"You'd better hurry. I've done what I could to stop the bleeding but Ned caught it in the chest. I seen wounds like that in the Great War. I don't think he can last."

"I'm on my way."

Tyler hung up and ran back to the kitchen.

"Oliver. There's been a shooting at the Cartwrights'."

"What the . . . ?"

"The POW escaped from the camp and went to the farm. Apparently the Land Girl has been killed and the son is badly injured. I'm going there immediately. According to John Cartwright, the Italian was the one doing the shooting."

Tyler headed upstairs to his room. "Contact Captain Beattie. Tell him we'll need a doctor and an ambulance at the Cartwright farm. Say we've located Iaquinta but there's been gunfire. One fatality, one injury. The POW isn't on the scene but he must be in the vicinity. Beattie should send a search party over there right away."

"My God, sir."

Tyler drove as fast as he could and he was at the farmhouse in fifteen minutes. John Cartwright was standing at the gate, holding up a storm lantern. The light winked in the dim light.

As soon as Tyler had stopped the car, John ran over to him.

"They're down in the barn. Susan is with Ned."

"Is he . . . ?"

"Barely alive but he's conscious."

Hurriedly, Tyler followed him.

The body of the young Land Girl was several feet away from the entrance. She was lying on her side. The entire right side of her forehead was a bloody, pulpy mess. Tyler stopped only briefly to check on her. She was obviously dead.

Farther inside, near the partition, Tyler could see Susan Cartwright kneeling beside her son, who was lying flat on his back. She had a towel pressed to his chest but it was already soaked with blood. As Tyler went over to them, he could hear the gurgling, liquid sound of Ned's lungs at every intake of breath. Susan looked up. Her face was sheet-white. Tyler dropped to a crouch next to her, and behind him John held up the lantern, which swayed in his unsteady grip.

"An ambulance will be here shortly," said Tyler. He gestured to Susan to move back and gently lifted the blood-soaked towel. There was a ragged hole in the centre of Weaver's chest and blood was pumping out. Tyler replaced the towel and applied pressure.

"Ned. Can you hear me?"

The injured man's eyes flickered open and he made a sort of grunting sound.

Tyler raised his voice. "Can you tell me what happened?"

Ned's eyes focused on him. "Are you a doctor?" he whispered.

"No, it's Inspector Tyler. The policeman you talked to before. A medic will be here soon. Can you tell me what happened?" he repeated. "Who shot you?"

"Itie ran at me. He grabbed the gun. Shot me in the chest." He struggled to lift his head. "How is Edie?"

"Not good, I'm afraid."

Ned sank back. "Is she dead?"

"Yes, Ned, she is."

Weaver licked his lips. "I'm thirsty."

Susan scrambled to her feet. "I'll get some water."

John grabbed her hand. "No water, Susan."

She shook him off in a fury. "Didn't you hear? He's thirsty."

Tyler looked at her over his shoulder.

"Your husband's right, Mrs. Cartwright. With a wound of this nature, he mustn't be given anything to drink."

Her face was contorted. "Stop questioning him, then. You're making him worse."

Tyler didn't want to say "This might be the only chance I get," but John did it for him.

"We must know what happened, Susan."

"He told you. Leave him be."

Ned's eyes fluttered. "Edie got in the way. Didn't mean it. Didn't want to shoot her. He came at me. Grabbed gun. Went off."

Tyler glanced around quickly. There was no sign of the weapon.

"Where's the gun?" he asked John.

"Haven't seen it."

Ned groaned and seemed to drift back into unconsciousness. Tyler thought that might be the end, but Ned spoke again, his voice so low Tyler had to put his ear a few inches from the man's mouth.

"He was outside. Came at me. Thought he was going to kill me. Only trying to defend myself."

Blood was trickling from the corner of his mouth and Tyler used the towel to wipe it away.

"Outside? Who do you mean, Ned? The Italian?"

Ned didn't respond. He managed to lift his hand. Tyler caught hold of it. It was icy cold.

"Do you know any prayers?" Ned murmured. "I'd like to go off with a prayer."

Tyler looked at John Cartwright, standing like stone behind him.

"He'd like a prayer."

John seemed incapable of speaking, but Susan immediately clasped her hands together. "Our Father, which art in heaven . . ."

Tyler turned back to Ned. His lips were moving as if he was accompanying her.

Susan continued, speaking fast. "Thy kingdom come, thy will be done . . ."

She hadn't finished when the barn door opened and three uniformed soldiers rushed in. The leader was white-haired and had doctor's flashes on his sleeve. The other two were young POWs. They were carrying a stretcher.

"Over here," called Tyler. "It's this one."

He moved out of the way.

Susan Cartwright was still kneeling in prayer. "You'll soon be right as rain, pet," she said.

Tyler thought that was extremely unlikely.

***

"Help. Help."

It was a child's voice, faint and feeble. Angelo froze. His thoughts were racing. Had a child fallen into a well or some such thing? Obviously the tree branch was preventing him from getting out. What could he do? Every minute of delay meant more chance that his own whereabouts would be discovered. He moaned.

In all likelihood he would be charged with murder. Edie was dead. He'd sprung at Ned, desperately trying to grab his gun. It had gone off, and the bullet had hit the other man in the chest. Angelo didn't even know if he was alive or dead. Even if he lived, Angelo knew he wouldn't stand a chance. Who would believe him?

He turned his bicycle.

The tiny voice floated out from the air vent.

"Is somebody there? Help! Please help!"

***

"He's still got vitals," said the doctor. "Let's get him to the hospital." He beckoned to the two medics who'd come with him. They were both young, frightened. "Put this man on the stretcher. We'll take him into Ludlow."

"I want to come with you," said Susan. "I'm his mother."

The doctor shook his head. "Better to follow behind us, madam. I will have to treat him as we drive."

"I'll take the lorry." Susan turned to John. "Will you come?"

"Of course."

Both of them followed the stretcher-bearers out of the barn.

The doctor halted in front of Tyler. "The girl looks to be beyond help."

"She is."

"Fill me in when you can. You can reach me through the camp. I'm Stevens."

He hurried off.

Because of the need to tend to Weaver, Tyler hadn't closely examined the nature of Edie's wound, but now he went over to her body. The right side of her forehead had been sliced off; the flesh gleamed red and raw. He could see brain matter. It didn't look like a bullet wound to him.

Edie was lying next to a post. There was a fresh gouge on one side where the bullet had sheared off a chunk of wood that must have flown straight at Edie and hit her full force. She must have died immediately. This bright young woman, the chatterbox with so much love and passion for life, had gone from the face of the earth.

***

Angelo dragged the branch away from the opening in the base of the wall. There had been no more cries and the silence drove him to move quickly. The branch was very heavy but he was able to move it sufficiently to clear the entrance. He bent down and shouted into the small opening.

"Hello in there! Are you all right?"

There was no reply.

He tugged at what appeared to be a loose plank. It was attached to a trap door, which he lifted up to reveal a narrow, dark opening and the top of a metal ladder.

"Hello," he shouted again, but there was only silence.

He turned so he could descend the ladder. At the bottom was a small, cave-like dugout. The light he'd glimpsed earlier was coming from a small lamp that was flickering faintly. He could just make out two boys lying on a cot.

Neither was moving.

***

Tyler stood at the threshold of the barn, watching as the morning light grew stronger. A cow inside mooed and he was jolted out of his reverie. Who was going to milk them?

After what seemed like an eternity he heard the blessed sound of a motorcycle and, sure enough, Agnes Mortimer came roaring down the road and into the yard. Mady was in the sidecar.

They quickly disentangled from the motorcycle, and Mortimer handed Tyler a brown envelope.

"Sergeant Rowell sent this, sir. It just arrived. He thought you would want to have it right away." It was stamped "TOP SECRET" in large black letters. When Tyler opened it, he found a second envelope inside, and within that, a single piece of paper. The message was handwritten, neat and small. Golden, he presumed.

> *The operative named Zechariah was with the Auxiliary for a while but he was released a year ago. Reason being, "not suitable." Unfortunately, I do not have a name for him. It was deleted for security reasons. Ezekiel is the code name of Samuel Wickers.*

Somehow, Tyler was not surprised. He could see Wickers enjoying the life of a commando with nobody to answer to except himself. So who was the unsuitable Zechariah? Presumably he would be aware of the location of the secret hideouts if he'd been in the Auxiliary Unit even if it was only for a while.

He addressed his constables who were waiting. "Constable Mady, stay here and guard this door. There's a corpse inside. Don't let anybody touch anything. There should be a contingent of soldiers coming from the camp any minute to search for the missing POW. Tell them they mustn't proceed until I get back."

"When will that be, sir?"

"Hopefully not long. Constable Mortimer, come with me."

"Yes, sir. Shall we take the motorcycle?"

Tyler hesitated. It was by no means his favourite form of transport but he didn't want to waste time fussing with the unreliable Annabel.

"All right. And this time you can speed."

"Yes, sir. Where are we going?"

"Up the hill. The Mohan farm."

They were at the Mohan place within five minutes. Tyler signalled to Mortimer to pull over near the front door. He could see that Sam Wickers and Tim were both having breakfast at the kitchen table.

Tyler had no idea what he might be walking into and, not for the first time in his career, he wished he had a weapon. Basically he was trusting his instincts. First, that Wickers was not a cold-blooded murderer, and second, that neither was the young Italian.

He knocked hard on the front door. Wickers opened it, and while he looked surprised to see them he did not seem particularly alarmed.

"Inspector, Constable Mortimer, don't tell me you've come to give me a report on my work?"

"No. I'd like to come in and speak to you in private."

"I was just about to go out and hunt us up some dinner."

"Don't push it, Wickers. You're not going anywhere. Let's just say we need to discuss a certain person."

"Who might that be?"

"His name's Ezekiel."

Wickers tensed. "Better I come out, then."

He did so and closed the door behind him. He had no coat but he seemed impervious to the cold.

Tyler nodded in the direction of Mortimer. "Don't worry. We can talk in front of my constable. I'll get straight to the point."

"Please do. I can hardly stand the suspense."

"Don't be so cheeky," said Tyler. "Fact is, I'm aware you're a member of the Auxiliary Units."

"Are you now?"

"Don't worry, I found out through proper channels. Chief constable and all that."

"Well, that's a relief. Wouldn't want you to read it in the *Ludlow Ledger.*"

"Cut it out, Wickers. I'm dealing with a serious situation."

"Sorry." Wickers seemed sincere for once. "What's going on?"

"As an Auxiliary, you would know about the hideout underneath the trough. Isn't that right?"

Sam nodded.

"That's where Jasper Cartwright's body was found. Did you dump him in there?"

Sam recoiled. "No. I did not."

"Somebody stabbed him with something that sounds suspiciously like a commando knife to me. Double-sided, sharp point. The kind you were most likely issued."

Sam rubbed his hands together to warm them. "Wasn't me. I don't fight with harmless old men."

"According to what I've heard, Jasper was a bit off his rocker. Did you run into him in the wee hours when you were poaching rabbits? Perhaps he threatened to tell on you."

"No. In my book, getting rabbits for those that need them isn't exactly a major crime. So what if word got out? We're at war, don't forget. Nobody cares." He rubbed his hands again. "I'm not going to stab somebody over a trifle like that."

"All right. I believe you. But what I'd like to know is if you did see Jasper? He was out wandering around in the storm."

Wickers shook his head. "No, I didn't see him. I know you don't have a high opinion of me, Inspector, but I assure you if I had run into the old man I would have taken him home."

Mortimer tapped Tyler on the shoulder.

"Excuse me, sir. Can Mr. Wickers provide us with an alibi? That would help enormously."

"I was about to ask that very thing, Constable," said Tyler.

Wickers grinned. "Matter of fact I can. Hope you won't be shocked."

"We'll try not to be," said Tyler.

"I wasn't home for the entire night."

"That's not what your chum said."

"Tim was trying to help, but I have a better witness who will vouch for the fact that I was nowhere near here on Monday night. If it's an alibi you're looking for, I've got one."

"Do tell."

"I spent the night, the entire night, with a lady-friend in Ludlow. I joined her about eleven and got back here at six. She'll vouch for me."

Tyler took out his notebook. "Lucky for you – if it's true. I'll need her name and address."

Wickers didn't answer right away. "Look, problem is she's married."

"Her husband wasn't at home, I presume, when you were, er, *visiting* this lady? Or was it a threesome?"

He caught a bit of a blush flit across his constable's face.

"What? No, course it wasn't," said Wickers, his voice indignant. "He works out of town."

"All right. I'll just ask her to confirm that you were together for the night. So? Who is she? Where does she live?"

Reluctantly, Wickers gave him the information. "You promise you'll be discreet? She's a good woman. She gets lonely is all. I don't want to get her into hot water."

Tyler wasn't going to be so hypocritical as to comment on marital infidelity. He put away his notebook. "All right, back to more important issues. We've got two young boys who've gone missing. We know they were making use of a hideout that was built by the Auxiliaries. It's not out of the question that they know something they're not supposed to. Frankly, Wickers, I fear for their safety."

"Good lord. You're not talking about the little Dutch kids, are you? Jan and Pim?"

"That's them."

"When you say they've gone missing, what do you mean?"

"They left their foster home yesterday, said they were going to London to see their Queen. They've vanished."

"Good lord," Wickers exclaimed again. For the first time, Tyler thought, the I-don't-really-give-a damn attitude dropped away. "They discovered me not too long ago when I was going into the hideout with some rabbits. I was careless, didn't realize they were out there playing at being Scouts. I put the fear of God into them, but also told them they could use the place as long as it was a deep secret." He bit his lip. "The Auxiliaries haven't been active for over a year. I didn't see any harm would come of it."

"Are there any more hideouts?" Tyler asked.

"One other, in the woods. It's not in good shape though."

"Did the boys know about it?"

"I mentioned it but I didn't show them."

Tyler looked over at his constable. The tip of her nose was red from the cold but she was listening intently.

"They might have gone there, sir."

"We'll check right now." Tyler turned back to Wickers. "Listen, son. I believe what you've told me, but there's something else I need to know. According to the chief constable there were two of you Auxiliaries in this area. One of them was discharged last year as unsuitable. Code name of Zechariah. What's his real name?"

Before Wickers could answer, Agnes Mortimer suddenly cried out, "Sir! Look. It's the POW."

Tyler twirled around. Emerging from the stand of trees on the ridge was Angelo Iaquinta. He was wheeling his bicycle. His arm was around one boy, holding him on to the saddle. The other boy was sitting on the crossbar and draped over the handlebars. Iaquinta was attempting to keep him in place with his other hand. Jan and Pim.

"Come on," said Tyler, and he set off on the run. Younger and faster, Wickers raced ahead, and Mortimer was close behind.

Angelo halted.

"Help. Please help me. The boys are sick."

Later, Tyler would credit Sam Wickers with saving Pim. Jan was looking green around the gills but he was still conscious. Tyler got him off the bike and carried him to the side of the path. Mortimer immediately removed her own coat and put it around Jan's shoulders. In the meantime, Sam lifted the smaller boy, who was pale and unmoving, off the handlebars and laid him flat on the ground on his stomach, arms above his head. He pressed on the boy's back, then pulled up his arms. Repeat.

Barely moments later, as if on cue, the cavalry arrived in the shape of an army lorry. The half dozen soldiers crammed in the back jumped out, rifles at the ready, all focused on Angelo. Tyler yelled at them to stay where they were.

"Situation under control."

Angelo made no attempt to get away but leaned on the bicycle watching anxiously as Wickers frantically worked.

It seemed a very long time before Pim responded but it was probably only minutes. His eyelids fluttered and a dribble of saliva came from his mouth. Wickers turned the boy's chin and he vomited yellow bile.

"Atta boy," said Sam cheerily.

Jan tried to stand up and go to his brother. "Pim. Wake up. Wake up."

Tyler held him back. "Take it easy, lad. Your brother's in good hands. He's going to be all right. Let the man finish his job."

Wickers had in fact stopped the artificial respiration. He turned Pim over onto his back and pulled him into a sitting position.

"Feeling a bit better, Scout?"

"Yes, Captain," whispered the boy.

"Keep taking some nice deep breaths for me, there's a chum," Wickers said.

Jan pointed at the group of soldiers and at Angelo. "They're not going to arrest him, are they?"

"I'm afraid he has to go back to the camp. He's a POW. You were very lucky he found you."

"A tree branch fell across the entrance. We couldn't get out. Pim started to get sick."

"You shouldn't have been in that hideout, young Scout. I told you we abandoned it ages ago. I didn't even know there was still a heater in there, but it was probably not working properly. Those things are bloody dangerous when they're faulty."

Nobody said, "You could both have died," but the words hung in the air.

Tyler had Wickers and Mortimer take the boys back to the Mohan farmhouse. Wickers gave Pim a piggyback ride. The boy was still ashen but alive. Jan looked wobbly but was all right with Mortimer taking his hand.

A corporal from among the soldiers came forward to take charge of the Italian. Angelo didn't resist, and at Tyler's request, he handed over the gun he'd taken from Ned. He had a wound in his left arm, but it had stopped bleeding and didn't look too serious. As the soldiers put him in the lorry, Tyler spoke to him softly.

"I'm sorry, son. I'm truly sorry about what has happened."

He made his way to the Mohan farm and was met at the door by Sam Wickers.

"We just got a message from the hospital. John Cartwright called. Ned died in the ambulance on the way."

"Damn. I didn't hold out much hope, I must say."

"Oh, and Inspector," continued Wickers, "I never got the chance to answer your question."

"Yes?"

"The real name of the other Auxiliary was Ned Weaver."

NUALA INVITED TYLER AND SERGEANT ROWELL TO come over on Christmas morning.

"You've got to come early because it will be torture for the boys to have to wait too long to open their presents."

She and Tyler had continued their relationship, but discreetly. Tyler left her bed in the middle of the night and grabbed a couple of more hours of shut-eye at home. He was starting to suffer from sleep deprivation, but so far it was worth it.

When he conveyed Nuala's invitation to Rowell, his sergeant grinned at him. "Might I suggest, sir, that you give yourself the luxury of staying through the night?"

"Hmm. I'm not ready to go public, Oliver. The boys are sure to wonder what I'm doing there."

"They'll be more interested in seeing what Father Christmas brought them. You can fib about dropping in if you have to."

Tyler had to admit, the idea of not having to go from Nuala's soft arms and bed into the cold night was quite appealing.

"I'll see what Nuala has to say."

It turned out she was ecstatic. He agreed to come when the boys were asleep and put his presents underneath the tiny tree that Nuala had decorated.

"I tried to do a sort of amalgam of traditions. I got a menorah for Hanukkah, and we're calling Father Christmas Saint Nicholas, which is what he's called in Holland. I don't want the boys to lose contact with their Jewish heritage, but they are determined to 'simulate,' as Jan calls it. So we're doing bits and pieces."

"Sounds good to me," said Tyler.

He'd hemmed and hawed about what to buy for Nuala and finally settled on a silver brooch in the shape of a Celtic knot. He'd bought the boys wooden toys that had been made by the Italian POWs. Jan's was a beautifully finished tank, and Pim's was a Viking boat. For both of them to share, he'd included a book on the English Civil War, which actually had a chapter describing coinage of the time. Their Elizabethan coin had been turned over to the local archaeologist, Mr. Reavill. The boys swore they'd found it on the road not far from the barn, and Tyler believed them. It seemed possible that Jasper had unearthed some sort of hoard in the field, but they had no way of knowing where that was. Tyler had shown the piece of paper he'd found in Jasper's box to the archaeologist, but he couldn't really help.

"It does look like directions of some kind but it could refer to absolutely anywhere. Maybe someday we'll have a way of better detecting these things, but for now we'll just have to wait around until the land yields up its secrets."

Tyler hoped that the boys would feel compensated for the confiscation of the coin by the chocolate medallions wrapped in gold foil that he'd brought them. He'd also been able to find some oranges, one for each child and one for Nuala. Under her instruction, Tyler wrapped the toys and put them underneath the tree. He noticed as he did so that there was a rather large package with his name on it, but he kept his curiosity in check. The sweets he stuffed into two old socks to hang from the mantel.

"I do want them to have a good Christmas," said Nuala. She shuddered. "I can hardly bear to think what a close call they had."

The problem had indeed been the faulty kerosene heater. There was no doubt the boys would have died from carbon monoxide poisoning if Angelo hadn't found them when he did. Tyler and Nuala talked about what to tell the boys if things went badly for Angelo, which they might.

"He's become their hero, second only to the Captain," said Nuala.

"Ah yes, Mr. Wickers."

As for Sam himself, after the drama of the boys' rescue he seemed a different man. He came to see them every day, even delivered some comics "from the Captain."

To Tyler's delight, a romance seemed to be gently developing between Agnes Mortimer, of long-established gentry, and Sam Wickers, of long-established farming stock. An unlikely match, but it reminded Tyler of himself and Clare.

Angelo Iaquinta was in prison, the civil one in Shrewsbury this time. He had filled in his part of the sequence of events that had been triggered by Jasper Cartwright's wandering in the night. The old man had come into the barn in the early hours of the morning. Edie had left long before. Jasper was carrying the metal case and started to mutter about hiding it, but he'd stumbled on something and the case had fallen from his grasp. At that point, Jasper turned tail and ran from the barn. Yes, Angelo had looked inside the case, he couldn't resist the temptation. He saw the gold wedding ring. It felt like a gift from God himself, and he took it.

Yes, he was very sorry when they found the old man's body but he hadn't dared say anything about their encounter. He'd hidden the case until he could sort out what to do. It hadn't occurred to him that Jasper might be in trouble until the next afternoon, and by then it was already too late to help.

The part following Angelo's escape from the camp Tyler already knew. Angelo had immediately made his way back to the farm so he could see Edie. They were embracing in the barn when Ned burst in with a revolver in his hand. Ned fired at him and Edie right away. No warning. Nothing. To Angelo's mind, Ned looked as if he had lost his mind. The first bullet grazed Angelo's arm. Edie tried to save her lover, to shield him with her own body. Angelo pushed her aside. Ned fired again and the second bullet struck the post, knocking off a big splinter of wood, which hit Edie directly in the head. When he related this to Tyler, Angelo wept. "I ran at him and tried to get the gun. It went off into his chest. I did not intentionally hurt him, even though he caused the death of my dearest love."

As Ned Weaver could neither confirm nor deny Angelo's version of events, Tyler examined the scene very carefully for as much evidence as he could find. Dr. Murnaghan confirmed that Edie had indeed been killed by a piece from the wooden pillar splintering off. Ned's wound was also consistent with Angelo's version of what had happened.

"What do you think will happen?" Nuala asked Tyler. "Surely they'll let him go."

"I'll testify for him, and Captain Beattie is prepared to go to bat about his good character, but who knows? We'll have to see how the prosecutor feels about the Italians."

Also working in Angelo's favour was Tyler's conviction that Weaver was the one who had stabbed Jasper and taken him to die in the bunker. They'd found a commando knife in his room, which Dr. Murnaghan was certain was the same one that had been used on Jasper. His gun was also army issue. The sad thing was that Ned, like Jasper, had his own stash of treasures. Dozens of toy soldiers.

It was Wickers who'd told them more about Ned's history.

"He seriously hurt his training sergeant. Wasn't even under enemy action. Apparently the sarge was a right wanker and kept riding Ned. One day, Weaver exploded and picked up a brick and slugged him. All swept under the carpet – didn't look good for the army. But Weaver was desperate to do his bit for the war effort. Took it hard being chucked out like that. He managed to get accepted by the Auxiliaries. He was healthy enough, physically, lived in the area. But he couldn't take that training either. Flew off the handle at the least problem. So he was set loose. Bit late, I thought. Weaver already knew the whereabouts of the hideouts."

Tyler had delivered the information to the Cartwrights. Once again they had gathered at the kitchen table. It was a painful session. Susan broke down and confessed that, in truth, she had heard her father-in-law leave the house shortly before dawn.

"I was so angry with him, I thought, 'Let him go. He'll soon be back when he realizes what the weather is like.'" She halted, swallowing back her tears. John said nothing.

"Did he come back?" Tyler asked.

"Yes. He pounded on the door. It wasn't locked but it stuck sometimes and he must have thought it was."

That accounts for the bruises on his knuckles, thought Tyler.

"I should have got up, I know I should, but I was so tired," continued Susan, her voice almost inaudible now. "And I knew he could get in if he wanted to." She stopped, obviously hoping for a response from her husband. None was forthcoming. "I fell asleep again," she went on. "Then I woke up because I heard somebody coming in. I assumed it was Jasper. My conscience was clear."

"But it wasn't your father-in-law. It was your son."

"It must have been," she whispered.

"Why do you think he went out at that time of the morning?" Tyler asked.

Her face was desolate. "I'm guessing he heard the knocking as well. Ned was always on the lookout for an opportunity to prove he was a soldier. He wanted an enemy he could defeat, a damsel he could save. He probably didn't even realize it was

Jasper. I think what he was saying in the kitchen that time was really about himself, not Angelo. Jasper in his madness went to attack him, and my son acted in self-defence."

They'd never know for sure, but what she said made sense given the nature of Jasper's wound. Weaver had probably panicked when he realized what he'd done, and he'd taken him to the one place he thought the body wouldn't be found. At least not for a long time. He hadn't counted on the boys.

The "if only"s filled the room. If only Jasper hadn't gone out to hide his treasure in such a storm. If only Susan had got up to let him in when she heard him knocking. If only John had heard him. If only Ned had got help immediately for the old man he'd only wounded.

Tyler felt that John Cartwright was also thinking these things. He felt sorry for the couple and the future of their marriage.

IT WAS SHEER BLISS TO STAY IN BED UNTIL SEVEN o'clock, when they were awakened by the boys going downstairs. They were whispering and tiptoeing, a surefire method of waking any sleeping adults. Tyler rolled on his side and looked into Nuala's sleep-rumpled face.

"Shall we get up and let the lads open their presents? You can supervise while I light the stove and make the tea."

This was in fact quite a procedure given the lack of electricity in the cottage, but Tyler wanted to experience what Nuala experienced every day.

Nuala kissed him heartily. "Sounds wonderful. Add some toast to that and I'll be in heaven. You'll find there are four eggs in the pantry. They're for us."

"Get up when you're ready. I'll look after things."

He got dressed fully before heading downstairs.

To preserve coal, Nuala had decided all activity should take place in the kitchen, and she'd stood the little tree in the corner. The boys had festooned it with paper chains. When he came in, they were standing looking at the socks hanging from the mantelpiece, each with their name sewn on them.

"Thought I'd come and help out," said Tyler. Not exactly lying but certainly with the intent to evade.

"Shall I let Mrs. Keogh know you're here?" asked Jan.

"No, that's all right, son, she knows."

At that moment, Nuala herself entered and saved him further prevarication. She was wearing her dressing gown. He'd thought of buying her a new one but truth was he liked the old plaid he'd first seen her wearing.

"Inspector Tyler is going to have breakfast with us this morning, boys. He's volunteered to get the stove going, then we'll see what Saint Nicholas brought us."

"I heard Saint N-Nicholas arrive, last night," said Pim in a conspiratorial tone of voice. "I think he's got a c-cough, though. He was moaning."

"Right," said Nuala, hardly able to keep from laughing. "The inspector will act as Saint Nicholas' helper and give out the presents." She picked up a blanket from the back of the chair and waved it at the boys. "Wrap up with this. I don't want you to catch cold. You can squeeze up together on the armchair."

They obeyed with alacrity. Anything to get Christmas moving along.

Tyler hurried with the lighting of the stove. "All right. Fire's going. Kettle's on the hob. Let's see what we've got."

The boys' excitement at opening their presents was heart-warming. Nuala had found a spinning top somewhere and given it to them as a Hanukkah gift. Jan said they'd played with one just like it when they were in Holland, the dreidel, they called it. He put it aside politely, and Tyler could see the memories were painful. His presents were well received, especially the sweets. Nuala seemed to like her little brooch and had him pin it on. *Whew.*

Finally the only present left was his. The boys watched curiously while he tore off the wrapping. No, not tore off. Peeled off. The paper was too precious and had to be carefully preserved. Inside was a plain box, and inside that a handsome dressing gown of blue wool.

"Matches your eyes," said Nuala. She lowered her voice. "You can keep it here if you like."

"Great idea," Tyler whispered back.

—

The boiled eggs, the toast with a slather of butter spread on it, the sweets – it was a veritable feast. Tyler felt happier than he had in a long time. He hadn't always enjoyed Christmas with his own children; there had often been such strain between him and Vera, it was hard to overcome.

Sometime in the late morning there was a knock at the door. It was Oliver Rowell.

"Just came to wish everybody a happy Christmas." He waved at the boys, who were on the floor playing with their new toys. "It's going to be a proper white one by the look of it. You'll be able to build a snowman."

Nuala greeted him warmly. She knew an ally when she saw one.

"Come in, Oliver. I've got a hot toddy just waiting for you."

"Delightful. What an admirable woman," said Rowell in his best Scrooge voice.

"The boys will love to show you their presents," said Tyler. "And I think there's something underneath the tree with your name on it."

In the nick of time, Tyler had remembered Rowell's wish for fleece slippers, and, with Dorothy's help, he'd tracked down a fancy pair.

"Who's minding the shop, by the way?"

"Constable Mortimer is on till three. I gave her short hours today. She's invited Sam Wickers to have dinner with her family." Rowell chuckled. "The lad seemed more nervous about the prospect of meeting the Mortimers than he would be at having to face a marauding horde." He handed Tyler an envelope. "Morning post arrived, sir. Don't want to spoil anything but this is marked urgent, so I thought I'd better bring it over."

Tyler stared at the all-too-familiar handwriting. Clare's. His stomach immediately knotted up. He could see by the franking it was much more recent than the one he'd read a couple of weeks ago. He walked away from the hearth and opened the letter. Rowell chatted with the boys.

December 19

Dearest Tom,

You'll never guess what has happened. I have been transferred to London so I am at the moment free to come and go. I can be with you! Forget everything I said in my last letter. I was in despair of our ever seeing each other again. I hope you didn't act on what I said!

I miss you so much, my dear Tom. If possible, I love you more than ever. I have been lucky to snag a room for us in Ludlow at the Feathers. I can be with you on Christmas Day for sure. I'll take an early train from London. Should arrive by noon. If you get this in time, meet me at the station. If not, I shall proceed to the hotel and wait for you there.

With much love,
Clare
P.S. Promise we will grow old together.

Tyler looked up to see that Nuala was watching him.

"It's from her, isn't it? Has she come back?"

"Yes," said Tyler. "I'll have to go. I'm to meet her at the train station."

Nuala was holding the new dressing gown over her arm. She held it out to him. "Perhaps you had better take this with you."

Tyler caught her hand. "I'm sorry, Nuala."

She shrugged, although her face was pale. "I'd meet Paddy at the station too if he came back."

He brought her hand to his lips and kissed her palm. She allowed it for a moment, then pulled away.

"You'll let me know what you decide, won't you?"

"That goes without saying."

"Go on then, before I throw myself at your feet and hang on to your legs. I'll tell the boys you've been called away on an important case."

Tyler got his coat and stepped out into the cold Christmas morning.

***

Up on the east field the snow fell slowly and steadily, blanketing the ground, until the raw patch of earth disappeared from view. Forty paces between the two hawthorn trees, ten paces south from the midway point, with Clee Hill to the north. Floating down the wind came the far-off jingle of a horse's bridle. The clay pot with its precious contents nestled deeper into the earth until it too vanished.

I called my good friend Enid one day a couple of years ago. She lives in Bitterley, a small village in Shropshire. We grew up together and stay in touch regularly. That day, she said she had a visitor and thought I would enjoy talking to him. On the line came Howard Murphy, a man with a strong Yorkshire accent. He is retired and loves going out with his metal detector to look for treasure, and he told me that in 2011 he had discovered something exciting in a field not too far from the village. In England, with such a depth of history, a Roman coin or a bit of Viking buckle is always being dug up in the fields. What Howard had found, however, was very unusual. It has come to be known as "the Bitterley Hoard," and it is one of the largest caches of Civil War coins yet found. Howard described it to me: a small clay pot, or tyg, as they are called; inside the pot was a leather pouch, mostly disintegrated by now; and in the pouch were 137 coins, two gold and the rest silver. The dates ranged from the reign of Elizabeth I (1558–1603) to that of Charles I (1625–1649). Not exactly a fortune, but a goodly amount nonetheless.

Howard asked if I would like him to show me where he'd found it. I jumped at the chance. Nobody really knew for sure where the money had come from or why it was buried in a farmer's field far from anywhere. There were theories, of course, but basically it was a mystery. Ha! What delicious bait to dangle before me!

I did some research: the area had been a hotbed of conflict between Cavaliers and Roundheads during the Civil War that had ripped up the country between 1642 and Charles' execution in 1649. Then, a few months later, I went to England and met up with Howard, who showed me where the treasure had been buried. As I stood in that grassy field on a bright summer's day, I communed with the long-dead man who had buried the coins, probably in haste, and not been able to return to claim them. I had some answers.

For the purposes of my story I have fictionalized the treasure ever so slightly: Jasper Cartwright removes one gold coin and two silver coins, reburying the 137 that were discovered nearly seventy years later. That's all.

I have been intrigued by the notion of this money reappearing during another terrible conflict. Not a civil war but a world war: 1942. Of course it has to vanish again.

The Bitterley Hoard is now in the protection of the Ludlow Museum, but in 2015 I was privileged to actually hold the treasure. Even though the coins are wafer-thin, they were heavy in my hand.

From all of this, I created *Dead Ground in Between*.

ACKNOWLEDGEMENTS

As always I am grateful to my good friends: to Enid (Molly) Harley, who made the first introduction; to Pam Rowan and Jessie Bailey, who are always so willing to find material for me. To Howard Murphy, for showing me where he made his discovery. And especially I must thank Peter Reavill, archaeologist and Finds Liaison officer for Shropshire and Herefordshire, who was happy to allow me to touch the coins, and discussed with me some possible reasons why they had been buried.

Derek Beattie kindly shared his extensive knowledge of Ludlow history.

Dennis Hunt gave me valuable information about his childhood on a farm during World War II.

Stanton Stephens at Castle Bookshop in Ludlow has been a wonderful supporter.

Special thanks to Jon Saxon of the *Ludlow Ledger*. Long may it thrive!

My friend, Peter Benne, himself a child of war, was most helpful with getting the Dutch children right.

My gratitude continues to my publisher, McClelland & Stewart, and my wonderful editor, Lara Hinchberger.